Time to
SHINE

MEL MENZIES

malcolm down
PUBLISHING

Time to SHINE

MEL MENZIES

British Library Cataloguing in Publication Data

A catalogue record for this book is available from the British Library

ISBN 978-1-910786-05-5

Cover Design by Esther Kotetcha Image supplied by Shutterstock
Printed in the United Kingdom
Typeset by Think-360

Malcolm Down Publishing Ltd
www.malcolmdown.co.uk

Mel Menzies
Facebook: https://www.facebook.com/mel.menzies
Twitter: https://twitter.com/MelMenzies
www.melmenzies.co.uk

Acknowledgements

Readers sometimes assume that novelists are drawing from real-life stories, and that the disclaimer stating that all characters are fictitious is, in itself, fictitious. It's true that new writers are told to 'write about what you know', and it would be equally true to say that most established authors of fiction (even if they are writers of fantasy) are attempting to convey the great themes of life.

So if asked if I had ever experienced anything similar to the plot of Time to Shine - a bad marriage, the prospect of divorce, recalcitrant teenagers, and the experience of counselling - I would have to say 'yes'. I've lived through the trauma. I've been on the receiving end of counselling. And I've survived. One might say 'triumphed'. By that I mean that I've learned lessons and, in doing so, I hope, have grown as a person. That does not necessarily mean that the stories or characters I write about are drawn from my own life experiences. What it does mean is that I have a passion to share the lessons I've learned.

As a consequence, in the days before accreditation was compulsory, I trained and practised as a counsellor. This does not imply, however, that I haven't also researched my subject for this book. Nor that I've ignored the wisdom and advice of those who have read the drafts of my manuscript, and have been kind enough to pass comment.

To that end, I'd like to express my thanks to my writing buddy, author and psychologist Angela Hobday, for her input and inspiration, as well as that of friends, ACW members, my book club and writers' group – all of whom have shown me enormous encouragement and support. Most of all, I want to thank my husband, Paul, for his enduring love, patience, wisdom and reassurance, and my daughters, Susie and Amanda, for their continuing contribution, care and affirmation.

Endorsements for Time To Shine

A beautifully written, well developed storyline makes this book hard to put down. Mel Menzies' insights into people, their feelings, dramas and worries had me nodding my head in agreement throughout.

David Scott
Newspaper management consultancy and journalism training

Being a psychologist myself, I love to read novels about psychology and counselling. This book does not disappoint.

Annie Try
Chartered clinical psychologist

I was gripped from the first page, and found the story riveting - never needing to sensationalise in order to keep the reader's attention.

David Grieve
Retired minister

CHAPTER ONE

SOMETIMES, WHEN YOU'RE counselling a client and she lobs a direct question at you, protocol requires that you bounce it back to her. A case in point is my two-o'clock this Friday afternoon, a mother of three, early-forties, by the name of Julia Worth. She's booked an appointment as a self-referral, and it's clear that she's desperate for answers.

'What do you think of divorce Mrs Adams?' she asks almost as soon as she's seated herself in the brown leather armchair opposite mine, in my first floor counselling room.

To gain time, I brush an imaginary crumb from my black work trousers, and push a stray strand of hair behind my ear. I could answer Julia in any number of ways: factually - it's the legal termination of a marriage; emotively - it's the upsetting and often messy end of an intimate relationship; cynically - it has the legal profession rubbing their hands together all the way to the bank; or experientially - been there, done that.

Instead, I ask, 'How do you mean?'

Not very original I grant you, but my aim is to get my client to open up.

A petite and attractive brunette whose dark eyes and full lips are crumpled with the ravages of distress and uncertainty, Julia looks me full in the face.

'Mrs Adams -'

'Evie,' I correct her.

'Evie,' she repeats. 'What I mean is that I don't believe in it. It's wrong. In my opinion, once you've made a commitment to marriage you should stick at it.'

She falls silent, leaning forward as if nursing an inner pain, her eyes welling with tears. I pass her the tissues and wait until she's ready to proceed. Behind her, motes of dust dance in the sunlight that streams through the ill-fitting lattice windows and lights up her face. From The Green below, at the heart of Exeter's city centre, I can hear the murmur of tourists imbibing the architectural and historical delights of the eleventh century St Peter's Cathedral.

Julia dabs at a falling tear. Naturally demonstrative, this is the part of my job I find hardest, having to restrain myself from reaching out and giving her a pat or a hug. I content myself by noting that, in stark contrast to my own drab attire, she at least looks well-heeled, if the fuchsia pink jacket and purple suede handbag are anything to go by. Small consolation, but if the marriage does end in divorce, at least she won't be destitute like some of my clients.

She straightens up, leans back in her chair.

'Trouble is,' she says, at last, 'my husband, Carl, seems to be convinced that I'm being unfaithful. I'm not. Not in that way, at least. But he's behaving abominably.'

Intrigued by the concept of multiple methods of unfaithfulness, I refrain from delving further at this stage.

'Have you tried to convince him of your fidelity?' I ask. Silly question, but it has to be posed. It never ceases to surprise me how many people shy away from confronting the truth.

'Oh, yes!' Julia is weeping properly by now. 'Most of the time he refuses to discuss it and tells me it's all in my head. At other times, he says, 'If you don't like it, you know what you can do.' I think he's trying to force me into leaving him.'

I scribble a note in my file. Could this be passive aggressive behaviour, I wonder? A well-known syndrome of manipulation, it takes the form of emotional abuse that is highly destructive, but gives the impression that the perpetrator inhabits the moral high ground.

'It all started when I became friendly with Hilary,' Julia continues. 'The new Chairman of the Board of Governors at my daughter's school. Carl hit the roof when the appointment was made. Went completely over the top. And he never misses an opportunity to make some scathing remark. It's bizarre. They obviously have history but, as I say, he refuses to discuss it.'

I raise an eyebrow. Could the said Hilary have featured in Julia's husband's life in some way that he would rather not be reminded of, I wonder? Some devious business deal on one side or the other? Or worse, perhaps, some adulterous behaviour one or other of them would rather keep hidden? I settle back in my chair and prepare to listen for the next three-quarters of an hour or so to Julia's account of the ups and downs of her marriage. Among women of her age, and mine, it's a familiar story.

'My parents had a very close and loving relationship,' Julia says, facing me from the other side of the cast iron fireplace. 'They did everything together. Everything. That's how they wanted it and that's what my sister and I believed was the norm. I guess I thought my marriage would be the same.'

She falls silent. Supposing her to be grappling with memories, I wait for several moments before nudging her on.

'And was it?' I prompt, at last. 'The same?'

Julia twists her shapely, well-manicured hands together in her lap.

'Carl has his own business. Engineering. He set it up himself. Went off to America - industrial spying he called it - brought back the first laser cutter in the country, and built up the firm to what it is today. It's his pride and joy; a legacy, he says, for our boys, Josh and Nathan.'

Through the window, I can hear the sound of organ music - probably a rehearsal for the next Sunday Service at the cathedral. Drowning out the usual low hum of human footfall and voices, it might, almost, I think, be a fanfare endorsing Julia's praise; an accolade for Mr Worth's business prowess.

'It was Carl's visionary way of thinking I admired before we married,' she continues, 'but it soon became clear that the vision didn't include me. Or at least, only when it suited.'

I nod, indicating my understanding. The old, old story, I think, momentarily abandoning my professional impartiality. Venus and Mars; Alpha male hunter-gatherer; Beta female support and home-maker.

'You say you were included "only when it suited" in respect of your husband. What did you mean by that?' I ask, recalling the notes I'd made.

Julia draws a sharp breath. 'I wouldn't want you to think that Carl neglects me. On the contrary. I have a very generous allowance, accounts at most of the major stores, and regular hair and beauty treatment.'

Even to me, to whom labels mean little and matter less, this much is clear. Julia is dressed head to toe in designer attire and adorned with Boodle-style diamonds, no expense spared. Slim and lithe, no doubt the result of hours of swimming, and pounding the running machine under the direction of a personal trainer, her skin, hair and nails are beautifully groomed and polished. She is the epitome of the successful businessman's wife.

It wouldn't do to jump to conclusions at this stage, but it may be that Julia's quick-fire defensive response to my question is motivated by guilt. Guilt that has, perhaps, been instilled in her by her husband? Guilt, I suspect, for what is perceived as a lack of gratitude on her part.

I smile and shake my head, reassuringly. 'I'm sure you want for nothing that money can buy.'

As I thought she might, Julia pounces on that.

'That's just the point, Mrs Adams - Evie. Sometimes I feel I'm just a walking clothes-horse. Nothing more than an advertisement for my husband's success.'

Julia pauses for a moment. She's clearly garnering some memory, some sense of recognition. Sure enough, she looks up and shares her thoughts.

'I remember once, some years ago, when I'd bought this lovely new sewing machine and I decided to do some dressmaking. Abi, my daughter, was only about seven at the time. I made matching outfits for her and me. Just simple little dresses in a Laura Ashley fabric. Abi loved that we looked the same. And it felt so good to be - creative for once.'

Anguish and regret are evident in Julia's eyes and voice. I think I have a pretty good idea why.

'And was your husband as pleased as your daughter was?'

Julia shakes her head. 'He was furious! Said it was a deliberate attempt to show him up; to undermine his role as provider.'

As I thought!

'How did that make you feel?' I ask, as gently as I can.

Julia considers for a moment. Then she bursts out, 'Like a puppet, with his hand up my back, making me do what he wants; what's best for him.'

* * *

Back at home, later that afternoon, Julia put her key in the lock and opened the front door. The black and white marble-tiled floor of the hall stretched before her, a grand entrance designed to impress visitors. She stepped over the threshold and closed the heavy oak front door softly behind her just as the grandfather clock struck four.

Wearing dark glasses to hide the ravages of her earlier tears, she'd driven straight home after leaving Evie Adams. The large period house, secluded and surrounded by an acre of grounds, was someway out of the city centre, and she'd encountered heavy traffic. Still, she'd made it. Plenty of time before Abi and the boys got home from school. Not that her absence would be the end of the world; they all had front door keys. Besides, she had the feeling, lately, that it didn't seem to matter much whether Mum was around or not.

She laid her car keys down on top of the polished oak chest against one wall, then went to hang her jacket in the cloakroom, opposite. She shrugged her shoulders repeatedly in a circular motion to relinquish the tension that gripped her, and let out the breath she was unaware she'd been holding.

The session with Evie Adams had been tiring but illuminating. Amazing really just how much she'd gleaned. Nothing new had actually been said, but Evie very cleverly seemed to ask just the right questions to highlight truths Julia had never seen before.

Had she, for instance, felt like a clothes-horse, as she'd declared herself to be? A walking advertisement for Carl's business acumen; his success? If she was honest, the thought had never occurred to her before this afternoon. It was only in response to what Evie had said - what was it now - something about having everything that money could buy? And suddenly, she, Mrs Julia Worth, wife of entrepreneur Carl Worth, had seen what she'd never properly seen before. 'Everything that money could buy' was not what she wanted; what she craved.

Showering her with gifts of clothes and jewellery had seemed, in the early years of their marriage, to be an affirmation of Carl's love. Time had shown it, in reality, to be the easy way out for him. She could see that now. It meant he didn't have to spend time with her; didn't have to make conversation with her; didn't have to get to know her needs; to understand her; to love her. And that, above all, was what she yearned for.

She looked at herself long and hard in the full length mirror on the wall. There were shadows under her large brown eyes, a slight droop to the corners of her mouth, and tiny furrows beginning to show on her cheeks. She turned sideways, straightened her shoulders, pulled in her tummy, lifted her chin and smiled. A definite improvement. She might be just the wrong side of forty, but she still had some attractive features, she thought.

Certainly that was the opinion expressed by some of Carl's colleagues - 'gorgeous as ever' - if they were to be believed. So why was Carl so offhand with her? And what could it possibly have to do with her friendship with Hilary? She turned from the mirror and made for the door.

'And just where have you been?'

Emerging from the cloakroom, Julia felt her heart miss a beat. At the far end of the oak panelled hallway, arms folded across his chest, Carl was leaning against the door jamb of the lounge. His dark hair, beginning to grey at the sides, was swept back off his face; his classic good looks were marred by the compressed line of his mouth, and the cold, inscrutable grey of his eyes. Tongue sticking to the roof of her mouth, and with a terrible, familiar sense of guilt, Julia found herself gabbling.

'What are you doing home? I didn't see the car.'

'Oh! Sneaking in were we?' Carl laughed, derisorily.

'No! I just hadn't expected you home this early. Good day at work?'

'As it happens, no! I had a phone call from Abi's school. They couldn't reach you. So I had to rush over there and take her to A&E.'

Julia grabbed the edge of the oak chest to steady herself. 'Oh, my goodness! What's wrong with her? Is she alright?'

Carl straightened, fixed Julia with an icy stare. 'She's okay. But that's not the point. Where were you? Why was your phone switched off?'

'I was - Where is she? I'd like to see her for myself.'

'As she would have liked to see you, her mother, had you not been gallivanting off. Somewhere that you're obviously reluctant to tell me about. Isn't that right, Abigail?'

Julia turned in the direction Carl was looking and saw her daughter, clad in her school uniform, at the top of the stairs. A fourteen year old mirror image of her mother, Abi's left arm was in a sling, her long brown hair dishevelled, her eyes red and tearful.

'Where were you, Mum?' she asked, making her way down the broad oak staircase as fast as she could, given that she was unable to hold onto the bannister. 'I kept ringing and ringing you.'

Julia hastened towards her, pulled the child into her arms, then partially released her as Abi cried out in pain.

'I'm so sorry, darling. I should have been there for you. What happened?'

Carl resumed his position, leaning against the door post, arms akimbo, one ankle crossed over the other, toe down on the carpet. Julia glanced in his direction. It was perfectly clear that he was making a show of being a spectator, but she was too concerned with Abi to be bothered.

'I dislocated my shoulder on the hockey field. It hurt so much!'

Unable to continue holding Abi in her arms without causing her further discomfort, Julia smoothed her hands down either side of her daughter's face and kissed her forehead.

'My poor darling.'

'Miss Staverton helped me inside and the Head called an ambulance. When she couldn't get hold of you, she rang Dad. Where were you Mum?'

There was an unmistakeable note of accusation in Abi's voice. Carl straightened up again.

'Yes. Where were you, Julia?' he drawled. 'We'd all like to know that.'

'I was in town.' Julia addressed herself to Abi. 'I'm so sorry, darling. Must have had my phone switched off.'

'Doing good for others were we?' Carl asked, a dramatised expression of intense interest lighting his face.

Julia flashed him a look in a silent plea for understanding and harmony. It failed. As it had, she realised, for at least half of the seventeen years of her marriage.

'Your mother had more important things to attend to, Abigail,' said Carl in tones which, if Julia hadn't known better, rang with sincerity. 'Things that wait for no man. Or daughter.'

He stood still long enough for Julia to catch the look of scorn on his face, then walked past her up the hallway and into his study without a backward glance. Despite her anguish, Julia made a mental snapshot so that she could describe the scene to Evie Adams when next they met.

I lock my counselling room and, with a sigh of relief, make my way downstairs. It's been a long day, and I must admit I'm more than ready for home. The evening air is sultry and the narrow streets around Cathedral Yard are heavy with the sound of footfall. Pushing my bike, I weave my way through hordes of last minute shoppers, plus those intent on enjoying the hospitality of the Ship Inn on Martin's Lane. The site of one of seven thirteenth century gateways into the Cathedral Close, the lane is too narrow to be more than a pedestrianised walkway leading to several upmarket boutiques on The Green. With scant interest in overpriced short-lived fashion items - or so I tell myself - I emerge, at last, onto the High Street, mount my bike and begin the cycle ride home.

The session with Julia fills my mind. Turning it over, I can't help feeling that the story she recounted to me has similarities to my own. We haven't yet established all aspects, but what she's said leads me to believe that her husband, Carl, has tired of the relationship, and that the harder she tries to put it right the more he's looking for a way out. In fact it's perfectly possible, as she intimated, that he's trying to force her hand.

What's not clear is why that should be? Could it be jealousy? Insecurity? Fear of having a dark secret exposed? Or perhaps, more likely, thwarted power? Which, itself, of course, might be rooted in insecurity? And where does Julia's new friend, Hilary, figure in this? Something odd going on there!

Obliged to stop at the zebra crossing outside Boots the chemist, my attention is drawn to a young couple with a bored kid in tow. They're canoodling as if they haven't a care in the world; as if the child were non-existent. Perhaps the mother's in a new relationship, I speculate, and the bloke isn't the boy's father? Poor little chap. He reminds me of myself at that age. He looks up with a sad, down turned mouth, and all the old memories crowd in on me. Swiftly expunging them, I wink, gave him a thumbs up which he returns, then cycle on as the crossing clears.

With the city centre once a fortified Roman settlement built on high ground, the journey home is downhill from here on. At least for a while. Freewheeling, I resume my appraisal of Julia's dilemma. Hadn't she said something about her parents being happily married, close and loving, doing everything together? And hadn't she finished by saying that she thought her marriage would be the same?

Perhaps that's the problem for many an unsatisfactory marriage, I think. We either rebel against what our parents stand for - as the boy outside the chemist might do. Or we allow our expectations to be unrealistically shaped by parental example. Negotiating the roundabout near the prison before heading off towards the army barracks, my mind turns to my own convoluted journey from wedded bliss to divorce. With a bit of a diversion for counselling along the way . . .

'So, Evie, tell me how you came to be married,' asked the counsellor to whom I'd turned for help when my marriage began to go wrong.

In my late-twenties at the time, I looked at Grace, seemingly so much older than myself, and wondered if she had the capacity to understand. Embarrassed with the memories I'd been asked to recount, I shuffled in my seat.

'My father used to say that marriage was the pinnacle of achievement if you were a girl. Marry well and you were made, he said. Drummed it into me.'

'And you believed him?'

'I thought I did.'

'But?'

'But - I guess I was kidding myself. And him.'

I stared ahead, trying to analyse the confused thoughts and teeming emotions of that time. 'I suppose, in reality,' I said, 'I just longed for independence. To escape from the controlling atmosphere of home.'

Grace nodded. Squirming under the searching gaze of my counsellor, I found myself unpacking that statement. Was my aspiration really any different to that of a million other teenagers, I wondered? Wasn't the adolescent struggle for independence a natural evolutionary process?

'And how did you meet, you and your husband?'

I fidgeted again. 'At a party in my home town, Sheffield. A friend's birthday. Pete was a police cadet. I fell for him big time. He was so different to anyone I'd ever known before.'

'And he felt the same about you?'

'I thought he did. I'm not so sure, now,' I admitted, tearfully. 'Perhaps it was just a matter of convenience for him, having a girlfriend who smuggled his washing into the family machine, and who could borrow the family car from time to time.'

I could have added that he might also have seen me as someone who had status and influence thrust upon me in that my dad was chairman of the local council. But I didn't. Because whatever the sentiments nourishing my alliance with Pete, they were irrelevant. They did nothing to alter the fact that the outcome was a failed condom, a shotgun wedding, and a father who all-but disowned me. Pete's move to the Exeter police force had followed swiftly. It was, I felt sure, the result of my father's machinations, because it effectively put me and my embarrassing condition out of sight of his cronies.

'So you got married,' Grace said, 'achieved the independence you craved; and what then?'

I cast my mind back. 'It didn't take me long to realise I'd simply swapped one sort of dependence for another,' I replied.

And a further ten years to admit it, I thought. Well it would, wouldn't it? I had no career as such. No aims in life. No idea what - other than parenthood - was available to me. And besides, my father had imbued me with all the old adages: Marry in haste, repent at leisure and You've made your bed, now you must lie on it, being the relevant ones here.

'I look back at that time and it's as if it wasn't me,' I continued in something of a trance. 'As if I was standing outside myself, looking at the child that was me and asking who she was, and how she could be at the altar making all those promises she barely understood?'

Seated in Grace's counselling room, I fell silent, following through on my train of thought. Who was that dreamer, the romantic who believed that if she loved enough, then love conquered all? And who was the boy who'd been told he was to have fatherhood thrust upon him, then had it wrested away? Forever. At least with me.

Coming out of my reverie, I realised that Grace was looking at me intently. Again, I squirmed with embarrassment.

'You said it didn't take you long to realise you were as dependent upon Pete as you had been on your parents,' said Grace. 'Can you tell me about that?'

'When I lost the baby everything seemed to unravel.' My voice broke. 'She was stillborn.' I fumbled for a hankie and, when I failed to find one, Grace passed me a tissue.

'That must have been difficult for you. For you both,' she said.

'It wasn't just losing the baby. That was bad enough. But I felt so guilty. She was the reason Pete and I had married. And suddenly she was gone.'

'But you weren't to blame, Evie. You were as much a casualty as your husband.'

I leaned forward, hugging myself. 'It didn't feel like that. Without the baby - there was no - no purpose to our marriage. Nothing to keep us together.'

'But you did stay together. For some years, I believe?'

'Ten.'

I fell silent again, summoning up the memories from the past. A decade of misguided hope, of wasted opportunities. What had driven me? Had my desperation to conceive again been fuelled by my need to be a mother? Or had I thought it a means of keeping Pete by my side? In my bed?

Whatever! It had failed on both counts. And failed dramatically.

But that afternoon in Grace's counselling room I was far from ready to admit to Pete's womanising, or my devastation.

'That first morning,' I continued, reverting to an earlier part of the story, 'I remember the casual way Pete kissed my cheek before setting off for work. In a funny sort of way, it gave me a sense of satisfaction; of security; of being properly married, a real wife now that the honeymoon was over.'

It had lasted all of a few moments, I recalled, a wave of self-pity engulfing me. Turning to watch his retreating figure, tall and lean in his police cadet uniform, my mood had changed, abruptly. The front door slammed behind him. Great waves of panic and home-sickness washed over me.

'It's a wonder I survived,' I continued, as if I'd voiced my earlier thoughts out loud. 'I knew no one here, in Exeter. I was hundreds of miles from home. And I was a teenage primigravida. It was winter, a dreary dark day, and the hours until Pete came home yawned before me. I think in that moment, if I'm honest, the eagerness I'd had for what I thought was independence began to shrivel.'

Grace looked up from her note-taking. 'How did that make you feel?' she asked.

'Well certainly not like running home to my parents!' I sat up straight, lifted my head and squared my shoulders. 'My father wouldn't have allowed it. Give up? Not part of my upbringing. Not part of his Yorkshire tradition, either. A soft southerner my mother might be, in his opinion, but he made sure that stoicism flowed through my veins.'

Stoicism! That's what I need now, I think, pedalling furiously as I change gear on my bike to begin the last lap: the hard slog uphill. Eventually, panting slightly from the exertion - despite the daily discipline I am not as fit as I should be - I arrive *chez moi*, dismount and push my bike up the garden path and into the tiny garden shed in which it is housed. The sweet fragrance of old-fashioned roses and early summer hollyhocks assails my senses and, even this late in the day, the gentle sound of bees in pursuit of nectar can be heard. Before I can insert my key into the front door lock, Pumpkin rushes towards me, tail held high, her green eyes aglow with anticipation. Purring, fondling, we greet one another in the usual way. And as I step into the narrow hall, my present day life embraces me, reminding me of all that is positive.

Things change, if you take action. This is what I need to impress upon the Julia Worths of this world.

'You said your husband believes you're being unfaithful?' I reminded her shortly before our session ended. 'Do you want to tell me about that?'

She shrugged, clearly embarrassed. 'It's just a feeling I have. Ever since I became friends with Hilary, Carl's been - really weird. Aggressive.'

'And you've no idea why?'

'All I do is help with the fund-raising charity at Hilary's church. Carl can't stand it. Sees it as some sort of betrayal, I think. As I said, the way he's behaving you'd think I was having an affair.'

'Really?'

'It's hard to explain,' Julia's face crumpled. 'His anger is totally irrational. He seems to be trying to make me choose between seeing Hilary or -' her voice petered out.

'Is this a man we're talking about? Hilary?'

'No! A woman.' Julia looked shocked. 'I don't mean an affair in that sense. It's not a relationship. It's - more to do with lifestyle, I think. What I mean is - well - I don't really know.' She paused, stared into space, then looked back at me, abruptly. 'I keep wondering if Carl's having a mid-life crisis. They do say that men can have a sort of menopause, don't they?'

'How do you mean?' I asked.

'Well, I wonder if it's to do with his father. I only knew him for a short time. He died about four years after we were married; the year Abi was born, I think it was. He was a barrister. Prided himself on his self-sufficiency, and made no secret of what he thought of anyone needy, or beneath him.'`

'So not the easiest of people to get on with?'

Julia screwed up her face in a non-verbal agreement. 'He certainly wasn't one to mince his words. He thought nothing of engineering as a career, and had no qualms in telling Carl so. It was all about brain being superior to brawn. That's what he used to say. He made it pretty obvious that he hadn't much time for his son.'

'And you? How did you find him?'

'As I say, I didn't know him for long. I suppose he must have been about - what - ten years older than Carl is now when he died. I remember there was a big to-do. Carl's mother sent for the priest to give him absolution. Last rites. And Carl went berserk. Went round the house yelling that if God forgave his father, he wanted nothing to do with either of them. God or his father.'

I felt puzzled, and said so.

'It was all to do with something that had happened when he was a schoolboy,' Julia explained. 'Something truly terrible. I know that from what his mother let slip at the time. But when I questioned her, recently, she refused to discuss it. Clammed up. Said it was all in the past. That what was done was done.'

'So, for some reason or other, Carl was not enamoured of his father?'

Julia frowned. 'It's hard to tell. I'd have said when we first met that he adored him. That he was the one person in the world he wanted to please. Or at least prove himself to. But - it seems I was wrong.'

'Oh? What makes you think that?'

'I remember Carl once said, following another blazing row when his father was still alive, that he never, ever wanted to be like him. I've not really thought about it much before, but I wonder now if -'

I waited. I thought I already knew what Julia was going to say, and sure enough I was right.

'The thing is,' Julia said, looking me straight in the eye, 'That's exactly what he's turning into. A mirror image of his father. At least with me. It seems that I can do nothing to please him.'

The clock on the mantelpiece struck the hour. Grabbing her handbag, Julia jumped to her feet, a look of panic on her face. She had evidently allowed no extra time for conclusions.

'Thank you for listening,' she said, breathlessly, and hastened towards the door. 'I feel so much better for having talked to you. But I need to get home now for the children.'

Aware of her anxiety, I sought to reassure her. We parted company with a speedily convened second appointment in the diary, and a sense of bemusement in my thinking.

Pondering the matter now, as I pause in the hallway to remove my coat and bicycle clips, I can only conclude that what's clear is a lack of clarity. More lies buried beneath the dark, airless, sub-soil of the past, I suspect, than appears in the neatly tilled surface of the present. Nothing new there, then!

On the face of it, it's not hard to see the parallels between Julia Worth's circumstances and my former life. Unilateral provision - one-sided giving - begets gratitude, which, in time, may turn to guilt. Guilt which, with a little encouragement, can be made to embed its roots in the insidious soil of contempt and power.

For me it was Pete's rescue of my 'damsel in distress situation' that evoked my indebtedness. Only for it to be followed by the guilt I'd expressed to

Grace when the baby - the reason for my rescue - was no more.

For Julia, it's clear that her financial and emotional dependence on Carl is the rooting hormone powder that's produced a burgeoning vine-like creeper, which requires increasing emotional support. The more Carl gives her, the more gratitude he expects, and the more guilt Julia experiences for having failed his expectation.

Moving down the hall to my tiny kitchen, I feel sure it's Julia's sense of dependency that needs to be addressed. She needs to become her own woman. To understand that in marriage, the sums don't stack up. It's not about two halves making a whole. It's about the union of one and one. Only then will love and respect be found to flourish. Only then will the relationship blossom and bear fruit.

Even so - I open the fridge door and peer in to see what's available for my meal tonight - even so, I reflect, I can't help but be intrigued. There's clearly something amiss with Carl's tortured relationship with his father. And what about the mystery of his hostility towards Julia's friend, Hilary?

CHAPTER TWO

JULIA PUT A glass of freshly squeezed orange juice on the breakfast table for each of the children, and glanced at Carl. He was flying out of Bristol, that afternoon, on a three day business trip to France and, despite everything, she felt a surge of pride. He looked every inch the part. The epitome of success. He rose from the table, shrugged on his jacket and straightened his tie.

'See you at the end of the week kids,' he said. 'And mind you look after that arm, Abigail Worth. No more venting your frustration on a hockey ball or beating up your brothers.'

Julia took in the scene before her. Josh, who at fifteen was dark and lean like his father, grinned broadly, while Nathan's plump, fresh features puckered with pleasure at his father's humour. Abi, meanwhile, stared wide-eyed and continued to twist her long dark hair between her fingers.

Sometimes Julia thought Carl had a better relationship with the children than she had, joking, handing out money at will, making decisions she was not party to. It all came so easily to him. But then he saw so much less of them than she did, and never had to do the disciplining that fell to her. As if to prove her point, a dispute began to take place before her.

'Mum, Josh has nicked my pen,' Nathan bleated, flicking cereal across the table at his brother.

'I have not, you freak,' Josh shouted, his face flushing crimson.

'You have so.'

'Have not.'

'Liar! Liar!'

'Stop it, you two. And Nathan, you clear up the mess you've made.'

'He has, too,' Abi intervened. 'Nicked Nath's pen. The one you and Dad gave him.'

Julia sighed. 'Joshua, you give Nathan his pen back before you go to school, or there will be no -'

The item, a black Schaeffer fountain pen, miraculously appeared on the table before she finished her sentence.

Julia looked at Carl in the forlorn hope that he might intervene. He seemed oblivious. Deep in thought about work, no doubt. Sometimes, she thought that was all that mattered to him. That she and the children were merely secondary considerations. Walk on parts.

She began to turn away to clear up the mess Nathan had created but stopped, suddenly. She could have sworn Carl had winked at Josh, as if to diminish the discipline she was endeavouring to mete out. One look at her son confirmed it. But then the grin on his face disappeared, leaving her uncertain. Was Carl taking his son's side against her? Or was she mistaken? She shook her head in an attempt to dislodge such feelings.

She couldn't blame Carl entirely for wanting a hassle-free relationship with his children, she supposed, especially in view of what she'd told Evie Adams the previous week. Carl rarely spoke about his father, and never about any malfunction in their relationship. But if, as she'd surmised, it had been lacking in mutual affection and respect - antagonistic, in fact - then naturally Carl would want to ensure a different outcome with his own children.

She pursed her lips. Having said that, she still thought his work schedule was at fault, the long hours piling on the pressure. He seemed, increasingly, to be involved in trips away from home. It might only be three days in Europe on this occasion, but he'd been talking, recently, about visiting some firms in Japan. That, he'd told her, would entail an absence of nearly three weeks.

Once upon a time, before the children were born, she would have gone with him and together they would have made it a working holiday. Nowadays - well, nowadays, she was a full-time mum and he was . . . She shrugged, imperceptibly.

'What time's your flight home on Thursday?' she asked, pulling a couple of paper towels from the kitchen roll and using them to wipe down the table. It was of cursory interest to her; she asked only out of a sense of duty, knowing from past experience what his answer would be.

'Lucy has the itinerary,' Carl replied, standing by the dresser and downing the dregs of his coffee. 'I'll get her to e-mail you a copy.'

Julia nodded. It seemed that Carl's PA knew more of his whereabouts than his own family. She took a piece of toast from the toaster, sat herself down at one end of the glass-topped table, and began to butter it.

'Could you get me some of that Tommy Girl perfume I told you about, please Dad?' Abi tilted her head to one side and spoke in an inveigling tone. 'From the duty-free?'

'And some duty-free fags for me, please Dad?' said twelve year old Nathan with a falsetto attempt at mimicking his sister.

'Cheeky!' Carl scuffed his younger son's hair affectionately with the flat of his hand as the boy ducked.

'And a bottle of Vodka for me, Dad?' Josh grinned.

Julia noted the banter with what would once have been pleasure but now had the effect of making her feel isolated. 'Would you like me to pick you up at the airport?' she asked, out of habit.

'No need. I'll have to drop into the office on the way back. We'll take a taxi.'

'We?'

'Lucy and I. She's going too. Need someone to carry the bags. Didn't I say?'

Picking up his travel bag and briefcase, Carl gave Julia a peck on the cheek before turning to the boys and saying, in what, ostensibly were jocular tones but seemed, to her, to be loaded with meaning, 'Make sure you keep an eye on your mother, and don't let her work too hard or stay out too late.'

He turned, strode across the granite-tiled floor and went out to the garage, closing the door behind him.

Julia stared after him. He'd said nothing previously about Lucy's accompanying him. It was only natural, she supposed. But still! It seemed to her to reinforce a change in emphasis.

Her gaze flickered around the large expensively fitted kitchen, and out through the patio doors to the manicured lawns that surrounded their house on the outskirts of the city. They'd bought it soon after Nathan was born, when Carl's business had taken off.

'I need somewhere grand enough to entertain clients,' he'd told her.

She'd thought the mortgage teeth-clenchingly high and had been worried sick for the first few years. But she couldn't bring herself to spoil his dream. Moulding herself into a hostess par excellence, she'd made every endeavour to live up to expectation. And she'd succeeded. Hadn't she? Even when the number of clients who visited had dwindled, as Carl increasingly wined and dined them elsewhere, she'd made no complaint.

Spacious and aesthetically pleasing, she had to agree it was an ideal family home, the tennis court providing a focal point for Abi and her friends, the field beyond an ideal place in which the boys might mess around. But despite everything, she had to be honest; lately it had felt more like a prison. And not only to her, but to the children, too. There's nothing to do round here, they complained. And it was true; they were too far out of town even to go to the cinema without involving one or other parent for a lift.

She glanced around the table. Usually, the children didn't 'do' mornings. Forbidden to have electronic devices to hand during mealtimes, they sat there in silence, spooning their cereal into their mouths, staring into space.

Her mind went back to Carl's parting remark. 'Make sure your mother doesn't work too hard or stay out too late.' Given that she had no paid employment, she thought this could only infer that it was her charity work he was calling into question; that she was not to be trusted; that she had to be watched. Instantly, she rebuked herself. She was becoming paranoid. Seeing duplicity where there was none.

The trouble was, though, that the boys were beginning to pick up on the tensions between her and Carl. Speaking to her as if she were the recalcitrant teenager and they the responsible parent, they were becoming tainted with an arrogance she deplored. She stood, and began to clear the table, re-wrapping open packets of cereal, wiping up the inevitable spilled milk and a sticky jar of marmalade. Josh, fifteen and already beginning to show a dark shadow around his jaw, grabbed the pot of jam before she could remove it, too.

'Hey, I haven't finished with that.'

'Don't speak to Mum like that,' said Abi.

Josh ignored her. 'You haven't forgotten I need a cheque for the trip to

Switzerland next term have you?' he asked, ladling jam onto his toast.

'I thought we said we were going to think about that,' Julia replied, turning to put things away in the larder and fridge.

'We did think about it, me and Dad, and we decided I should go. So I'll need it this morning.'

Ignoring the grammatical *faux pas*, Julia turned, leaning back against the worktop to look at her eldest son. His shock of black curly hair was longer than was permitted at St Cuthbert's, the fee-paying school that both boys attended, but the smugness in his eyes told her that he dared her to pass comment.

So this was how it was to be, was it, 'me and Dad' making the decisions and Mum meekly complying? She knew, for her son's sake if not her own, that she should fight this. What sort of mother would she be if she allowed Josh to develop into the kind of piggish lout who thought it okay to put her down and, by extension, all other women? What sort of relationships might he establish with the opposite sex if she did nothing?

'I think your father and I ought to talk this through,' she said. 'I've no objection to your going to Switzerland, *per se*, other than that it's the same week we told Granny we'd take her to Spain.'

She and Carl had bought a luxury apartment some years ago in Marbella, and had been so often to stay that they now felt almost part of the local scene. The arrangement to take Carl's widowed mother had been made when Julia noted how depressed she'd become when her little Jack Russell died.

'Wha'ever!' Josh fixed his mother with the sort of look you'd give when scraping your shoe free of dog mess. 'We'll see what Dad has to say about that.'

He stomped from the table, knocking Julia's unfinished piece of toast to the floor, and left the room. Julia stared, helplessly, after him.

'You shouldn't let him get away with that, Mum,' said Abi, retrieving the fallen toast. 'You should stand up for yourself. That's what you're always telling me.'

Julia smiled at her daughter. 'Quite right!' she said, smoothing down Abi's hair and dropping a kiss on the top of her head. 'You're a person of great value. And don't you let anyone convince you otherwise.'

She turned away. Hypocrite! She must learn to practice what she preached. She was sure that was what Evie Adams would advocate.

* * *

Arriving for work early one morning soon after my meeting with Julia Worth, I park my bike, as usual, in the passage at the side. My counselling room, one of several used by practitioners in the group, is on the first floor of one of the ancient buildings in Cathedral Close. Once the site of Roman baths and a basilica in the first and second centuries, this whole area at the heart of the city of Exeter continues to be a haven for both locals and tourists in pursuit of relaxation and renewal. With nearly two thousand years of history at my feet, I am firmly of the opinion that the angels must have been smiling on me when they made this my place of work. By anyone's standards it's awesome.

Supported, collaboratively, by a couple of GP's surgeries in the city, several local churches and, of course, the therapists themselves, the practice is thriving, the clientele plentiful and varied. Each of us has their own mentor or supervisor to ensure high standards of professional procedure, but obviously there are times when, with all due respect for confidentiality, we discuss aspects of our work with one another.

Having secured my bike, I turn and bump into my colleague, Guy Sampson.

'What do you think makes a man dissatisfied with his lot, when he appears to have everything?' I ask without preamble, voicing the question that's uppermost in my mind.

Guy is one of the kindest men I've ever known: a gentle giant, with an invalid wife and plenty of reason for self-pity, but no hint of it. Behind a bewhiskered face, he sports the twinkliest blue eyes anyone could imagine

'Whoa!' he replies with a smile. 'That's a big question.'

I grin. Is that a subtle reproof, correcting my lack of finesse? Not that I'm offended. Guy's the sort of bloke that women find attractive on two fronts: he's a shoulder to lean on, but he also brings out all your maternal instincts.

'So?' I turn to retrieve my personal belongings from my saddle bag.

Guy's grin broadens, takes on an air of teasing. 'As someone who has everything, my only dissatisfaction is that there are others with little or nothing.'

I'm a little flummoxed. Guy appears to have so little, so how can he say he has everything? There's simply no comparison between him and the Carl Worths of this world. Before I can comment, he relents.

'I take it that by *everything* you mean money and status?' he asks. 'But there are other riches in life.'

I'm not sure I'm any the wiser. Even if Guy means richness of life options and relationships, he'd still be lacking, in my opinion, given the restraints Nancy's disabilities must impose upon them. Frowning slightly, I begin to mount the stairs.

'Add a beautiful wife and healthy kids to the money and status mix,' I continue, 'and -'

'And why should he want for more?' says Guy from behind me.

'Exactly!'

We arrive on the first floor landing. Guy's room is before mine. He unlocks his door. 'Want to come in and tell me what this is all about?' he asks.

In the sunlight I can see that his greying hair and beard need a trim, and his jacket either a trip to the cleaners or the recycling depot. Poor man! It must be tough being a carer at home and counsellor at work.

Guy opens the door, goes in and dumps his things on his desk.

'I've got some gourmet coffee. Gift from a grateful client.'

'Now you're talking!' I follow him in, cross the room and look down from the window at the early morning hustle and bustle taking place on The Green, while he fills his coffee machine with water and measures out the ground coffee beans. Leaning against the windowsill, I chat inconsequentially for sometime, while the coffee brews.

'It's just that I have a new client,' I say at last, turning away and taking a seat, 'and there's something strange going on. She mentioned a new friendship she's made, which seems to have inflamed her husband. He appears to have taken an intense dislike to this woman. But there's more to it than that. I can't help feeling that something's happened in the past. Something that's been hidden. And now it's raised its ugly head -'

Calmly, quietly, Guy continues to lay out mugs, milk and sugar as if it were some regular morning ritual; which it probably is, now I think about it; a sliver of time away from his invalid wife, in which he can attend to his needs, his pleasure. He purses his lips, looks thoughtful, and says, as he passes me a mug-full of steaming, swirling, aromatic liquid heaven,

'Sounds to me as if he might be having a crisis of confidence. Male menopause? Is he the right age?'

I sip my coffee. 'That's just what my client suggested.'

'There you are then.'

Not entirely convinced, I drop my gaze and stare at the floor trying to recall my first impressions.

'You're religious, aren't you?' I ask, more as a statement than a question. 'I mean - you go to church?'

Guy nods, looks as if he's going to say something, but refrains.

'My client seems to think that her husband views her involvement with this new friend and the charity she runs at her church as if it were - I don't know - a sort of unfaithfulness? I'm not sure whether he's jealous of the time she spends away from home. Or whether it's something deeper than that. A betrayal of values?'

Guy seats himself on the office chair in front of his desk and swings himself round to face me.

'Could be either,' he says, slowly. 'Religion can be one of the most divisive things on earth. You've only to look at the wars being waged around the world at present to see that.'

'Mmm.' I'm still not convinced. 'This is the C-of-E I'm talking about. I thought it was meant to be all about love?' I sip my coffee, closing my eyes to savour the flavour.

'Indeed it is. But that's a radical concept. Love implies relationship. There are those who find it,' he shrugs, 'shall we say - threatening.'

'Threatening?' I open my eyes. 'That's a strong word.'

Guy nods. 'You talked about the possibility that your client's husband might find her involvement with her friend a betrayal of values. *His* values. So the things that once united them might now be the very things that divide them. He may well feel that, through her friend, she's now challenging - perhaps even condemning - what he stands for.'

'Mmm. So possibly even more threatening,' I say slowly.

'Exactly!' Guy responds.

I stare at the ceiling, relishing the coffee, thinking through what Guy has said. Love? A relationship? Perhaps Julia's right. Perhaps her husband does view her new allegiance as infidelity.

Julia folded her arms. It was Thursday evening and, determined to make amends for what she saw as feebleness on her part, she waited up for Carl's return from his business excursion in France. The subject of Josh's school skiing holiday in Switzerland during half term had to be raised. She was going to get to the bottom of it come what may. Abi was right. She should stand up for herself. How, otherwise, could she ever be a good role model for her children?

Nathan had gone to bed sometime ago, complaining of a sore throat. Abi had followed soon afterwards, and Josh, Julia sighed, well, Josh would do his own thing no matter what.

Julia watched the ten o'clock news in the homely chaos of the family room. On impulse, she then moved into the lounge, choosing to say what she had to say in there. A large south-facing room at the back of the house, it was furnished with pale almond coloured carpet, antique furniture and Carl's art collection on the walls. With the curtains drawn across the French doors and the window on the adjoining wall, an aura of calm prevailed. Just what she wanted.

Arriving home at ten past eleven, Carl was clearly surprised to find her downstairs at all, let alone in a room reserved more for entertaining than *têtes à têtes*. Julia greeted him with a kiss, asked about his trip, and waited for him to be seated before repeating what Josh had said at breakfast on Monday morning.

'I thought we'd agreed we were going to think about it; talk it through together?'

'Mmm? What's that?' Carl asked from behind the newspaper he'd retrieved from the magazine rack.

He'd left his briefcase in the study next door, and had removed his jacket and tie. He looked tired but somehow - Julia couldn't put her finger on it - somehow exhilarated? Negotiations with the French must have been more successful than he was letting on, she thought. A sense of guilt permeated her mind; was this the right time to be making demands of him? But if not now, then when? She proceeded with caution.

'Josh. And his school trip. He says you agreed he could go.'

'Did I?' Carl put the paper down; he looked genuinely surprised.

Julia frowned. So that was it! Josh was trying it on. She shook her head.

'He is the limit. I'll have to have words with him. Or perhaps it would be more appropriate if you did?'

Seated in one of the easy chairs to the side of the fireplace, she looked across the expanse of carpet between them. Carl was slumped on the sofa, one leg raised on the seat, but carefully, so as not to soil it with his highly polished leather shoe. He shrugged.

'Well, I may have told him he could go. No harm in it is there? In fact, now I come to think about, he asked for a cheque that morning while I was getting the car out of the garage.'

Julia looked down, folded her hands in her lap, then stiffened her fingers. A pulse throbbed in her temple, and her neck felt taut. She rolled her head from side to side, then looked across at Carl.

'He asked me, too. You didn't give him one?' She kept her voice low and even. 'What about the trip we've planned with your mother?'

Carl leapt to his feet, strode across the room to the sideboard, poured himself a Scotch and said, with his back to her, 'Well you can hardly expect a soon-to-be sixteen-year-old to spend his holidays with Granny, can you?'

He was clearly irritated. Julia shrank back in her chair. He doesn't want to come home to this, she thought. He thinks I'm smothering Josh. And perhaps I am. The old familiar sense of guilt kicked in.

'You may be right. But I wish you'd discussed it with me,' she said, looking down again at her hands.

Savouring the double malt, Carl returned to his seat.

'I did discuss it with you. You've forgotten.'

Her head jerked up, involuntarily. Had he? He was always telling her she'd forgotten discussions he insisted they'd had; appointments he'd made that affected her; decisions they were supposed to have reached together - none of which she could recall. Was he being perverse? Or was she losing the plot?

She lowered her eyes, aware that Carl was staring at her.

'Look,' he leaned forward, sitting on the edge of the sofa, legs apart, hands on his knees. 'I've a lot on my plate at present. Work. The thing I do that keeps you and the kids in the lap of luxury.'

His voice dripped with sarcasm. Julia shifted, uncomfortably, in her chair. He did work long hours for them all. She had no right to complain. How would she feel if the situation were reversed? Carl begrudged his family nothing that money could buy.

The thought reminded her again of her session with Evie Adams. 'I can see you lack for nothing,' she'd said. And it was that statement that had triggered the realisation in Julia that she lacked the one thing she craved. Love. And respect. Something you earned. Something she'd lose once again if she missed this opportunity to clear things up.

'So - what about your mother?' she asked, trying and failing to control the wobble in her voice.

Carl didn't hesitate. 'I'm afraid you're going to have to go without me,' he said. 'I've another business trip coming up. Something rather big in the offing.'

Julia felt her jaw drop. Carl's mother was not the easiest person in the world. If her only son couldn't manage to be there for the week, he'd have to cancel it. She opened her mouth to tell him.

As if on cue, Carl's mobile burbled, signifying an incoming text. He took it from his pocket, looked at the screen for a moment, then indicated that he was going to his study next door.

'Got to check some papers,' he said, and walked out of the room leaving the matter of his son and his mother unresolved.

It's Friday again and Julia has arrived for her second appointment.

'So, how have things been this week?' I ask.

She looks thin and browbeaten, dark shadows beneath her eyes, her shoulders sagging beneath the designer denim jacket. Nevertheless, she takes a seat and looks me full in the face.

'It's been terrible! My eldest son, Josh, seems to think he can walk all over me, encouraged by his father. And I got home from here last week to find that my daughter, Abi, had had an accident and the school had called Carl because they couldn't get hold of me.'

I purse my lips to indicate my sympathy. 'Not good! Is your daughter alright?'

'She's okay; bit shaken up and upset when I didn't respond because my phone was off, but we've made it up now.'

'And your husband?'

'He was furious! And so sarcastic. It's as if he enjoys putting me down in front of the children.' Julia falls silent, her eyes downcast, twisting her hands in her lap.

'In what way did he put you down?'

'He was going on about my having 'more important' matters to attend to than the children.' She gestured the quotations marks with her fingers. 'I think he's feels that - well, I suppose he's right! If I hadn't been here, seeing you -'

'I see. You mentioned Carl's view of your new friendship last week. Would you like to tell me more about that?'

Armed with what Guy has told me - his perception of the strains Julia's new-found allegiance might have brought to her marriage - I feel I can bring some intelligence to the matter.

Julia hesitates, clearly unsure as to where to begin. 'Well,' she says at last. 'As I told you, Hilary's the new Chairman of the Board of Governor's at Abi's school. That's where I met her. She's a very nice person. A bit older than me. She invited me for coffee. We got to know one another. And we've become friends. But Carl seems to bear her some sort of grudge.'

'Is there a reason for that?'

Julia shakes her head. 'I have no idea! I can't get to the bottom of it. He refuses to talk about it other than to make cutting remarks about her, and the time I spend with her. The only thing I can think is that it has something to do with the fact that Hilary is what Carl calls a 'do-gooder'. She helps organise the local food bank, and raises funds for a couple of charities. One to do with overseas aid and another for the homeless. I've been helping her lately. Doing a bit of baking to sell at events.'

I nod as several pieces of the jigsaw look as if they might be falling into place. Still, it wouldn't do to jump to conclusions.

'So why would that affect your husband?' I ask.

Julia twists her hands in her lap.

'He despises anything like that. It's not charity *per se* that he looks down on. More to do with what he calls "pie-in-the-sky thinking", "life-ever-after". That sort of thing. I don't know why. He won't talk about it. It could be something to do with his father. I believe he was a church warden. Lay reader. Something like that And from what I can gather - as I told you last week - he actually wasn't a very nice person. Certainly as far as Carl was concerned.'

Aha! I scribble in my notebook.

'And what about you?'

'Oh, my parents weren't the least bit religious. Though for some strange reason they sent me to a convent school.'

'And you don't know why?'

'No idea. I believe my grandmother paid the fees. Perhaps she felt that convent discipline was better than most. And I suppose it was.'

'Was it a good experience?'

'Some of the nuns were very kind; lovely people. But the religious side of things, rosaries and catechism, all the pomp and ceremony -' a slight frown furrows Julia's brow. 'I was going to say it turned me off.'

She lapses into silence, a bemused look on her face.

'I sense a *but* coming up,' I prompt her.

Julia pauses for a moment, adjusts the front of her white silk blouse, and sighs. The sun is streaming in and the heat is building up.

'Shall I open a window?' I ask, rising to my feet and crossing the uneven floor. Down below, on The Green, in front of the cathedral, there's some sort of pageant taking place. As I seat myself, once more, the murmur of voices can be heard, and then a bugle being played.

'What I was going to say,' Julia fidgets, clearly uncomfortable with her thoughts, 'was that I realise now that my time at the convent might have had a more positive impact on me than I used to think.'

She fiddles with the vivid green silk scarf at her throat which even I, a devout advocate of second-hand clothes shops and make-do-and-mend, have to admit - albeit reluctantly - sets off Julia's burnished locks to perfection.

'What makes you say that?' I ask.

Julia sighs. 'Hilary called in one morning a few months ago about some baking I'd promised to do. I was rather upset. Carl and I had had a row. She did all the usual things, made me sit down and have a cup of tea, comforted me, reassured me.'

Julia stops. I wait, convinced that there must be more. She looks down at her hands. Picks at a roughened cuticle.

'A few days later, she asked if I'd like to accompany her to morning service,' she continues, without looking up. 'Carl was away. The children are never up that early at the weekend. Seemed like a good idea.'

'And was it? A good idea?'

'It was -' she shrugs, hesitantly '- different. Very friendly.'

I sit in silence, waiting for her to continue. The sound of drum beats drifts through the open casement window, and a fly buzzes, trying to find its way out. Julia pushes her hair back from her face.

'I've been a couple of times since. And once or twice I've been to Hilary's in the evening with some of her lady friends who meet regularly together. After all, Josh is nearly sixteen now. As long as he has my mobile number, I figure he's old enough to keep an eye on the other two. And everyone's so nice. Understanding.'

Julia's face flushes. She's obviously on the defensive. I smile, to put her at ease.

'It was only ever meant to be when Carl was away on business,' she continues. 'But one evening, he came back earlier than expected. Must have been a couple of months ago. Walked in about ten-ish and found the children still up watching some film on TV. He was furious.

'I know! I should have been back sooner. I usually am. But we'd been talking at Hilary's about the correlation between love and forgiveness. One of her friends had been reading a book, a real-life story of a Dutch woman who was sent to a concentration camp for helping the Jews to escape the Nazis and endured years of abuse, yet had this amazing power to forgive the very people who had incarcerated her. It was so moving!

'I ended up in tears. And out it all came. Carl's indifference to me. His being away so much. The way he puts me down in front of other people. I didn't know them that well, the other women. But they were so kind.'

As she recounts her story, Julia is close to tears again.

'So, you found solace. Friendship. Understanding. Nothing wrong with that,' I reassure her. 'Of course, marriage is different for everyone. But it doesn't mean that you have to live in each other pockets. You're entitled to have your own life.'

Julia nods, clearly relieved to find someone who understands.

'After all,' I continue, 'a lot of men play golf, or snooker. It's perfectly acceptable to have exclusive friendships and activities. There's a school of thought that says it actually enriches a marriage. Gives you something fresh to talk about, together.'

Julia looks alarmed.

'Oh, I couldn't talk about my new friends to Carl,' she protests. 'He'd think they were either wimps or fanatics.'

A musical fanfare followed by the sound of applause drifts in through the open window. The unintentional irony is not lost upon me. I suspect Carl would be well pleased, if he'd heard it.

'He's no time for any of it,' Julia continues. 'They're just after your money, he says. Spongers! And they're not getting any of his when he's worked hard all his life for it. But I don't see any harm in my baking a few cakes and cookies to help raise funds for the homeless, here and overseas, do you? It's not as if we can't afford it.'

She shivers; rubs her arms.

Deep in thought, I don't respond immediately. From what Julia has said, it would appear that her husband's views are somewhat extreme. Why else would he object to his wife's attempts at fund-raising? I rein in my speculation. Could there be some connection between Carl's father and Hilary? Some corrupt moral issue that calls into question their professed church allegiance? Something dire enough to justify Carl's hostility?

There must, I feel sure, be more to this than meets the eye. But now is probably not the best time to broach the subject. Conveying sympathy for Julia's discomfort, I rise from my chair, cross the room, and shut the window.

CHAPTER THREE

INSIDE AN OAK-PANELLED office in the financial sector of Exeter's city centre, Carl Worth signed the papers before him with a flourish, and pushed them across the leather topped desk. Leaning back in the plush leather chair in which he was seated, he gave a smile of satisfaction.

'All done,' he said, replacing the cap on his rhodium trimmed Cross fountain pen and clipping it in the inside pocket of his jacket. 'Time I wasn't here.'

He rose and shook hands with his bank manager, Miller. They'd been at school together. Termly boarders, two small boys cowering under a strict regime. And later two angry young men, helpless in the face of an injustice. The bonds they'd forged were inseparable.

This morning, barely a week after Carl's return from the Continent, they'd struck a business deal that was mutually beneficial. The warmth and enthusiasm as they embraced and bade their farewells was notable.

'Everything okay with you?' Miller asked, an awkward concern peppering his tone. 'It's the anniversary coming up soon, isn't it?'

'Yep! Twenty-eight years. I'm timing the launch of the new factory to mark the occasion. Hope you'll be there?'

'Naturally! Erm - is that twenty-eight years since - the death? Or the verdict?'

The naivety and stupidity of Miller's question rendered Carl almost speechless. Painful memories rained down on him, ripped into his chest, opened the old wound. He flinched, then drew a breath and allowed his anger to reinflate his lungs.

'Now why would I want to commemorate a miscarriage of justice perpetrated by my tyrant of a father, Miller? Use your head! It's Spud's memory I want to honour.'

'Of course!' Clearly embarrassed to have miscalculated the date of events, Miller clapped a hand on Carl's shoulder.

Carl forced himself to relax. 'In fact, I'm planning to set up an apprenticeship in Spud's name. But keep schtoom about that at the moment, will you.'

'Of course!' said Miller, again. 'Great idea.'

Carl turned and left the office. Running down the steps, he emerged into the pedestrianised shopping area of Princesshay and headed off towards Cathedral Close and his favourite watering hole, where he was meeting a colleague for lunch.

A sense of well-being swelled within him. Heck! More than that. Munificence. Largesse. Pride of achievement. That was more like it. Catching sight of himself, dark-haired and debonair, in a shop window, he liked what he saw. The Saville Row suit, hand-made shoes and silk tie said it all.

Memories of his beloved Welsh grandmother filled his thoughts. She'd have been proud of him.

'Pity your Da didn't live long enough to choke on 'is words,' Nain had pronounced when he'd won his first major contract with the Ministry of Defence, making a component for armoured vehicles in Afghanistan. And she'd given a robust and unequivocal opinion as to how unfavourably her only son's career in defending criminals from their just deserts compared to her grandson's achievement in defending 'our brave soldiers'. If only, Carl thought, they were both still alive to see him now.

What he was about to do, as he'd explained with great seriousness and devotion on a regional TV news programme earlier that week, would bring employment to a deprived area; help hard-working families; revive the local economy.

'So it means nothing to you that the development of this new industrial site will mean the destruction of cherished woodland?' the presenter had asked, having explained, beforehand, that the question was mandatory, as far as her producer was concerned, and no aggression was implied on her part.

'Of course it matters to me,' he'd replied, revealing that his Nain had lived here, in this very town, and that what he was planning was partly a testament to her, but concealing - for the time being - that this was also the site of his school friend's death. 'But what matters more,' he continued, 'is the income that this industrial site in general, and my factory in particular, will provide for the hard-hit residents in the area.'

Not only would he provide employment for the community, he'd continued, he would be as one among them; drinking in their local taverns; eating in their restaurants; spending his money in a manner that would benefit them all.

The news item had brought a mixed reaction. A handful of job applications, a fistful of angry letters from some of the community. But he'd win them over soon enough. And not for the first time. Mr Affable, that was the Carl Worth his friends knew and loved. One of the things he'd learned in life was that a charm-offensive would get you far. He waved to the butcher, his pal Steve, as he crossed the road.

'Great fillet steak last week,' he called. 'Have to order another soon.'

Have to settle the bill soon, too! The good thing about including the butcher on your dinner party list was that it earned you credit. He waved again, and strode on.

Of course, he thought, ducking to enter the dark interior of The Ship Inn on Martin's Lane, expansion would also buy him more fillet steaks, increase his workforce and his bank balance. Perhaps, one day soon, he might even float on the stock exchange? What would his father have made of that, then?

Impatient with himself, he erased the thought from his mind. All that was of secondary importance, hardly worth a mention. For now, he was more than happy to exploit every government grant that was going simply to open a second factory. What mattered was his status in the business world. Not some stupid wish to impress his dead father.

'Expanding into Wales and linking with colleagues in France will bring in a whole new customer base,' he'd told Miller. Adding, silently, 'pat on the back, Carl Worth!'

The silver BMW M2 coupé that was currently sitting in the showroom with his name on it was his just reward, he thought now. He couldn't wait to take it for a proper spin, foot to the floor, wind in your hair. That would bring Julia back into line. To hell with her puny fundraiser friends who seemed to have stolen her affections and filled her head with all sorts of nonsense. He'd show them a thing or two about providing for the masses.

The ebullience he'd experienced earlier deserted him. He felt irritable. He wished Julia had retained the panache that had so enticed him in the early years of their marriage. Had he misjudged her then? Where once she had been carefree and confident, she now seemed to have shrunk into herself. So much of her time, these days, was spent whining about irrelevancies. Moralising about undeclared business perks that were no concern of hers or the taxman's. Suggesting that their lifestyle was too extravagant and that some of their income might be put to better use helping others. Silently, but obviously, rebuking him for his generous gifts to the kids.

All this prancing on principle went against the grain. Who was it said that religion was an opiate for the masses? Whoever! They were right. If there was one good thing he'd learned from his father's behaviour, it was that he didn't need God as a prop. And neither - given the lifestyle he, Carl Worth, provided for her - did Julia. It did nothing for his street cred.

Once upon a time, she'd hung on his every word. Nowadays, she did nothing but complain that he didn't discuss things with her. The truth was he'd like nothing more than to enlarge upon the plans he had for the Welsh factory. But unlike his PA, Lucy, he knew Julia would only feign an interest and change the subject as soon as possible.

Julia's interest, like his mother's, had rapidly waned, though she was quick enough to spend what he earned. The look of guilt on her face had not gone unnoticed when he'd reminded her of his largesse the other evening. And quite right, too. She'd a lot to be thankful for. And once the Welsh factory was up and running, there would be yet more.

He ordered a pint of bitter and asked for the lunch menu. Taking a seat at the bar until his colleague arrived, his thoughts turned again to the deal he'd brokered with Miller. For a second, he felt a stab of guilt. But as experience had shown, guilt was best staunched before resolve became extinguished.

He pulled back his shoulders, sat taller on the bar stool. Yes! Putting the house up as collateral against the bank loan was more than justified. He'd just have to pick the right time to tell Julia, if indeed, he did tell her. Given the fuss she'd made over the cheque he'd given Josh for his school trip - And the way she'd reacted to the news that he was going to be unable to accompany her to Spain with his mother - Yep. Perhaps silence was the better option. Especially as they were dining with friends that evening.

Julia shifted, uncomfortably, on her seat. The couple at whose home she and Carl were dining that evening, cackled with laughter.

'You look like the cat that got the cream tonight, Carl,' said Dave. 'Won the lottery, have you?'

He poured a fine Pinot Noir into their glasses and Laura passed the vegetables across the table. Julia spooned broccoli onto her plate, watching Carl's face as she did so.

'Yes. Haven't you heard?' Laura added. 'He's taking us all on a cruise next month.'

Julia felt bemused. It was clearly a joke, but did they know something she didn't? Carl and Dave had been at uni together and, though Julia got on well enough with Laura, she considered them Carl's friends rather than hers. There was something about this evening's humour that made her feel uncomfortable.

She looked across the table at her husband. She hadn't noticed earlier, but now that Laura had drawn attention to Carl's demeanour it was glaringly obvious. Ever since the debacle over the cheque Carl had given Josh, and the indifference he'd shown when it came to absenting himself from the Spanish holiday with his mother, she'd felt a little depressed. Vacillating between anger for the way in which Carl seemed to delight in putting her down, and anger with herself for deserving to be put down! Nevertheless, friendship and good manners required that she make an effort now.

'Carl's got some big deals coming up,' she said, injecting a degree of pride into her voice. She helped herself to sautéed potatoes and a courgette cut in half lengthways and baked with a sprinkling of cheese and breadcrumbs on top. 'He was on the Continent last week, and he's even talking about going to Japan.'

'Japan?' Dave lifted his eyebrows and said, suggestively, 'All those Geisha girls! How are you going to cope with that, Julia?'

Julia looked to Carl to answer, but he was busy selecting the vegetables Laura was offering him. She would have to respond herself.

'Oh, I'm all in favour of husband and wife not living in each others pockets,' she said, repeating Evie Adam's advice to her the previous week, but without letting on where it had come from. 'It enriches a marriage if you each do different things. Gives you something new to talk about when you're together again.'

'Carl's encounter with Japanese Geisha girls might be enriching for him,' Dave chortled. 'But I wouldn't have thought it would be for you, m'dear.'

'What's all this about *enriching a marriage*?' Carl said smoothly, lifting his wine glass to his mouth. 'Not more of your do-gooder drivel is it, Julia?'

Julia felt herself flush.

'Marriage Enrichment is a national organisation,' she said. 'I've been looking it up on the internet. It's all about listening and expressing feelings; learning how to give and receive positive feedback; and resolving conflicts. They do seminars. You start by focusing on the positives, then you look at the changes you want to make in your relationship.'

Julia looked down at her plate, pushed a piece of tarragon chicken onto her fork and put it in her mouth. She'd said too much. Too soon. Or at least in the wrong place. She'd meant to bring this up quietly with Carl, at home, in the hope that he'd agree to go on a seminar with her. As it was - she glanced across the table - the scorn glittering in his pale grey eyes said it all.

'Sounds like marriage guidance,' said Dave, quaffing back the wine. 'Watch out Carl, you'll be divorced in no time and she'll be suing you for your millions in alimony.'

'It's not at all like marriage guidance,' Julia protested. 'This is for good marriages. To make them better. Not failing ones.'

'Sounds just what Dave and I need,' Laura smirked. 'He never *listens* to me. Do you, darling? I *expressed my feelings* about the three stone diamond ring I fancied and there was lots of *conflict*. Because I didn't have any *positive feedback*.'

She waved her ringless right hand around the table to demonstrate her point.

'Mmm? Wha-do-you say?' Dave grinned, cupping his hand around his ear and aping deafness.

'There you are!' Laura laughed. 'Perhaps we ought to sign the two of them up, Julia. Before Carl goes off to Japan. Unless, of course, he's going to take you with him?'

Carl turned to Laura. 'Sadly, I'm not going anywhere as exotic as

Japan. At least for a while yet,' he said. 'But I am planning to open a second factory on a new and expanding industrial estate in Wales. All in its early stages at present, but it's linked to a government initiative intended to encourage enterprise in deprived areas.'

'Good on you,' said Dave, raising his glass. 'I'll drink to that.'

'And me,' said Laura.

Julia obediently lifted her glass to her lips. She felt sick. Carl had said nothing of his plans to her. Nothing! As if she had no interest in his work. As if she were a nobody in his life. And where was he getting the money from? Only this week Steve, the butcher, had sent a third reminder about outstanding invoices going back six months or more. How was that to be paid? And the children's school fees were coming up. What about them?

She daren't ask. He'd only say he'd already told her. Like an automaton, she raised her glass and drank his health. Three more days till she saw Evie Adams again. She wished she didn't have to wait that long.

A phone message from Julia Worth awaits me when I arrive at the office on Thursday morning but when I attempt to return it there's no reply. She's not conveyed anything material in what she's said, and the only clue to her state of mind lies in her stilted tone of voice. Unfortunately, I'm in no position to follow through.

One of my clients, a woman with an abusive husband and drug-addicted son, recently suffered what she's reported as a fall, as a result of which she's broken her leg. A GP referral, whom I've been seeing for some months, the woman is now finding it difficult to travel into the city centre. Consequently, I've agreed to go to her home once a fortnight on what would, normally, be my non-contact day. Making up the time for filing and paperwork shouldn't prove too difficult, and I'm anxious that she shouldn't miss out.

Trouble is, she lives on the far side of Exeter, almost as far south as where the M5 crosses the canal and river and, therefore, too far for me to cycle. As my car is currently out of action, having failed its MOT, I shall have to ride to the coach station and take a bus from there. It's a lengthy journey, but needs must.

I arrive mid-morning and make my way down one of the side streets to Daisy's home. It's easy to see why drugs have taken hold on this estate. Relatively affluent it might be, but there's precious little sense of community, and still less to occupy the needs of adolescents. I can imagine, only too well, what a stroll in the park it must be for the drug barons to fill the vacuum.

Daisy's home, like every other in the neighbourhood, lies behind net curtains. Shrouded in isolation. She's been referred to me by her doctor following a series of broken limbs alleged to have been accidents, and though she's been happy enough to attend appointments in my counselling rooms, it's clear that she's not comfortable with my visit. Aware of the curtain twitching that accompanies my arrival, I can understand why.

Nervous, eyes darting from side to side, she shuts the door hurriedly, concerned that nosy neighbours might put two and two together and make five; frightened that my presence might further jeopardise the tenuous relationships she has with husband and son.

It's not my job to persuade anyone to walk out of a situation like the one that Daisy is facing; my aim is only ever to help clients bring clarity to their problems; to see for themselves what options they might have to resolve them; and to regain sufficient self-esteem to make wise choices and activate decisions. Daisy sits before me wringing her hands, too uptight to benefit from my probing. The session does not go well, and eventually we agree that further meetings will have to wait until she has sufficiently recovered to make the journey into the city.

Two hours after arriving, and awash with tea, I board the bus back to the city centre. All being well, I should have plenty of time on my return to Cathedral Close to follow through on Julia's call, and for a good couple of hours of paperwork. Setting aside my disappointment at having failed to move my client on, I assume an air of cheerful nonchalance.

'Morning!'

Greeting the bus driver with a broad grin, I deposit my briefcase on the floor between my feet and rummage in my shoulder bag for my purse to pay my fare. Dough-faced, he is unresponsive. Knead him and prove him, stick him in the oven to cook, and he'd still fail to rise and show a little humour, I suspect. Deflated, I turn from collecting my ticket and begin to make my way up the aisle to take one of the few vacant seats at the back of the bus.

And then I see her. Bosomy Barbara from the Post Office. One time resident of my neck of the woods. Pete's new, younger model. His wife of three years, since he dumped me for her.

The bus lurches off. I almost lose my balance. I catch my breath. Of course! This bus route runs down to Topsham where Pete now lives in the cottage this woman inherited from some rich maiden aunt. Close to the point where the rivers Exe and Clyst meet in extravagant collaboration before pouring themselves into the sea. I bet it's worth a fortune. In fact, I'd go so far as to think that Pete . . .

No! I mustn't think like that. I spent a year in therapy when it all happened, precisely to rid myself of such thoughts.

Nevertheless, my blood runs cold. My heart races. My hands feel clammy as I grasp the pole to steady myself. I have to pass this woman, with her blonde hair and floral smock top, to reach my seat. Needless to hope she hasn't seen me. She looks me full in the eye before turning away. Recognition dawns. It's of no consolation that, if anything, she looks worse than I feel. A deep flush suffuses her face, then she blanches. Frantically, she scrabbles at her feet, lifts a large shopping bag onto her lap, and proceeds to investigate its contents.

It's clearly a ruse to distract attention from herself; to disguise herself - and her condition. But it's too late. I've already seen. And if my heart was racing when I first set eyes on her, it's now competing with Olympic gold medallist, Mo Farah. For what I've seen is the pits. Bad enough to know that Pete dumped me in favour of this woman. Worse still to see the outcome. The shopping bag on her lap does nothing to conceal it. Bosomy Barbara is pregnant.

Seated, tense and silent on the bus, I work out my strategy. The ethical principles of counselling and psychotherapy, as laid down by the British Association for Counselling & Psychotherapy, require practitioners to seek supervision for appropriate personal and professional support and development. Naturally, one of the first things I plan to do, on my return to Cathedral Close from Daisy's, is to ring my mentor, Grace.

But as I enter the building after an arduous cycle ride from the bus station, I encounter my colleague, Guy, on his way down the stairs. My state of agitation must be plain to see.

'Whatever's up?' The concern in his voice has me close to tears. 'Come on,' he continues, linking arms with me and turning me around. 'I'm taking you for a cuppa. No ifs. No buts.'

We cross The Green and head for The Royal Clarence Hotel. Built originally as Assembly Rooms in the 18th Century, it became England's first ever hotel soon after. Someone once told me that at the time it was under the management of a Frenchman and, given its continuing charm and elegance, I'm not surprised. Even in my current state of distress, I'm overawed by its splendour.

Leading me to a table in the window, Guy orders tea - Earl Grey, no less. With his untidy facial hair and tired clothing, his appearance seems completely out of place; yet, at the same time, he is clearly at ease. For the first time since I set eyes on Bosomy Barbara on the bus, I find a smile on my face.

'That's better,' he says. 'No need to talk unless you want to. But I have time on my hands. No clients beating down my door.'

'I've just been to see one,' I explain when the waiter has brought the tea, served in a silver pot, real china cups and saucers and - sneaked in for Guy's benefit, I suspect - a naughty plate of muffins.

'I thought Thursday was a non-contact day for you?' Guy indicates that he's happy for me to be mum.

'It is!' I reply, lifting the teapot while marvelling at how unused I am to the concept of wielding a tea-strainer and such posh receptacles. 'Long story.'

Guy nods, evidently unwilling to quiz me further; but the pain inside me swells to bursting point.

'I had to go and see a client on the other side of town. Terrible history. Shared the bus journey home with the wife of my ex. She's pregnant.'

To my horror I find that simply saying the word out loud has reduced me to tears. Through my mind flashes the whole scenario of her swelling stomach, the child developing in that secret place within her, her labour, the adoring expression on Pete's face as his baby comes into the world, its first steps, first words, first day at school... It's all too much. Way too much. The teapot wobbles in my hand and I bang it down harder than I intended on the table.

'I'm so sorry.'

Struggling to stifle my sobs in my hankie, I'm acutely aware of the embarrassment I must be causing Guy.

'Nothing to be sorry about,' he says, with such kindness he sets me off again. 'We have the lounge to ourselves. Everyone's out enjoying the sunshine.'

It's true. Mercifully, we're alone. When I have my tears under control, Guy passes me my cup.

'Drink up,' he says. 'There are medicinal properties in tea, said to calm frazzled nerves.'

I gulp down the hot scented liquid and Guy pours me a second cup.

'It was such a shock,' I explain, knowing that he's cognisant of the full story of my miscarriage and divorce years later. 'Silly, really, because I always knew it was me that was unable to conceive, and not Pete's fault. Why would I not expect Barbara to be pregnant? But it just seems so unfair.'

Guy purses his lips in empathy. 'It's hard when those who've wronged you cause you such distress. You're not alone in finding it unfair.'

'It's the thought of what might have been. What will never be. The child I can never cradle in my arms.'

I'm off again. Guy puts a hand on my arm, sits in silence until my tears are spent.

'They say time heals,' he says, offering me a muffin and tucking into one himself, 'but that's a fallacy. Grief - especially when it's for the loss of a child - is never done.'

There's a sadness in his voice that tells me he's not speaking as a counsellor-observer of such loss, but as one who has experienced it.

'Has it happened to you, too?'

He nods. 'We lost our little girl in the car accident that put Nancy in a wheelchair.'

Did I know that? Have I forgotten?

'I'm so sorry.'

He shakes his head. 'As I say, the grief is never done with. You learn to manage it. But it's like a hidden spring. Liable to burst forth when you least expect it. It's hardly surprising that your encounter this morning would be a trigger.'

Filling my lungs, I turn away and stare through the window. The cathedral looms large, its Gothic beauty supposedly a monument to the glory of God, but in reality, for people like me, more of a tribute to the ingenuity, dedication and skills of the craftsmen who brought it into being.

'It's not that I'm jealous,' I begin, then I see Guy looking at me over his glasses and retract. 'Well - yes I am, jealous. Why couldn't it have been me all those years ago?'

Guy wipes his mouth free of muffin crumbs, crumples his paper serviette, and drops it on his plate.

'Thing is, there are tens of thousands of men and women who will never have children, and millions more who have them and lose them. Often in horrific circumstances; wars, disease, violence.'

I lean forward to speak but Guy has anticipated my protest.

'I know. I know,' he says. 'I'm not putting that forward as a comfort, nor as a reprimand; merely as fact. In my day, we were brought up to count our blessings. Sometimes it's hard to find any. But it does help. I count the fact that Nancy still lives and loves me a blessing; the fact that I work in such a beautiful place and have you as a colleague; the fact that I know, from the feedback I receive, that my work has a positive effect in the lives of others.

'You are a person of great worth, Evie. Just as you are. With or without a partner or offspring. So don't let the enemy - the voices-off stage - tell you otherwise.'

I'm crying again, but they're tears of gratitude; gratitude that I have a friend in Guy; thankfulness that I have a life, and that it's a good and fruitful one. He's right. Years of therapy for myself, and training to help others have taught me that. It may not always feel like it, but I am a person of merit. And I won't let anyone tell me differently. Lifting my cup to my lips, I avail myself, again, of the medicinal qualities of the tea Guy has bought me.

CHAPTER FOUR

BACK IN THE office following afternoon tea at The Clarence with Guy, my mind is full of what he has had to say. It's all very well him applying the principles of transactional analysis, in which the fundamental value of each person is respected regardless of the behaviour they might display, but that behaviour still needs to be addressed. In reminding me that I'm a person of worth, he has shown me what's known as 'unconditional positive regard' and I'm grateful. Nevertheless, I need to acknowledge the negative thinking patterns that my encounter with Bosomy Barbara has induced, and activate change in myself. If I can't do it for me, I can't do it for Julia, Daisy, or any of my clients.

Abandoning the office work I'd planned, I return home early afternoon, settle myself on the sofa with Pumpkin purring on my lap, and ring my mentor, Grace. Fortunately, she's in, and she's willing to talk there and then. Or rather, to listen! I explain the circumstances of my visit to Daisy, my car being out of action, the necessity of making a bus journey, my encounter with Pete's new partner, Barbara.

'It was such a shock,' I finish. 'But I can't imagine why. Why would I not expect her to be expecting? It's absurd.'

Stroking Pumpkin's silky fur and eliciting signs of pleasure in her is therapy beyond compare for me. Her feline warmth on my lap warms my heart, too.

'The point is,' says Grace, 'how do you *feel* about it now that you know?'

From the sofa I can see out of my sitting room window, through the net curtain to my tiny garden and beyond, to the pavement. My neighbour's young son - a little younger than my daughter would have been now, had she lived - is learning to ride his bike, wobbling past in a manner that looks destined for disaster. I hold my breath as he disappears from view.

My vision shifts. Beside the fence that divides my garden from next door's, are the hollyhocks I planted the year I moved in, now flowering gloriously in the late afternoon sun. I'm reminded of when I was little, playing with my cousins in my parents' large, walled garden, where we used to collect the seed heads and marvel at their resemblance to minute circular sliced loaves. To my mind they were fairy bread; tiny miracles.

'The child in me wants to wallow in self-pity,' I tell Grace, my voice rising. 'To stamp my foot and shout and scream. It's not fair. Why her? Why not me? Why did I have to be childless?'

At the other end of the phone, Grace is silent. She knows me well enough to be aware that I will have conducted an internal debate in my head, in which I will have countered those feelings with other, more positive ones. I know, too, that she understands me well enough to allow me the freedom to acknowledge those feelings, because honesty is paramount to my healing.

Smothered emotional responses abounded in my family and, therefore, in my life script. The proviso instilled in me by my mother 'to be a good girl' dominated my thinking in such a way that the subconscious story I wrote for myself from infancy complied with this. In adulthood, with the help of therapy, I've broken free of the mould; I've moved to a place of autonomy.

Pumpkin jumps, suddenly, from my lap to the floor and proceeds to wash herself, licking her paw and smoothing it over the otherwise unreachable parts of her head. It's a picture of my cleansing: washing away the constraints of past expectations, of being my parents' daughter, Pete's wife, one of society's childless single women; revealing the woman I am today. *Allowing me to be the Me I'm meant to be,* I think.

'You know what,' I tell Grace, rising to my feet and peering out of the window to reassure myself that my neighbour's son remains intact,

'I'm okay! Had my pregnancy proceeded and my marriage remained intact, I would never have gone into therapy, and never had a career as a therapist.

'And just think! As the crazy mixed up kid that I was then, I'd have been sure to have passed all my hang-ups onto my child. The world is probably a better place because that didn't happen.'

The young cyclist reappears, no broken bones, still wobbling like mad but still aloft on his saddle.

'And I hope,' I continue, 'well, I like to think that the person I now am, as a result of what happened to me, is a force for good in the lives of others. My clients. The Daisy's and Julia Worth's of the world.'

Grace voices her agreement and I turn away from the window. Bringing her ablutions to an end, Pumpkin trots across the room, tail held high, the look on her face as she turns towards me one of complete confidence that I'll come running, open the door for her and let her out. Oh, well, I think, bidding Grace goodbye, being slave to my cat is one up on any of the other nomenclatures with which I once was labelled. Hastily, I run to do the bidding of my mistress.

Friday morning brings a deluge of rain, plus a phone call from the garage to tell me that the bill to bring my car up to road-worthy standards will run into the high hundreds. I've no option but to accept both situations, and don my waterproofs for the journey to work by bike.

It's a hard slog battling against the elements, first freewheeling down to the barracks, then the muscle crunching strive uphill to the city centre. A quick glance at my reflection in the shop window as I push my bike down Martins Lane tells me I resemble the proverbial drowned rat. My only consolation is that Guy looks a bigger drip than I when we arrive together at our counselling rooms in Cathedral Close.

Wonderful location that it is, there are no parking facilities nearby and he's had a fair old walk in to work from one of the municipal car parks. But it gives us a laugh as I apply the hairdryer I keep at work to our lank locks, clothes, and his beard.

'There's something rather surreal about watching the steam rise from your head,' I tell him. 'Aren't you worried? Could be that brain box of yours evaporating.'

'Nope,' he responds, with humour. 'What you see before you is the George Stephenson of brain power, fuelling up and raring to go.'

I'd forgotten that Guy is a locomotive nerd. I blow the hairdryer in his face before switching it off.

'Well it's not a modest one, that's for sure,' I tease him.

The rest of the day passes uneventfully. Julia Worth is my third and last appointment, due to a cancellation. Looking over my notes in the moments before her arrival, I see she's told me enough about her marriage and herself for her husband's manipulative behaviour and her guilt complex to be glaringly obvious.

'Yes, I do feel guilty a lot of the time,' Julia tells me when I begin to delve. 'That's why I tried ringing you earlier in the week to see if you could give me some advice. Sorry. I know I shouldn't presume upon your time.'

I wave her apology aside.

'I'm so undeserving of all that Carl does for us,' Julia continues. 'And I know he deserves my gratitude. I promised to love, honour and obey. To be a good wife,' she shrugs. 'So I just try to get on with it.'

Despite the rain - how do some women get away with it - she looks immaculate. Her hair shimmers in the overhead light which the dullness of the day has necessitated, while mine fizzes and bubbles around me. Her black slacks and killer high heels are in stark contrast to my creased trousers and loafers. But these are mere observations on my part, and I feel no envy; only a fervent hope that by the time we finish, be it weeks or months from now, she will have been set free to be the person she was meant to be.

'What do you understand by the concept of submission?' I ask, following up on her statement.

She looks surprised, a small frown on her face, as if she's never thought it through. 'Well,' she looks down at her hands, twists the wedding ring on her finger. 'When you make your marriage vows you promise to be obedient, don't you.'

'So submission and obedience are synonymous?'

'Yes. I'd say they are.'

'What about obedience and capitulation? Defeat?'

Julia frowns, clearly uncomfortable with the way this is going. I try a different tack.

'I'm not trying to catch you out, Julia,' I explain, gently. 'We're just trying to establish how far submission and obedience go. For instance, does it mean that if your husband asked you to steal you'd do so?'

She laughs, her nerves jangling. 'Of course not! That would be breaking the law. Carl knows that. And the ten commandments.'

I'm no believer, myself, and religion plays no part in counselling practice, but I am aware of the basic tenets of Christianity.

'Supposing he simply asked you to falsify a tax return?'

'No!' Julia shakes her head. 'I wouldn't do it. And neither would he.'

'What about if the two of you dined out together and he put it down to business expenses?'

Bingo! I can see by the look of confusion on Julia's face that I've got her thinking.

'That has happened,' she admits, with a certain reluctance. 'Frequently.'

'And how have you dealt with it?'

Julia hesitates.

'Whatever you tell me, I'm not going to stand in judgement or condemn you for it,' I assure her.

She sighs. 'I suppose, until recently, it didn't even occur to me think about it.'

'And now?'

Julia hesitates. 'It makes me very uncomfortable. I told Carl how I felt, recently. We ended up having a terrible row. Shouting. Name calling. It was awful. So not what I want from my marriage!'

I smile, full of sympathy. It's clear that this is a point of contention between Julia and her husband. A difference in values. A change that has manifested itself as a result of - what? Julia's friendship with the Hilary woman? A recognition of the effects of her convent school discipline? The occasional morning service? Whatever it is, I feel sure that this is probably at the root of Carl's sense of betrayal. I lean back in my chair and cross one leg over the other.

'Supposing I tell you that we all operate from three different ego states, Julia: Parent, Adult, Child. You and I are talking Adult to Adult. But if I started speaking to you in a Parent ego state that elicited a Child-like response from you, perhaps as -'

'But Carl doesn't do that. He's a good provider. For me and the children. I'm lucky to have so much.'

I'm aware of the clock ticking on the mantelpiece and that Julia's time will soon be up. What's more important, though, is that she understands what she has just done. I sit forward, clasping my hands in front of me and resting my elbows on my thighs so that I can look up into her down turned face. She's fighting it, but I know it's beginning to sink in.

If I'm right, Carl is taking the Parent role at all times in their relationship in order to elicit just the sort of response that Julia has manifested here, today. Having, for years, been the Nurturing Parent, in which he is the provider, his expectation is that she will operate in Child mode, the good little girl syndrome, in order to boost his ego.

Her new allegiance to a different set of values, gained from - Hilary? church? - has set that awry. From what I've seen and heard from Julia, my guess is that while continuing to operate in Parent mode, Carl has now switched to Critical Parent state. We're back to the scenario of his feeling that his authority has been usurped by Julia's church allegiance and that he has to regain authority.

Julia lifts her head and looks me full in the face. I sit back in my chair. I can see in the depths of her dark brown eyes the dawning of recognition.

Julia finished icing the cake she'd made earlier and stood back to inspect her handiwork. Tomorrow, Friday, would be Josh's sixteenth birthday. The six days since she'd last seen Evie Adams had passed uneventfully, but with another appointment next day, she wanted to be sure she had everything ready well in advance. She wiped her fingers on a damp cloth and turned the cake around to view it from the other side.

It was a chocolate sponge, large and rectangular in shape; enough to feed the family, plus Josh's three closest friends, who were going to be staying over, before Carl took them all on to a motorbike scramble on the Saturday, somewhere near Honiton.

Julia nodded to herself, pleased with the result of her efforts. Using a white sugar paste icing, she had carefully rolled it out to cover the entire cake. On top of that, she'd placed a similar layer of rolled black icing, but with a rectangle, nearly the size of the cake, cut out of it, so that it formed a frame around the white icing.

Onto this white background, she'd carefully piped a number of small, square, coloured images. Top left was a green one with a white cloud; next to that was a white one with black figures representing Josh's date of birth; and next to that a yellow one with ruled lines. Others included a clock, a tiny board game, and a bookcase. Along the bottom were three blue squares, one of which contained a small white envelope, plus a red square with white music symbols. They were too small to add the words that should be there, but she hoped it would be obvious to all that the cake represented an iPad.

Abi, her arm now out of a sling since Julia had taken her to see their local GP, had come across the cake that morning before school and asked about it.

'You're not to tell Josh,' Julia replied. 'We're giving him a mini iPad for his birthday. Daddy's picking it up on his way home from work this evening.'

'Ooh, he'll love that,' said Abi. 'Does that mean that I get to have one when I'm sixteen?'

'Cheeky!' Julia said, affectionately. 'I thought you'd be wanting a prom frock, or a trip to a beauty salon?'

Remembering the look of delight on Abi's face, Julia felt a thrill of pleasure. She was so fortunate to have such a lovely daughter. The boys, too, of course, though over the last year they'd been steadily growing away from her. It was a natural enough phenomenon, she supposed, but it troubled her to see how little respect they had for her these days. Their complete disregard for her authority was becoming ever more flagrant, and Carl seemed to do little, or nothing, to support her.

'They're okay!' he argued when she again tried to bring up the subject of Josh's school trip. 'Nothing wrong with them. Don't want them to grow up being wimps, do you? They're just learning to be men.'

Julia wasn't so sure. Were arrogance and misogyny desirable aspects of manhood? Not in her book. And where did this collaboration between her husband and son leave her?

She wasn't a hundred per cent sure that she'd understood, but Evie Adams had seemed to imply that Carl was behaving like a parent with her. Being a figure of authority. Expecting her to fall into line with unquestioning childlike obedience. Given that he didn't do that with the boys, did that mean that he saw them as equals? And did it follow that they, too, saw themselves in parent role to her role as child?

Shaking her head at the recalled discussion she'd had with Carl about the boys learning to be men, she sincerely hoped not. She'd met men like that before: arrogant and self opinionated. She'd no wish for her boys to end up like that. But what could she do to avert it? It seemed pretty well inevitable that your children would play one off against the other if parents didn't present a united front.

Frustrated with the enormity of the problem, she took the cake out to the cool room, off the kitchen, and hid it in a cupboard. And only just in time! As she emerged, Josh and Nathan appeared in the kitchen, threw down their school bags, and made for the fridge.

'You're back early,' Julia retorted. 'I've only just finished my lunch.'

Their ties were askew, the top buttons of their shirts were undone while the tails hung outside their trousers and they looked thoroughly dishevelled.

'Burst pipe,' said Nathan, his voice and face full of childish excitement. 'Swamped our classroom and the canteen. Gushing out it was.'

'A burst pipe in the summer?' Julia found it hard to believe.

Josh kicked the fridge door closed and turned, a can of coke in his hand.

'Seems some pathetic nerd with a pickaxe decided to dig up the friggin' playground and hit the mains,' he said.

'What?' Julia felt faint. Was this a copycat American school murderer wielding a pickaxe?

'He's kidding, Mum,' said Nathan, heading for the cool room. 'Have you got any cookies?'

'Not in there!' Julia said, sharply.

Nathan turned, a mischievous grin on his face. With his light brown hair, fair complexion and rounded features, he was much less like his father than Josh; more like Julia's side of the family, in fact.

''What are you hiding, Mum?' he said. 'Come on Josh. Let's go look.'

'No! Please don't.'

'Something to do with Josh's birthday tomorrow?' Nathan asked. 'Come on Mum, what have you bought him? You haven't hidden his new bike in there?'

Julia frowned. 'Bike? What bike?'

Furious, Josh turned on Nathan. 'I told you not to say anything.' He threw his empty coke can at his brother.

'Stop it, you two!' said Julia. 'It's only a cake in there. But - yes - it is for tomorrow, and no, I don't want you two tucking into it today. Understood?'

'Okay! Okay! Calm down,' said Josh, in condescending tones that sounded, to Julia, just like his father's.

Unwilling to engage in an altercation with the soon-to-be-birthday boy, she ignored his rudeness, stooping to pick up the empty coke can from the floor to hide her concern. Behind her, the boys skulked off to their rooms, glowering, and she was left with no explanation for the supposed burst pipe, their early return from school, nor for the enigma of the 'new bike'. Taking a cloth from beneath the sink, she wiped the floor clean where drops of coke had been spilled. Then she busied herself washing up her icing equipment and clearing up the kitchen before Carl returned.

It was during a visit to the men's room at the Golf Club that evening, when Carl realised he was going to be well and truly late home for supper. Hardly surprising, he thought, though he supposed he should have rung Julia. He pushed his fingers through his hair in an attempt to brush the thought aside.

If he was honest, he was finding his wife's association with Hilary Bankster an ever-increasing source of irritation. An internet search earlier in the day had revealed something of the woman's background. A highly successful teaching career in Canada had preceded an equally rewarding decade in management. Until her return to the UK two years earlier and her appointment as Chairman to the Board of Governors at Abi's school.

But it was the omissions he found most telling. There was nothing pre-emigration. Nothing to link her to those earlier events in Wales. Nothing to impugn her reputation. It was as if her infamy had been airbrushed from her CV.

Standing before the mirror as he washed his hands, Carl squinted at his reflection. Was his drive the result of his father's machinations, he wondered? Or despite them? To whom or to what did he owe his achievements? A determination to prove himself better than others? He nodded, affirmingly. From this angle he could see signs of silver at his temples. He dipped his head the better to see them. They added, rather than detracted, he hoped, to the image of success. Straightening his tie, he went in search of the others.

He'd spent most of the afternoon filling in some of the finer details of his proposed expansion into South Wales, and discussing strategy with his business manager, Frank. Naturally, Lucy had been there to take notes, and at his suggestion the three of them had then called in at the Golf Club to toast their endeavours with a bottle of 2004 Moet & Chandon. It was, he told himself, a show of appreciation; an act of bonding.

The Golf Club was his domain. Reeking of the old Imperial order of his grandfather's era, it was somewhere he was well-known and respected; somewhere he wined and dined lesser clients, those who didn't quite merit the five-star treatment. Aware that doing so served the dual purpose of making his employees feel valued, plus reminding them, graphically, of their boss's status in society, he'd taken Frank and one or two others there as his guests, from time to time. But never Lucy.

He frowned at the omission. There was something very agreeable about entering the bar with a good-looking young woman at your side, and she was certainly a head-turner, no doubt about it. He nodded to acquaintances seated in groups around the room, and exchanged a few words with closer friends, before leading his guests to a table.

When the waiter had poured the champagne, they drank one another's health, and congratulated each other on their accomplishments and their altruism in bringing employment to a deprived area. At last, realising how late it was, he made a move.

'Can't stop,' he apologised, draining his glass. 'I need to get off.'

They left the building together and walked outside to the car park.

'Sorry to break up the party,' Carl said, shaking Frank by the hand. 'I have a birthday present to collect for Josh. Taking him to the Devon Classic Scramble on Saturday.'

'Enjoy!' said Lucy. She fished in her bag and brought out a small gift-wrapped package, which she pressed into Carl's hand. 'For Josh,' she said. 'Wish him happy birthday from me.'

Carl felt touched. Lucy had been with him for a couple of years now and had excelled in keeping him up to date with personal events, as well as his business appointments. This, however, was the first time she'd sent a gift for one of the kids. Poor girl. Thirty-something and unmarried. In the wake of a broken long-term relationship, he thought it remarkably kind of her to bother. Surely, even in front of Frank, it warranted a peck on the cheek without raising an eyebrow?

'That's very kind of you,' he said, leaning forward. Her skin felt silky warm; he squeezed her arm; whispered his thanks. Tall and lithe, she was a natural blonde, in stark contrast to Julia's small frame and dark hair. She was, also, a woman after his own heart: a go-getter in a supportive, not competitive, way; an Alan Sugar apprentice par excellence.

A sudden sharp shower terminated the farewells and Carl's ruminations as each dashed for their respective cars. It wasn't until he reached home, after calling in to pick up Josh's present, that the comparison in demeanour really came home to him.

'Coo-ee,' he called, summoning the family to the back door as he stepped into the kitchen from the garage. 'I'm back.'

As expected, the boys had been watching for his arrival from their bedrooms. With a wild flurry of adolescent feet pounding down the stairs, Josh appeared in the hall, loudly demanding the presence of his sibs.

'Quick! Quick! Dad's home with my birthday present.'

Julia emerged from the family room.

'Well you're not having it tonight, are you?' she said as he ran past her. 'I haven't even wrapped it yet. And your birthday's not until tomorrow.'

'Don't think you'll be able to wrap this in paper, Mum,' said Nathan, running past her down the hall.

'What's happening?' Abi asked, lagging behind the others.

Carl stood waiting at the door until they were all assembled in the kitchen.

'Bah boom!' he announced, and flung open the door between kitchen and garage. 'Happy birthday for tomorrow, Josh.'

Shiny and new, the 50cc motorcycle gleamed in the fluorescent light from the garage. Josh, closely followed by Nathan, rushed forward, went to mount the bike, then hesitated.

'Can I?' he asked, a look of pleading on his face.

'Course you can,' said Carl. 'It's yours.'

'Oh, Dad!'

Josh flung his arms around Carl's neck, before turning and seating himself on the bike. In that brief moment of embrace with his son, Carl looked across the room to where Abi, mouth wide open, stood with her mother. His lip curled. The look of confusion and anger in Julia's eyes filled him with triumph. Immediately, it was replaced with a sense of fury. Enough to make him want to turn on his heel and go back to the sweet, silky warmth he'd encountered in the golf club car park.

CHAPTER FIVE

JULIA SLEPT THAT night in the spare room. The intimacy of sharing a bed with Carl was too much for her to bear. She shuddered at the thought. Where once she had felt that she must be at fault, that Carl must have good reason for his dissatisfaction with her, she now felt only anger.

How dare he! How dare he go behind her back. How dare he give their son - the child she had carried in her womb, brought into this world, and nurtured thereon in - what she could only think of as a lethal weapon. With the power to maim. To kill himself. Perhaps to kill others.

She thought back over the evening. The look of triumph in Carl's grey eyes when Josh had thrown his arms around him had not escaped her. It shrieked of power. Of putting her in a place of helplessness. What had he said when she'd raised the fact that the gift they'd agreed upon had been an iPad? He'd addressed himself not to her, but to Josh.

'You'll have to humour Mum, Josh, and take care. I told you she wouldn't like it. That she'd worry.'

Too right Mum didn't like it!

Josh had had the grace to look slightly ashamed. 'Sorry, Mum. But it is the best present ever, thank you.'

Why was he thanking her? Had Carl implied that she was party to this, albeit reluctantly?

'Are you allowed to ride it on the road?' Abi asked, her tone of voice echoing Julia's incredulity. 'Won't you have to take a test?'

'It's only a 50cc-er,' Nathan replied. 'I'm gonna get one when I'm a bit older.'

'You can ride it at events,' Josh explained, running his hands lovingly over the red handlebars and wing mirrors. 'Dad says he'll get me some lessons and a provisional licence, but you can't go on the road 'til they know you're okay. Isn't that right, Dad?'

'You have to complete a CBT course - compulsory basic training,' Carl replied.

'And then he can go on the road? At sixteen?' Julia felt faint.

'Yes, once he's got through the course. But he'll still only have a P licence until he's seventeen, and he can't go above thirty miles an hour.'

Fast enough to kill yourself, thought Julia, especially if you factor in the combined speed of other vehicles in a contra direction. She hugged herself, rubbing her arms in the chill air from the garage and moved away from the open door.

'He can't take me on the back, either,' Nathan said, screwing up his face. 'But he's gonna let me have a go off-road. Aren't you Josh?'

Julia caught Josh's eye before he looked away, clearly embarrassed.

'We'll see,' he replied.

'Josh! You said you would. You promised.'

The sound of Nathan's voice, petulant and immature, struck Julia like a wet fish slapped hard against her face. She was about to make some retort when the telephone rang. She picked up the handset. It was for Josh, of course; his paternal grandmother. He took the phone from her and turned away. It was immediately apparent from his excitement that she had been in the know about the bike, had, perhaps, contributed to it in some way.

And so, too, of course, had Nathan been in on the secret. It dawned on her, suddenly! His comment about the bike being hidden in the cool room earlier that afternoon had made that clear. She felt herself become tearful. It appeared that only she and Abi had been kept in the dark.

Unable to tackle Carl in front of the children, she'd turned on her heel and gone upstairs to run a bath. Abi had come looking for her, but by that time, as if in an attempt to wash away the past, she was steeping in hot water and fragrant bubbles. She stayed there until the water was too cool to be comfortable, until her skin was beginning to feel like that of an over-ripe peach. Blow Carl! Let him dish out the meal she'd cooked for him and the children. Let him worry about their table manners. About clearing up afterwards. About the children's homework.

When she emerged from the en-suite into the bedroom, clad only in a white towelling gown, Carl was waiting for her.

'Come on love. You know I was never wholehearted about an iPad for Josh.'

He reached out to pull her into his arms. Furious that he should think it so easy, she brushed him off.

'How could you? Without even discussing it with me?'

'I knew you'd worry. I was trying to shield you.'

'To shield me? I'm not a child! I'm a responsible adult. Don't you think that as Josh's parents we should have talked this through. Adult to adult?'

'What's the point?' He matched her tone. 'Whatever I suggest, you don't want to know.'

'That is not true. And you know it.'

'You have no interest in anything I have to say. Besides, you just want to mollycoddle the boys.'

Wise, now, thanks to Evie Adams, Julia stood her ground. 'I want them to grow into responsible young men.'

Carl snorted. 'And what sort of young men would that be? Namby pambies? Mummy's boys? Pie-in-the-sky wimps?'

'The sort of young men that show some respect for the women in their lives.'

'Well heaven help them if they end up with the sort of woman I got landed with.'

The row had gone on and on, getting nowhere and ending only when Abi, red-faced from crying, came to the bedroom door and begged them to stop.

'Tell your mother, not me,' Carl snapped. 'All I did was to fulfil my son's dream of owning and riding a motorbike. You'd think I'd given him a poison chalice. Or been an absentee father who was too busy indulging himself to be bothered to think of his boy.'

'Poison chalice?' Julia nodded. 'It might as well have been. The way you put me down in front of our children. It has to stop.'

'Stop it, Mum,' Abi yelled. 'Stop it Dad.'

Carl turned on his heel and left the room. A few moments later, Julia heard the car start up and head down the drive. She turned to comfort Abi, but Abi was having none of it. Sickened with the way things had gone, Julia dragged herself across the landing to the spare room, threw a sheet and duvet on the mattress, locked the door and climbed into bed.

It's Friday, I've finished my lunch and am trying to do a little work-related housework - filing and dusting - before my afternoon sessions begin. Armed with the healing my teatime chat with Guy brought me, following my encounter with Bosomy Barbara a fortnight ago, I'm feeling relaxed and ready to deal with Julia Worth's visit, whatever it may bring.

For some reason, she missed her last appointment. Just didn't turn up. Instead of a phone call, all I received was a handwritten card of apology a few days later, which promised an explanation the following Friday. Today.

'I'm so sorry,' she says when she arrives in my counselling room and presents me with a bunch of white lilies, from the florist, no less! 'It was unforgivably rude of me to leave you dangling like that.'

I shake my head, grateful for her unexpected kindness and generosity, but wondering where on earth I'm going to find a vase.

'Not at all. I knew you'd have good reason.'

I show Julia in and excuse myself to go to the tiny kitchen on the landing, fill a jug with water, stick the lilies in, and return with them to my room.

'Of course, nothing's really unforgivable,' Julia says having clearly been pondering her statement in my absence. 'Are you a believer?'

With a name like Evie Adams? I think not! Weren't they two of the most notorious sinners of all time? A bubble of laughter wells up inside me. Hastily, I suppress it.

''Fraid not.' I place the vase of flowers on the mantelpiece between us. 'Not that I'm ignorant of such things. Nor am I prejudiced in any way.'

Is that true? With my back to Julia, I frown. I suppose, if I'm honest, I have my own views of creation and the meaning of life. Vague, unformed and unobtrusive though they are, they could hardly be said to be compatible with church stuff. I just take care not to allow them to influence my counselling techniques. Seating myself, as usual, with my back to the window so that Julia's face is not in shadow, I take out my notebook and client file.

'So what happened last week?' I ask.

'I'm afraid I was in rather a state and wasn't up to going anywhere.'

With remarkable composure and detail, she recounts the story of the motorbike Carl has purchased as a birthday gift for Josh, stressing that it was behind her back; the ensuing row with Carl; and Abi's distress.

'The thing is,' she concludes, 'next day, when I was on my own in the house and had time to think, I realised that what you'd said the week before made sense. Not that I could remember it all. But I think it was something about acting as adults. Or as parent and child?'

She regards me, earnestly, seeking confirmation, and a sense of satisfaction floods through me. No guarantees of where this will end, but now, five weeks into therapy, I feel we're beginning to get somewhere.

'It's not about *acting* a part,' I reply, picking up on her interpretation. 'More about learned behaviour. For instance, the Parent state is ingrained in us by the adults we encounter when we're children. So that's our own parents, aunts, uncles, and grandparents, as well as our teachers, neighbours - any figure of authority, really. We become conditioned to interact with others in certain ways. Thus, depending upon our conditioning, we might find ourselves adopting a nurturing habit, or an authoritarian habit.'

Julia fidgets in her seat. For the first time since she began counselling sessions with me, she looks alert and interested.

'I think that's what Carl's been doing,' she says. 'He talks down to me all the time. As if I'm a nobody. As if I'm one of his minions. He puts on this act of being the Big Boss.'

Julia stares into space, lost in thought.

'As I say, Julia, it's not an act. It's learned behaviour. And it's relevant to us all. We're all conditioned by the adults around us when we're children.'

Julia puts her head on one side the better to think through what I've said, and for a moment her face is obscured behind a veil of long dark hair. Eventually, she straightens up and says, looking into the space behind me,

'I'm not sure my childhood has had that much of an influence on my behaviour as an adult. My parents, particularly my stepfather, were very strong on discipline - hence the convent school I told you about. I never seemed to meet the standards they required of me, so I spent most of my childhood being grounded, or having my pocket money stopped.'

She refocuses, looking at me intently with a slight frown on her face.

'I was determined I wasn't going to be like that when I started a family. Without falling into the trap of going completely the opposite way to my parents and not meting out any discipline, I wanted to be approachable to my children. In a way that my parents weren't to me.'

A smile hovers on my face. 'I can understand that. But don't you see, Julia, your childhood conditioning *did* have an effect on your adult behaviour. It made you determined not to follow suit. Instead of the Authoritarian Parent, you became the Nurturing Parent.'

'Oh! So you mean -' a look of enlightenment dawns in Julia's eyes. 'You don't actually become a mirror image of your parents then?'

'Not necessarily.'

'But rebelling against what they stood for is still a manner of conditioning?'

'Exactly! The values that were instilled into you as a child may influence your behaviour as an adult in either a positive or negative way, but the fact remains that they do have an effect. You can't be indifferent to them.'

We continue to talk around the subject until a sudden flurry of rain beats against the window pane behind me. The hum of human voices rising from the Green begins to disperse as the people gathered there run to seek shelter. I rise and cross the room to shut the window.

'So what about the Child and Adult?' Julia asks, behind me.

I turn, and make a face. 'I think our time is up. Besides, you've enough to think about for this week. I'd suggest you keep what you've learned to yourself, for now, and next week we'll follow through on the other ego states.'

Julia looks disappointed.

'Just be an observer,' I advise her as she stands and pulls on her jacket. 'See what you can glean from the way you habitually behave in response to those around you. And the way they respond to you.'

'Perhaps I could keep a journal?' Julia's face lights up. 'Record some of my observations?'

'Excellent idea,' I agree, showing her to the door. 'See you next week.'

Next week turns out to be that evening!

Making only a meagre living from my regular counselling, I'm fortunate enough to be able to add the income from one corporate client who pays me a retainer so that I'm on hand for any emotional catastrophe or work-related blips that might arise among his employees. In addition to that, I'm expected to put on a seminar once a year focussing on such matters as better management skills or, perhaps, improving client relationships and customer services.

Bruce is a pretty philanthropic sort of bloke and, over the years, we've struck an acquaintanceship that surpasses that of a mere business associate. As a result, he's included me in the works' Christmas party in the past, as well as in one or two meetings among senior management, where the professional opinion of a therapist might be deemed valuable. Of course, it's probably all tax-deductible, but that's the cynic in me speaking out of turn. The *real me* appreciates the trust conferred on me by my client, I remind myself. The *real me* is exhilarated by the opportunity to enjoy a more up-market ambience than exists *chez moi!*

This Friday, I've been invited to the Golf and Country Club to be wined and dined as part of an elite management group looking into various aspects of expansion. I'm aware, as I don my best frock, purchased from one of the High Street charity shops, that this evening might, also, involve waist expansion and necessitate the letting out of seams. Or more probably, knowing my absence of sewing skills, the purchase of another charity shop frock.

Alighting from the taxi I've had to book, my car still being off-road, I take in the grand portico entrance beneath which I'm standing, and the stucco Georgian style building stretching away on either side, and thank heaven that I was unable to come under my own steam. The taxi will be booked to expenses with Bruce so will cost me nothing. By comparison, my clapped out Ford Fiesta would have cost me my street-cred among the elite company I shall be keeping. Instantly, I give myself a mental slap on the wrist. Life may not have given me much in the way of material assets, but this way of thinking is not at all in line with my usual courting of contentment.

It's not until I've met up with the rest of my party and we're seated in the opulent splendour of the light and airy bar, that I set eyes on Julia. She has her back to me, which means I have the freedom to study her, and boy, what a vision stands before me. Her hair is swept up in a chignon, revealing a long white neck, and she is the picture of elegance.

Chatting with another couple at the bar, she appears to be husbandless herself. Casting my eyes back and forth down the length of the room, I can see only groups of men, or couples. Then behind one of the arches that divides the currently empty restaurant area from the bar,

I spy what I take to be a clandestine meeting *à deux*.

Out of sight of Julia and her companions, indeed most of the people waiting to dine, a man, a ubiquitous tall dark and handsome Mr Darcy-type, is whispering what I can only suppose are sweet nothings to the tall, slim blonde at his side. Almost instantly they part, with a soft kiss on the cheek. But not before a large bouquet of red roses has changed hands. Clutching them behind his back, Mr D then swivels on his heel and makes his way back to the bar.

Julia Worth looks up as he approaches. I'm holding my breath. No! But yes. Involuntarily, my breath is expelled. It's clear, from the body language I can discern and the fact that the flowers are proffered to Julia, that Mr Darcy is, in fact, Mr Carl Worth. So that's the way the wind is blowing!

'What are your thoughts, Evie?'

Bruce's voice breaks through my reverie. With what I hope is admirable professional aplomb, I turn back to the matter in hand.

'Well clearly, if expansion is going to mean relocating personnel, it would make sense for me to talk with the wives and families beforehand, in order to obviate any major emotional disruption.'

Everyone nods in agreement. Then the waiter arrives with the menu, while on the periphery of my vision, I see Julia and Carl being shown to a table.

The moment Julia reached home, she looked out a vase, a shimmering crystal *objet d'art* she'd inherited from her grandmother, and filled it with water.

'They're beautiful,' she said to Carl, removing the bouquet from the pastel coloured tissue paper and cellophane in which they were wrapped. 'Thank you. I thought you'd forgotten.'

Carl hovered at the kitchen door.

'Would I forget our wedding anniversary?' he asked, head down and penitent, looking like a retriever that had been reprimanded.

'It's actually on Sunday, not today,' said Julia. 'Hence the lack of anything from me as yet.'

Carl nodded. 'I know! Just thought I'd show my keenness by being premature.'

'I thought dining at the Golf Club with Frank and his wife was just a business arrangement,' said Julia, cutting stems and placing the roses in the vase.

'Well there you are, then. Surprise, surprise!'

'Thank you!' Julia smiled, turned from her flower arranging, crossed the room and gave Carl a peck on the cheek. It was clear that despite, or perhaps because of, the upset over Josh's birthday present, he was making an effort, and she appreciated it.

Following her last session with Evie, she was more determined than ever not to allow Carl to rile her. Consequently, although business had figured quite highly in conversation between Carl's manager and himself, she'd taken it as simply par for the course. She and Frank's wife had chatted between themselves while the men talked shop, and Carl had not only ordered champagne, he'd proposed a toast 'to my beautiful wife'. All in all, they'd enjoyed a thoroughly convivial evening.

The surprise celebration had been surpassed only by Julia's surprise at encountering Evie Adams at the Golf Club. Somehow, perhaps because of Evie's habitually drab appearance that did nothing for the prettiness that lay hidden in the soft round contours of her face, she'd never imagined her frequenting the sort of places at which she and Carl wined and dined.

It was only as she'd made her way down to the dining room at Carl's side, that she'd seen Evie. She was with a group of men - another surprise - and it looked as if she was holding forth and they were willing listeners. Julia felt her cheeks burn and her footstep falter. Hoping that Carl would be unaware of her discomfort, she passed swiftly by, thankful that even though Evie was facing her and couldn't have failed to see her, she had kept on talking and didn't even glance in their direction. When Evie's party eventually came into the dining room, Julia noticed that she sat so that she was facing away from Carl and herself. Consequently, it was only during a chance meeting in the Ladies' Room, that they exchanged greetings.

'Celebration?' Evie asked, applying soap to her hands from the Evelyn & Crabtree dispenser when she emerged from the cubicle.

'Wedding anniversary on Sunday,' Julia replied. 'Thank you for ignoring me. It might have been difficult to explain you away.'

Evie smiled. 'No probs,' she said. 'I'm here with a client who's paying me an exorbitant fee, so I owe him all due attention. Lovely flowers, by the way.'

'They were! I had to ask the bar staff if they'd put them in water until we finished dining. Mustn't forget them when we go home.'

They'd then bade one another farewell and returned separately to their respective tables.

It didn't strike Julia until she was clearing the breakfast things on Monday morning when Carl was back at work and the children at school, that there was something rather odd about Carl's producing an expensive florist's bouquet at the Golf Club. How had he smuggled them in? She'd seen nothing in the car, and he could hardly have hidden them in the boot because he'd have had to go outside again, to the car park, to retrieve them.

She shook her head. Perhaps he'd had them delivered direct to the Golf Club to add to the surprise? Tucking a couple of packets of cereal under her arm, she carried them and the dirty bowls across to the worktop to be put away in the larder and dishwasher respectively. Whatever sleight of hand had been required to magic the bouquet into being, it had more than achieved its purpose, she thought.

CHAPTER SIX

THE SCHOOL TERM draws to a close with the uncharacteristically English forecast of a long hot summer still to come. Standing by my desk so I can consult my diary, Julia tells me that with the advent of the school holidays the following week she will be unable to attend counselling sessions quite so frequently. Besides, she informs me, apart from the incident over Josh's birthday present which was something she now realises she has no option but to accept, her relationship with Carl seems to have improved somewhat.

'You saw the flowers he bought me,' she says on what will probably be our last meeting until the autumn school term. 'And it turned out that what I thought was going to be a business meeting with his manager was, in fact, a surprise anniversary celebration.'

Setting aside my concern for the eternal naivety I encounter among the wives of errant husbands, I smile and murmur a spurious but expected congratulations. If she's right and Carl has, indeed, turned a corner then I'm delighted. If, however, the evidence of my own eyes proves correct, then Julia is to be pitied. Only time will tell which.

What remains key to the whole problem, in my opinion, is the Hilary enigma, plus Carl's history with his father. But how to get answers on either subject when Carl refuses to throw any enlightenment on them and Julia remains in the dark? That's the real mystery.

I look up from my diary. Julia's complexion has taken on a new sheen, and her softly bronzed limbs, clad in short skirt and strappy top, shimmer as she seats herself.

'So, it sounds as if you two are getting along better,' I begin.

'Much better!' she responds, leaning forward as if to emphasise her point. 'I've been looking into marriage enrichment, reading up on it, and talking to one of Hilary's friends who sets up groups around the country. Carl refuses to contemplate going to a meeting, but I've been trying to practice some of its concepts on my own.'

I'm puzzled. 'That must be difficult given that the basis of marriage enrichment is about feedback and affirmation between the couple.'

Julia nods. 'Yes. But I've been trying to do what that old song says and *accentuate the positive, eliminate the negative* - you know the Bing Crosby / Bette Midler one.'

'And you think that's working, despite being somewhat one-sided?'

'Oh, without doubt. The more I find to be positive about, the better Carl responds.'

My brain is whirring. Unable to share in Julia's excitement, I remind myself to make a note later, in Julia's file. Is there some sneaky reason for Carl's apparent change of heart? Or is he merely satisfied that Julia's Child mode - the good little girl - conforms to his expectation?

'And have you been taking on board what we talked about in respect of submission?' I ask.

'Oh, yes. Because I realise now, since you pointed it out, that being a good wife doesn't mean I have to live in Carl's pocket, or agree with everything he says and does. I still have to be true to myself. To my opinions.'

Julia's features relax. I suspect she's ticking off the questions I'm asking her as if they're tests she's passed; giving herself what, in the trade, we call 'positive strokes'.

'Actually,' Julia continues, 'from what I've read, and heard from Hilary and her friend, I think the idea of being two whole individuals who are united - rather than two halves - underpins the whole concept of marriage enrichment. I remember you said something along those lines. That you have to build some separate activities into your marriage or it becomes stale.'

'Absolutely!' I nod. 'You have to keep your relationship fresh.'

Julia's face is flushed with enthusiasm. 'I explained that to Carl. And though, as I said, he still doesn't want to join a marriage enrichment group, he does seem to have changed his outlook. He's happy to go along with the idea of us having more time to ourselves. To pursue outside interests.'

The cynic in me is wary. 'Just as long as you *are* united,' I remind Julia. 'You don't want to end up each going your own separate way.'

'Good heavens, no! That would defeat the purpose.'

'And Carl agrees?'

'Of course. His head's just full of business things at present, so he doesn't always think things through. I realise now, I have to be patient. To be prepared to allow the ideas I put to him to have time to sink in.'

'So you're able to talk to him about your other activities - the charity and fund-raising - are you?'

Julia flushes. 'Mmm - not exactly. But I can understand that. As I said, he needs time to come round. And I need to give him that space. Hilary's been very supportive in helping me to see that.'

She's clearly looking for affirmation and, despite my reservations, I feel I must be encouraging at this stage.

'Well, I'm impressed! It sounds to me as if you're on the road to recovery and are learning the concept of Adult to Adult transaction.'

Julia straightens up and beams. 'I have you to thank!' she says, adjusting the strap of her sun top. 'But you told me you were going to explain the Parent Adult Child thing to me. You've helped me so much already, I'd like to understand that properly.'

I lay my notebook down on the adjacent sideboard, and lean forward to flick the switch that will set a small fan in motion to cool the room.

'PAC. I think we covered some of this last time we met,' I begin. 'Remember I said that all human interaction tends to fall into one of three ego states? The easiest way to remember it is to think of the Parent state as *taught* - the conditioning we receive from our parents; Adult state is *thought* - when we think through and rationalise our situation then determine the action we'll take; and Child state is *felt*. It's an emotional state, in which we respond in an angry, petulant, or despairing manner. Or perhaps with undue obedience.'

Julia is silent for a while, thinking through what I've said.

'So when I was responding to Carl in the way I did when I first came to you, I was in Child state?'

I nod. 'I'd say that's possible.'

'And he was in Parent state, telling me what to do. Ticking me off whenever I did something he saw as undermining him. Like the dressmaking I did. Or going to Hilary's?'

'Yes.'

'And that made me respond emotionally. I'd feel angry. Or despairing. So I was behaving in Child mode?'

'It doesn't *make* you respond in any particular way, Julia. We all have the ability to make *choices* in our lives. But not everyone realises that. It's about becoming self-aware, so that you have control of the way you respond to others.'

I speak slowly and deliberately, intent upon getting the truth of this across to her, reducing the complexity to simple layman's terms.

'This branch of psychology is called Transactional Analysis. In other words, it's a study of how humans relate to one another. An analysis of the transactions between them. Once you understand that you have the power to decide how you will interact -'

'Yes, I can see that.' Quick to learn, Julia is excited about the truths we've uncovered. 'So I can *choose* to respond as an Adult, and hope that Carl will do likewise?'

'Indeed. But you can choose to respond as an Adult whether or not he continues to behave in Parent or Child state. You've depicted some of his behaviour as being in Parent mode, but I wonder if his response to things like the dressmaking episode you told me about was the result of his feeling threatened? In other words, an emotional response. That of the Child.'

'Oh, Evie, I could hug you. You've been such a help to me.'

I wave her praise aside.

'The past year has been a nightmare of confusion and despair,' she continues, her cheeks glowing. 'I've sometimes felt as if my marriage was like a forest. And I was lost in the middle of it with no idea how to find my way back out to civilisation.'

'You're not alone in feeling like that,' I assure her, leaning back in my chair and crossing my legs.

Julia smiles and her eyes light up.

'Now,' she says, 'because of what you've told me and shown me, I feel I can understand. I can see a pattern. It's a bit like being given a map. So even though I'm still in the forest, I believe I can find a way out. Instead of feeling lost I feel there's hope.'

To my acute embarrassment, but immense pleasure, Julia gets up from her chair, leans forward, wraps her arms around me and kisses my cheek. My only concern, as she seats herself again, is that I hope to goodness she's right and I'm wrong. I may have given her the map to get out of her forest, but who's going to be waiting for her at the other end? Carl? Or will he have galloped off into the sunset with whoever it was that he was whispering sweet nothings to at the Golf Club?

Carl was on a roll. Barely able to wipe the Cheshire cat grin from his face as he peered at himself in the bathroom mirror that morning, he nicked his chin while shaving. He dabbed at it with a piece of quilted toilet paper, at the same time mentally ticking off the list of successes he'd notched up in recent times.

First off was his relationship with his daughter. He felt sure that being on hand to take Abi to the hospital when she'd dislocated her shoulder and was unable to reach her mother had raised his credibility in her eyes. Plus-points for Dad; shame about the minuses for Mum! It had not been a major incident and the sling had soon been discarded; but the gratitude and affection Abi had shown him over the ensuing weeks had taken a markedly upward turn, despite the upset caused by his recent row with Julia.

Then there was Josh's motorbike, the cause of the row with Julia, but nonetheless an inspired gift in Josh's eyes, on the eve of his birthday. The visit to the Devon Scramble that had followed on the Saturday with a handful of his school friends was the icing on the cake.

'I shall soon be taking part,' Josh had told his pals, full of excitement.

What dad's heart could fail to melt in response to the love and gratitude in his son's face? And how very different from the relationship he'd had with his father! Carl felt himself stiffen before the bathroom mirror. Relationship? There had been none. With birthdays a term-time event, he'd spent every one at boarding school. The customary greetings card and fountain pen, or the like, had been left with Matron, and his parents had 'indulged' him with a stilted phone call on the day. That was it.

He grimaced. If there was one thing he was determined to accomplish in this life, it was to lavish his kids with all that had been lacking in his life. They would want for nothing. Pity Julia seemed intent on thwarting him. Had she really thought they would be attending motorbike scrambles merely as observers? Where would be the fun in that?

Of course, he realised now, you couldn't expect a woman to understand. He'd been livid when she'd stormed off to bed in the spare room. He'd taken the car, headed for the motorway and driven like a maniac for a good hour or more, before returning to Exeter and bedding down in the office. Lucy, what a star she was, had been the impeccable PA when she'd arrived at work next morning. She'd asked no questions, but instantly produced a washbag containing unused toiletries, plus a fresh shirt and tie, still wrapped in the cellophane in which they'd been purchased.

'You never know when these things might be required,' she'd said, leaving him to his own devices in the men's room. And he'd marvelled at her perspicacity. He was one lucky bloke.

And then there was the celebration at the Golf Club. Metaphorically speaking, Lucy had again saved his life. Originally, he'd intended the dinner to be a low-key business affair.

'Bottle of Bologna or similar, best way to show our wives that we're going up in the world,' he'd said to Frank when they'd signed the relevant papers at the solicitors' office. 'No need to alarm the women by giving out too much information.'

With his mind abuzz with business, Carl had completely forgotten his wedding anniversary that weekend. But Lucy, what a Wonder Woman she was, had rung him on his mobile and reminded him. Now how many women would do that?

'Did you find the bouquet I ordered for Julia?' she asked. 'You were on the phone when I left the office, so I didn't have a chance to let you know.'

'I wondered whose it was. Thought they must belong to the cleaner, and I was over-paying her.'

'Never mind. I'll bring them over to the Golf Club,' Lucy had said. And bless her cotton socks, she had.

'You ought to join us,' he told her when she texted him to say she'd arrived, and he'd met her out of sight of his party. But she wouldn't hear of it: gate-crash your celebration? Nah! Not her style.

Dabbing again at the cut on his chin, Carl rinsed off his razor and towelled his face dry. Being able to present Julia with a bouquet of roses just before announcing Frank's involvement in his expansion into Wales had proved to be inspirational. She'd blossomed. And changed. Back to the old Julia: sweet and feminine in her gratitude and affection.

True, she was still knocking about with that damned woman, Hilary, and her bunch of do-gooders, but he was coming round to the idea. It kept her occupied while he was busy. She'd spoken about the need for married couples to have relationship enriching experiences, occasional separate ventures so that they had something fresh to converse about. Perhaps it was no bad thing. Given that he was going to have to be away a good deal setting up the new business, it would give Julia an interest in his absence.

As for him, he'd have plenty to think about. And plenty to do. Accompanied by his trusty PA, Lucy, of course.

The trouble with terraced houses, and I guess with semis, is the proximity of your neighbours. Okay! I know that people like Julia Worth would tell me you're meant to love your neighbour as yourself, but that doesn't say a lot. Deprived of sleep by the neighbour from hell, you're not going to love them much. Or yourself for that matter.

Not that the couple next door are neighbours from hell. On the contrary. They're delightful, but they've recently reproduced. And while modern builds are like cardboard boxes, even one-hundred-year-old substantial brick built properties like mine have adjoining walls that behave like the skin on a drum. Every sound is magnified. Reverberates.

I waken, that weekend, to the hum of next door's washing machine - they're on a special tariff so everything that happens tends to happen in the dark - followed by a thud and a crying baby.

I lie there, cocooned in my bed. I've been dreaming. About my baby. The tiny scrap of humanity that left my body all those years ago. Before her time. And the thud from next door has featured in my dream. Seconds before I wake. It's my baby's body. Dropping to the floor. The miniscule hands and fingers outstretched. Clutching. Trying to take hold of life. And failing. The mouth open. Wide. Screaming. A silent wail for help.

It didn't really happen like that, of course. But I am wracked with guilt. For my child. For that life denied. For my inability to provide. To nourish. To hold on. To impart safety; security. I am wracked with guilt. For my husband. For his loss. For wrecking his manhood. His chance to father a child. I am wracked with guilt - and half awake. Overwhelmed with the pain of memory. Throbbing with the thought of that swollen belly on the bus; of knowing it contained Pete's child; of imagining the future.

The washing machine next door, energised by Economy Seven as perhaps Bosomy Barbara was, builds to a crescendo of whirring parts, a screech of triumph as it wrings every last drop of moisture from its contents. On and on. Eventually to stop. The baby next door quietens.

I am fully cognisant. I breathe deep and slow. Meditate. Recite my mantra. Dissipate the tender ache inside. I am liberated from sadness. From my slumbers. From my bed. My usual Saturday begins.

This, I think as I go downstairs in my pjs, is where counselling comes into its own. The practice of person centred therapy founded by Carl Rogers that I've studied over the years requires a steady development of self-awareness. This is what I've been trying to bring about in Julia Worth. Because it's only as we arrive at a greater understanding of our feelings and actions that we can hope to effect changes in our lives. Changes that are more than skin deep. Changes that affect our inner being and, in so doing, eventually influence our outer behaviour.

I put on the kettle to make myself an early morning cuppa, greet Pumpkin and pour milk in her dish as she returns from a night of debauchery in the neighbourhood. And I feel, suddenly, so thankful for what I've learned. The memories of loss and the grief that ensue may never be fully expunged - and nor should they be. But in acknowledging and dealing with them, the devastation they can wreak can be avoided.

Seating myself on a stool, and scooping up my silky, slinky cat, I bury my face in her fur. The truth of the poem that says it's better to have loved and lost than never to have loved at all fills my heart and mind. *I am a better person for having experienced that loss,* I murmur. Purring away on my lap and surveying me with eyes half-closed in ecstasy, Pumpkin offers me her complete agreement. She is, I've long ago decided, one highly intelligent moggy.

Unexpectedly, although it was only yesterday that I saw her, I have a phone call from Julia. Given that she told me it was doubtful she'd be able to see me during the school holidays, my instinct is to expect the worst. It's just as well I don't voice my fears, however, because it immediately becomes apparent that she's far from down.

'Evie, I wonder if you'd be kind enough to accompany me to a concert at the cathedral this evening?' she begins. 'I'm so sorry it's such a last minute invitation. I bought the tickets ages ago thinking that Carl would want to come, but it seems he has something else on.'

With the phone clutched to my ear, I'm in a dilemma. First I'm not very well up on classical or religious music; second, what is Carl Worth up to on a Saturday evening without his wife; third it's deemed neither advisable nor ethical to socialise with a client; and finally, tickets for events at the cathedral cost the earth. Well! It's the earth to me. I guess for people like Julia it's barely a sod or a shovelful.

'I'd love you to be my guest,' Julia continues, perhaps sensing my hesitation. 'The lilies weren't much of an apology for missing a session. I know you have to invoice me for a missed session -'

'Only half the usual fee,' I interrupt.

'But even so,' Julia continues, 'you'd salve my conscience if you'd agree.'

Put like that, how can I refuse? After all, it's not as if we're going to get much chance to fraternise at a concert, and neither shall I be beholden to my client, since this could be considered payment in kind.

We meet on the Cathedral Green at the Great West Door that evening, and are ushered down the main aisle.

'Did you know that the roof is the longest medieval vault in the world?' Julia whispers. 'Incredible, isn't it, to think that such architectural skill existed so long ago. And that it's still standing today!'

I did know and, like Julia, marvel at the enduring beauty of our surroundings.

'And to think, all this was built to inspire us with a sense of God's greatness. Incredible, isn't it?' she continues, as we take our seats right down at the front.

I nod, politely. I suppose it must be. If you believe. It's not that I don't. Just that I -

The orchestra, the Bournemouth Symphony Orchestra, no less, begins to warm up and the audience - or should it be congregation? - falls silent. There, beneath the Gothic splendour of vaults and pillars, carvings and ancient stained glass windows, I find myself slipping into some other world for the next hour or so, immersed and mesmerised. A glance at Julia reveals that she is as rapt as I. And by the time the choir begins Handel's Hallelujah Chorus, we are both lost for words.

Perhaps, I think, there might, after all, be something in the concept of a God who is capable of inspiring such wonder and awe. If so, then he is certainly due the applause and standing ovation we offer at the end of the performance. A tear runs down my cheek, and I'm in no haste to brush it away.

CHAPTER SEVEN

JULIA STOOD WITH her back to the kitchen sink contemplating recent events and those yet to occur. Summer had come and gone, the half-term holiday in Marbella with Carl's mother had passed better than expected, and Josh, moody and unpredictable these days, seemed to have enjoyed his school skiing trip. Now, with October drawing to a close, Julia was looking forward to the opening of Carl's Welsh factory.

With critical aplomb, she surveyed the results of her mammoth cooking session. If only for sheer quantity, she thought it worthy of the Great British Bake Off. Her chorizo and chilli mini pizzas were spicy enough to fizz like Catherine wheels; her vol-au-vents light enough to be the puff of wind from which they derived their name. Her only concern was whether the fancy fillings might be too sophisticated for those for whom they were intended - Carl's employees.

When Carl had first mentioned the advent of the new factory in Wales at Dave and Laura's, she had to confess she'd felt a mixture of pride and dismay. Pride in the altruism he'd displayed, bringing work to deprived areas. Dismay because it would mean he'd be away from home more than ever. But she'd known better than to ask him to spell out his plans. Any interest she might have shown, or comment she had to make, would have been seen as counterproductive.

He'd then expanded on his plans during their anniversary dinner at the Golf Club towards the end of July, dropping the news into the conversation as casually as if it were no more than a redesign of the firm's logo or the purchase of new office furniture. There, in the company of Frank and his wife, Julia had felt suffused with delight. Where other men might have shouted it from the rooftops, it seemed to her that Carl took his business acumen with such humility it could command only admiration.

Yes, fear had gripped her too. Plagued with financial concerns, she'd asked him, humbly, to enlighten her. But once he'd explained his motives, and the increased business this would bring in via exports to France, she was right behind him. How could she not be, when he told her that the bank manager was so supportive? She'd made up her mind that she would do everything possible to affirm him.

The revelation had also clarified much of the acrimony that had passed between them earlier in the year, she thought.

'Getting the factory ready for a grand opening is the reason why I shan't be able to spend any time in Marbella with you and the kids,' he'd explained. 'And it's why I thought it best for Josh to go on his school trip so you wouldn't have to juggle the demands of a sixteen year old with those of my mother.'

Suddenly, all the upsets before the summer holidays had fallen into place. The sense of shame this had induced in her, left Julia full of contrition. How could she have been so selfish? There was Carl, going all out to be public-spirited, to bring work to jobless families, and all she could think about were her own self-seeking desires.

Determined to make up for her lapse, she'd insisted on undertaking the catering for the office party Carl was planning.

'I'm laying on a coach to take the Exeter workforce over to meet that of the new Welsh factory,' he'd said, a few weeks ago. 'I want there to be a sense of unity and collaboration between them. If we're to make inroads with exports into France, then co-operation between the two factories is crucial.'

Julia supported the concept whole-heartedly, hence the catering project. There would be no mass-produced shop-bought produce for Carl's workforce; only the best delicacies she could create. She'd even purchased large plastic containers and hired a refrigerated van to ship the stuff over to the new factory. She was determined to do him proud.

The only fly in the ointment was Josh's continuing resentment. It had simmered throughout the summer and now, with his first half term in the sixth form behind him, was at boiling point.

'What the heck was the point in Dad buying me a motorbike if he's no intention of taking me on scrambles?' he'd yelled at Julia one morning, his vehemence making her wince.

Given the hurt that was so clearly in evidence, she found it difficult to reprimand him for his bad language and attitude. Instead, she'd tried reasoned explanation. But even at sixteen, he simply refused to see that his father had little or no time at present.

'So what you're saying is that I don't count? The only thing that matters to Dad is blinkin' work?'

'That's not true,' Julia said, ignoring the profanities in her effort to calm him down. 'Your father loves you very much. And so do I!'

The look of pain and anger in Josh's eyes were like fiery darts in Julia's flesh.

As summer progressed, she'd tried again and again to help him see reason, but to no avail. To be honest, and against all previous expectation, it had been a relief when the time came for Josh to leave for his school skiing trip. Having time alone with Abi, Nathan and her mother-in-law in the Marbella flat, had proved to be a much needed respite. They'd swum in the pool, sunbathed on the beaches, and spent time admiring the stately buildings in La Plaza de los Naranjas, as well as visiting the shops, art galleries, bars and bistros. Without Josh sulking around, the atmosphere had been harmonious and fun. Sadly, however, it was clear, on their return home, that neither time nor space had succeeded in stabilising Josh's thinking.

Remembering it all now, Julia sighed. She could see both viewpoints. The sense of rejection in Josh's demeanour was like a wound in her side. At the same time, he had to understand that he could not always be the centre of his father's world.

She pushed her hair back from her face. The afternoon sun was beginning to stream through the French door windows of the kitchen, glinting off the granite worktops and the glass-topped table on which the party food was spread. With no concept of the appetite-size of the eventual consumers, she only hoped that what she'd made would prove to be sufficient.

Glowing with a sense of achievement, she packed away the last batch of culinary delights, sealed the lids and placed them in the freezer. Only a couple of days to go before they'd all be devoured, she thought. By an appreciative workforce, it was to be hoped! Grateful, not to her, but to the employer to whom they were indebted. It was, after all, what Carl deserved. The thought stopped her in her tracks. How far she'd come in the last few months! And it was all down to Evie Adams' expert guidance.

One of the things I used to love doing at the weekend - before my ex, Pete, and Bosomy Barbara made it difficult for me by moving to the area - was to don my hiking attire, take the short train ride down to Exmouth, and walk the beginning of the Jurassic Coast. Nowadays, it's Sidmouth that I head for, where the Triassic rock, at two hundred and thirty million years old, is said to yield rare fossils of desert creatures.

Not that I've come across any! But that's because I can't tear my gaze away from the view. The red sandstone cliff-face that winds its way around this section of the coast glows like the gemstones of a necklace in the low-angled autumn sun. And from my vantage point at the top of Jacob's Ladder - a steep stone staircase up the cliffs - the sea shimmers before me. Spread like a sequin-spangled cloak in the hands of an opera star, it looks as if it has been flung across the curvaceous lines of Lyme Bay, from Portland Bill through to Hope's Nose, and Start Point beyond. Feasting my eyes on it, I can't help feeling that the longer journey is more than worth while.

I'm sitting alone, after my walk, in the window of a tearoom on Sidmouth seafront one Saturday near the end of October, when who should walk in but Daisy, my client with the abusive husband and drug-addicted teenage son. My astonishment at seeing her here, in an up-market resort some thirty-five miles from home, may appear to be a little snobbish; but the fact is that she's never struck me as the type to go sightseeing, unless the sight she was intent upon seeing was rich in merry-go-rounds and kiss-me-quick produce, or their modern equivalent. Surreptitiously, I study Daisy for a moment. Her leg now appears to have mended, and she's accompanied by a woman of similar age, who promptly heads off to the Ladies' Room.

In the far corner of the crowded restaurant, I bury my head in the menu so as to give Daisy the opportunity to slip out, ostensibly unnoticed. I wouldn't want to embarrass her by giving her cause to have to explain me away to her companion. However, it appears that my sensitivity is unfounded.

'Hell-ow!' she calls, with enough volume and excitement to make heads turn.

I raise my head, smile and lift my hand in greeting. Taking that as an invitation to join me, Daisy manoeuvres her plump self between chairs and tables, across the room to where I'm seated. She lowers herself onto a chair opposite me.

'I'm ever so glad I've seen you,' she says in a stage whisper, swivelling from side to side to ascertain whether, or not, she is being overheard. 'I'm livin' up 'ere now. Didn't 'ave time to let you know. It all 'appened so fa-ast. M' brother's taken me in. 'E manages the farm shop for the big 'ouse. 'E's taken me on as the cleaner. It's ever so nice up 'ere.'

Her chins wobble with emotion, and her eyes glow with relief.

'That's great news, Daisy. And your husband?'

'I've left 'im. Couldn't stand it no more. An' my boy, Jem, 'e's left an' all. M' brother got 'im a job as farm labourer. Just as long as 'e don't touch the pot again. There's no drugs up 'ere, see. It's too posh.'

Daisy's companion has emerged from the Ladies' Room and is looking around for her.

'Gotta go,' says Daisy getting up from the table and waving. 'That's m' sister-in-law. Bit of a dragon, but she's got a 'eart of gold.'

'Comin',' she calls, before turning back to me. 'Thanks ever so much for wot you done, Miss Evie. I'm ever so grateful. If it 'adn't bin for my doc sendin' me to you, I don't know what I've done. Probably bin buried six foot under by now.'

She flashes me a smile that plumps her cheeks into two red cushions, then proceeds to negotiate her way across the room to the door. Basking in a satisfied glow, I raise my hand to bid her a fond farewell, then lift my cup to my lips in a toast to her future.

Like so many women subjected to violence, Daisy had allowed herself to be brain-washed into believing herself worthy of nothing better. Shame and a lack of self-worth had her convinced that she was to blame. But now, it would appear, the cowed creature I was called upon to help has blossomed. She's clearly taken on board all I've encouraged in her and become her own woman. While the breakdown of a marriage can never be seen as ideal, the myopia in Daisy's vision has been cleared. She's stood back, surveyed the scene objectively, and taken the option that was best for her.

A sense of satisfaction takes a hold of me as I finish my tea and make ready to leave for home. Like the Jurassic cliffs that have stood the test of time, the Daisys of this world are what make my job worthwhile. Her new-found independence will see her through, I hope. Now, if only Julia Worth, whom I haven't seen for several weeks, turns out as good as Daisy, I shall be well pleased.

Julia took a suitcase down from the top of her wardrobe in readiness for her visit to Wales for the opening of the new factory. She was still puzzling over a conversation she'd had with Carl two days earlier. While packing his case for him, she'd come across a brass plaque on which the name and date of the factory opening had been engraved, together with the words, *In memory of 'Spud' - Maurice Piper - the best friend any boy could want. RIP.* Beneath that was what Julia presumed were the dates of his birth and death, twenty-eight years earlier.

It had been wrapped in what looked like a school scarf though, never having seen a single photograph of Carl during his schooldays, it was not one she recognised. Intrigued, she'd stood there reading the inscription, when suddenly Carl had come into the room.

'What are you doing with that?' he asked and, snatching it from her hand, he wiped an imaginary finger print from the brass.

Immediately, Julia felt guilty and embarrassed. 'Sorry. I didn't mean to intrude. It was lying there in your case and I thought I'd better investigate before packing for you. What is it?'

'Just something I'm taking down to the new factory,' Carl said, his voice inexplicably hoarse, his eyes fixed on the object in his hand.

'Someone you knew well?' Julia asked. 'Someone from school?'

He nodded.

'He must have been someone special to have you commemorate him in this way?'

Carl didn't answer.

'How did he - ? What caused him to pass away so young?'

Carl rewrapped the plaque, replaced it in the suitcase and slammed the lid shut. 'What indeed?' he'd said, full of venom. And he'd turned on his heel and left the room.

Julia couldn't get over the look of hatred on his face, nor the bitterness in his voice. What could have caused such loathing? Twenty-eight years ago Carl would have been - what? Seventeen? So who was this Maurice Piper? And how come he'd died so young? There were no answers, and she presumed, since it was nowhere in sight, that Carl had taken the plaque with him when he'd left for the Welsh factory two days ago.

Abi came into the bedroom and sat on the king-size bed in the lotus position.

'Why haven't you and Dad gone to Wales together, Mum?' she asked.

Deep in thought, Julia was only marginally aware of the critical tone in her daughter's voice. Lifting a black Honiton lace cocktail dress from her wardrobe she held it aloft, her head tilted to one side.

'Too dressy?' she asked, as much of herself as of Abi. She replaced the garment and raked along the row of hangers in search of something more appropriate.

'It just seems a bit mean of Dad expecting you to find your own way over there,' Abi continued, turning to lie on her side with her feet curled up beneath her, and her head propped up on her hand. 'I mean, you haven't been to the factory before, have you?'

'Mmm?' Julia held a second dress - a simple, full length black silk crepe - at arm's length to assess its suitability. 'No. But Daddy's given me good instructions, and I've got the SatNav.'

With her free hand, Abi began twisting her long wavy hair into strands that hung down the sides of her face.

'Okay. But that doesn't explain why he didn't take you with him yesterday.' She sat up, suddenly. 'No. Not that one. The emerald green silk. The one with the sticky-out skirt. Makes your waist look tiny. And it brings out the red in your hair.'

'I have red in my hair?' Julia dipped her head to look more closely in the mirrored door panel of the wardrobe.

'Course you have. And it's natural, too. Unlike some people's! You need to wear the big square emerald ring Dad bought you too; and the matching earrings. Then you need that frosted burnt orange nail varnish to set it off.'

Julia sat down on the edge of the bed and ruffled her daughter's hair.

'My! Are we turning into a fashionista?' she laughed.

Abi swung her legs down in front of her and stood up. The fuchsia pink satin throw and white Egyptian cotton bed linen were crumpled where she'd been lying. She smoothed them with her hand, puckering her mouth.

'I'm just looking out for you, that's all.'

Julia mimicked her daughter's pout, rubbing her thumb over Abi's mouth as if to erase hers.

'I know you are, darling. And I appreciate it. Daddy's gone on to get things ready at the factory. If I'd gone with him, I'd have had to leave you and the boys with Granny for an extra day. Not a good idea, eh?'

Abi pirouetted away from her mother.

'I s'pose. But I bet you that Lucy's there with Dad.'

She threw herself forwards, full length on the bed. Julia turned her over, put her face down close to Abi's and looked at her, reproachfully.

'Of course Lucy's there! She's Daddy's PA, isn't she. It's her job to see that everything runs smoothly. That's what she's paid to do.'

Abi continued to glower.

'We ought to be kind to her, anyway,' Julia went on. 'She split up with her boyfriend, recently, and I don't think she and her parents get on.'

Still no response from Abi, who looked only slightly mollified. Julia stood up, went back to the wardrobe and picked out the Chanel style dress Abi had indicated she should take.

'Now come on,' she said. 'Tell me what shoes you think I should wear with the emerald green silk? You've clearly got a talent for this sort of thing.'

With a studied show of reluctance, Abi dragged herself from the bed and went to her mother's shoe cabinet. After a moment's search, she extracted a pair of platform shoes with three inch stiletto heels.

'It has to be these,' she said, handing them to Julia. 'You've got to stand head and shoulders above all the other ladies. Show Lucy who's boss.'

Julia smiled, indulgently. For some unknown reason Abi appeared to have a grudge against Lucy, whom she'd only ever met on rare visits to her father's office. She couldn't imagine why! Lucy came across to her as a thoroughly likeable and hard-working sort of girl. An ideal PA for Carl. Perhaps she ought to invite Lucy round so Abi could get to know her better? Yes. That's what she'd do. She felt sure the younger woman would be a good role model for her daughter.

If there was one thing in which Carl revelled it was a party! And a party of his own making, when the invited guests were the very people who relied on you for a living - well - that had to be the best. Here in the once industrial area of Wales, with the steel works in Port Talbot, he knew he was on to a winner. Add to that the Severn Bridge link with the M5, and ferries to Roscoff or Cherbourg close to hand in Pembroke and Plymouth, and it was a no brainer. The generous subsidies from the British Government to help some of the poorest communities were, quite simply, the gold dusting on an already extravagant package.

He looked around him, contentedly. The factory building was spanking new, laid out like an aircraft carrier with plenty of outside parking, on a busy industrial estate, set in the once thriving coal fields of South Wales - *De Cymru* - and surrounded by the wooded beauty of Monmouthshire. By the end of the week, the building would be filled with the accoutrements of his industry: machinery - electronic and mechanical; profile cutters; conveyor belts and AGVs. Today it was filled with his workforce and their spouses and partners, plus local and regional media: journalists, radio and TV presenters and cameramen.

They'd arrived yesterday morning, he, Lucy and Frank, to set everything up. Hired tables and chairs were set around the perimeter of the factory, while a bar, manned by local caterers, flowed as freely as the nearby River Usk. On one wall, an industrial size screen displayed film taken previously of the Exeter factory at work, plus a Skype connection with their French counterparts. By the time the three of them had returned to their hotel for dinner and a celebratory bottle of champagne, they were physically shattered, but mentally elated.

Aloft on a gantry platform that morning, Carl quietly congratulated himself. If the idea was to impress, which it was, it had surpassed expectation. Looking down on the heads of his workforce, old and new, English and Welsh, Carl addressed them in ringing tones in both languages.

'Welcome Ladies and Gentlemen, friends and family. Thank you for coming to our gathering today. *Croeso foneddigesau a boneddigion ffrindiau a theulu. Diolch i chi am ddod i'n cyfarfod heddiw.*'

Reverting to English and drawing on various news items he'd researched, he played on his Welsh heritage, linking them together in a way that was both inclusive and humorous.

'My Great Aunt Bets may once have had the honour of serving Lloyd George with tea and Bara Brith,' he began, 'but I assure you she was not responsible for the asbestos contaminated tarantula that was reported to be on the loose in Cardiff earlier in the year, nor for the death of Nick Boing, Cardiff's 22 stone sheep, nor for the blanket-wrapped, jacket potato fed chimps that braved the snow at Swansea last winter. In fact, Aunt Bets would be more likely to be serving the people of this region by getting her hands dirty here, in our fantastic new factory, rather than worrying about furry friends of the four-legged or eight-legged variety.'

As he'd intended, the humorous references to real local events were an ice-breaker par excellence, drawing great guffaws of laughter, and bonding the men with one another and, crucially, to him. He continued for a further ten minutes, reminding his workforce of the meaning of altruism - they were to be the means of bringing growth and prosperity to the region; of the strategic demographics of their workplace, with international airports at Cardiff, Bristol and Exeter; ferries connecting them with Ireland and Europe; of the faith he placed in them, and the sense of partnership he aspired to between labourers and managers. Laying it on thick, he pointed out the part his wife had played in providing the spread they were about to consume, stressing the 'family' nature of his business.

It was an exercise in garnering every last drop of gratitude and loyalty from his employees, and he felt sure, as he stood down, that he'd succeeded. There was certainly plenty of applause as he introduced the Secretary of State for Wales, and still more as the MP prepared to do his stuff. Standing in the limelight of a media frenzy, Mr Jones took a moment to draw attention to the plaque Carl had had erected inside the factory entrance.

'In commemoration of a young man, Maurice Piper, affectionately known to his friends as Spud, who died twenty-eight years ago today on this very spot, and whose story some of you may recall.' He then cut the ribbon, declared the factory open, and proposed a toast to its ongoing success.

'Thank you,' said Carl, holding a hand-shake with the MP long enough for the photographers to get a good shot.

'Well done,' said Frank to Carl before he began to mingle with the multitude. 'You sold it to 'em good and proper.'

'You were brilliant,' Lucy breathed, softly, adding, as Frank turned away, 'in more ways than one.'

'Watch it,' Carl hissed, but it was said with a smile on his face, a warm suffusion of memory inside, and a brief squeeze of Lucy's arm as his wife advanced upon them.

'Darling,' he said, turning to Julia whose face he perceived as gratifyingly full of admiration and adoration. 'Let me introduce you. Lucy you know, of course. And Miller, our bank manager.'

'You must be very proud of what Carl has achieved,' said Miller, taking Julia by the hand. 'And all in honour of our school friend, Maurice Piper.'

Carl frowned at Miller in an attempt to warn him off.

'Oh yes, the plaque he had engraved,' Julia said turning away from

Carl. 'I hadn't realised the young man had died here. Nor that the date was so special. Remind me of the circumstances.'

Again Carl flashed a look of warning at Miller, but again it went unseen, and he had to turn aside as the Secretary of State spoke to him.

'Maurice - Spud - died a horrible death at school. Could have been a devastating scandal for the school. But Carl's father -'

Carl intervened, swiftly taking hold of Julia's elbow and leaving her no option but to turn in his direction.

'Julia, you haven't met our honoured guest, the Secretary of State,' he said, firmly.

The greetings that took place were mutually warm and satisfying and, as Julia dutifully made small talk with the minister, before turning to include Lucy, Carl was aware of a sharp prick of conscience. No one could doubt that his wife remained a good looking woman despite the ravages of childbirth and advancing years, but she couldn't hold a candle to the bloom of youth that was evident in Lucy's peaches and cream complexion and firmness of flesh.

Naturally, Julia had impeccable taste in style and attire, but much of that, it had to be said, was down to his wealth and generosity. Lucy had enjoyed no such advantage. Yet despite the obvious chain-store element of her clothing, she somehow managed to exude an air of raw and tangible allure behind a facade of demureness and capability that befitted the PA of a flourishing businessman.

'Mrs Worth,' Lucy said, grasping Julia's hand in both of her own. 'What a wonderful spread you've provided. Carl must be over the moon. You must be such an asset to his business. I couldn't begin to compete. I'm the world's worst dunce in the kitchen.'

Carl dipped his head to hide a smile. With a few well-turned compliments, Lucy had shown all the cunning of a wily fox, reducing Julia to the housewife that she was. Julia, of course, was disarmed.

'It's Julia, Lucy! No formalities, please. They're not bad, the vol au vents, are they? I was pleased with the result. Naturally, I made the pastry with butter. But of course, I couldn't begin to do what you've done here -' she waved her hand aloft '- organising all this. I don't know what Carl would do without you.'

Carl didn't know either. Nor why he found his wife's self-effacing demeanour so irritating and his PA's shrewdness so laudable. He held up his hand to terminate the exchange.

'Now, now, you two. No time for any further mutual admiration.

We have a workforce to meet and greet.'

'Of course,' Julia smiled. 'But you must come round for a meal with us, Lucy. I have a daughter who would love to meet you and get to know you.'

Carl felt rather than saw the quick glance Lucy flashed his way. He knew he'd have to put a stop to Julia's plan. An uncomfortable stab of conscience arrested his sense of well-being. He'd overstepped the line with Lucy and he knew it. Enjoyable didn't begin to describe the frisson of delight he'd experienced with her the night before when, after Frank had retired, she'd accompanied him to his room. Ostensibly for a nightcap, they'd both known what it would lead to.

Though neither would admit to it openly, the inevitability had been spelled out weeks before. Perhaps even as far back as the business trip to France. But however predictable, there would be repercussions. A guilty conscience was something he'd simply have to learn to live with. Carl knew, with the hunger of an addict, that there would be no turning back now.

CHAPTER EIGHT

APPEARING AT THE door of my counselling room one Friday lunchtime, Guy issues an invitation for a fortnight's time.

'Nancy's nephew is coming to visit us from America at the beginning of December,' he explains. 'She wondered if you'd like to come and dine with us?'

Looking up from my desk, I marvel at the generosity of spirit to be found in Guy's wife, Nancy. Invitations from the Sampsons are not infrequent, and I have the impression that Nancy feels sorry for my 'single plight' - which is ironic given her own disabilities. Wheelchair bound since the car accident she endured years ago, she remains serene and capable.

'Wouldn't she rather have them to herself?' I ask, taking it for granted that there will be a wife accompanying the nephew. 'I don't suppose she sees them that often.'

Guy grins. 'A touch of the Barbara Streisand's going on m'thinks.'

Shaking my head, I reveal my confusion.

'Matchmaker, matchmaker...' Guy bursts into song. 'I think Nancy's hoping you'll show Scott the sights.'

'Oh, he's on his own?' Stupidly, I feel myself blush as I realise my surprise sounds more like pleasure. I turn away to hide my embarrassment.

Guy becomes serious.

'He is. Recently divorced.' He sinks into the leather armchair normally reserved for clients. 'The thing is Nancy has an appointment with the consultant on Saturday, which I shall have to take her to, so it's going to be a bit miserable for Scott without us for company. I know it's a big ask. But you couldn't -'

'Course I could! You and Nancy have done enough for me over the years.' I scoop up a couple of files from my desk, open my filing cabinet, and lock them inside. 'What sort of things is he interested in?'

Guy's face lights up. 'Oh, he's quite easy going. Just the typical American thirst for history: cathedral, canal, quay, Roman underground passages. Anything, as long as there's no retail therapy involved. So I understand.'

'Retail therapy?' I rasp, opening my eyes wide to ape a humorous horror. 'What possible therapy could there be in shopping?'

Guy laughs, rises from the chair and ambles off to his own room ready for his first client of the afternoon. Basking in the glow of friendship, I flick through the diary on my desk and write myself a reminder of Guy's invitation.

My next appointment is Julia Worth. I can see the moment she arrives that it would be useless making small talk and asking how her holiday in Marbella went. The distraught look in her eyes says it all. She takes her usual seat by the fireplace, in which a single-bar electric heater burns.

'It's Josh,' she says, as soon as I seat myself opposite her. 'My eldest. The sixteen year old. He's in the sixth form now. We were summoned to see the Headmaster. At least I was. Carl's in Wales, busy with the new factory.'

I grimace in sympathy and wait for her to proceed.

'Apparently, Josh had a fight with another boy. Our butcher's son, whom we know well. Broke his nose.' She falls silent, twisting her hands together in her lap, a tortuous demonstration of how she feels.

'Isn't fighting par for the course with boys?' I ask. 'A natural outcome of all that unused testosterone?'

Julia is not amused. 'It was pretty full on. Neither the Head nor I can get to the bottom of it. Josh just clams up. But Nathan, my youngest, hinted that it was something the other boy said to Josh. Something damning about his father.'

'It could just be jealousy,' I say, again trying to lighten Julia's mood. 'I remember doing the school run for a friend's children years ago and they spent their whole time boasting about whose house was biggest and best, whose dad had the smartest car, who had the most holidays abroad. It went on and on, until one little girl who'd said nothing, burst out *Well my mummy's got a bigger bottom than yours*, and we were all reduced to tears of laughter. I was laughing so much I nearly lost control of the car.'

Julia gives a wan smile. 'I think it's more than that,' she says. 'You remember I told you Carl bought a little motorbike for Josh's birthday in July? The idea was that they'd go to scrambles together. But Carl never seems to have any time for anything, these days. I've tried to explain to Josh but -'

She breaks down, and I hand her the customary box of tissues and wait for her tears to abate. She shudders and looks at me, pleading for answers.

'I think Josh may be smoking pot. I've caught him a couple of times with his head out of his bedroom window. I just don't know how to handle it. What to do?'

I purse my lips and exhale slowly in a gesture of sympathy. 'Does the school know?'

Julia shakes her head, her eyes wide with alarm. 'They've already threatened to suspend him.'

'Threatened? Does that suggest they've no evidence?'

Julia squirms. 'I don't know. I was too upset to ask. Besides, I wouldn't want to alert them to the possibility if they don't know.'

'Well, have your tried asking Josh? Does he admit to it?'

'No! He just keeps swearing. Yelling at me. Telling me his father doesn't care about him.'

I make a note. 'And what does your husband have to say to that?'

Julia pauses. 'Well, that's just it. Carl's hardly around at the moment. I keep trying to tell Josh that his father's got a lot on. And that it's only temporary. But I'm beginning to wonder if that's true. I suspect he's going to have to spend more and more time in Wales. And in France.'

Head down, I scribble in my file. When I look up, Julia is staring into space. In comparison to her usual immaculate appearance, she looks a little dishevelled; her mascara smudged; nail varnish chipped; her hair wind-blown; her winter boots muddy and in need of re-heeling. I note these things non-judgementally, merely as an indication of her state of mind.

'Does your husband not have business partners who could take on some of the workload so he could spend more time at home?' I ask.

Obviously miles away, Julia appears startled. 'Carl was a sole trader before he opened the Welsh factory. He's taken Frank on as a partner now. Frank manages the Exeter factory, but I think it's in name only. Carl always jokes with friends that he runs too fast for anyone else to keep up with him.'

'And there's no one else?'

'Frank's a dear,' she replies, 'but I don't think he has the right qualities to take on any more. I don't want to sound critical, but I'd say he has enough on.'

'So! Who's going to be managing the Welsh set up?'

Julia twists the wedding ring on her finger then smoothes her hand over her skirt. 'Carl has a PA. Lucy.'

I wait, but she's fallen silent. 'And Lucy's helping with the new venture?' I enquire.

'Lucy's everything you'd want in a PA. Brilliant! She never misses a thing. I think Carl finds her indispensable.'

'You think...?'

'I'm sure he does. I'm sure she is. Don't misunderstand me, Evie. I think Lucy's wonderful. A real asset.'

I dip my head to hide my expression. I'm reminded of earlier sessions, first when Julia wouldn't hear a word against Carl and then later when it was her mother she defended.

'But?' I ask.

Julia hesitates.

'It's just that you sounded as if there was a 'but' coming?'

Julia lifts her hand with a dismissive gesture. 'But Abi, my daughter, seems to have taken a dislike to her.'

I raise an eyebrow. 'Oh? Why would that be?'

'I've no idea! I even suggested to Abi that we might invite Lucy round for a meal one evening soon after the Welsh factory opened. But, frankly, I almost felt ashamed of my daughter. She was on the point of being downright rude.'

Julia shifts, uncomfortably. She attempts a smile. 'Oh, dear! Telling you all this makes me realise what a dysfunctional family I have.

Neurotic me. Angry Josh. Suspicious Abi. Nathan, the youngest, seems to be the only one who's normal. And how long's that going to last, I wonder, with adolescence only a year away?'

'And Carl?' I ask.

Julia looks startled, as if her husband were no longer a consideration when it came to family matters. Again, she waves a hand, dismissively. 'Oh, he's just trying to make life better for us all,' she says.

It's clear she has a long way to go before she reaches a place of clarity and honesty; before she can be said to see the way forward.

'So what do you think I should do about Josh?' she asks.

What indeed? I stand, and lean forward to switch off the electric fire.

'Would you like me to see him?' I ask when I take my seat again.

'Goodness, no! I'd never hear the last of it from him. And he'd be sure to tell Carl.'

'Would that be altogether a bad thing?' I ask in the hope of provoking her to think it through.

'Evie! You know what he was like about my seeing Hilary. Doing the fund-raising and everything.'

'But did that stop you?'

'No... But I don't talk about it any more. And I don't go to events regularly. Only when Carl's away.'

It occurs to me to wonder why, with a savvy friend who could advise her, Julia continues to come to see me.

'So what do your new friends think of the situation?' I ask, instead.

'Oh, I haven't told them about Josh. But as far as Carl's concerned-' she looks sheepish. 'Look, Evie, I know you don't agree. But I think they're right. Trust and meditation are the best way forward. Better than confrontation.'

I assume as placid and accepting an appearance as I possibly can. 'And will the Headmaster agree to trust and meditation rather than confronting and suspending Josh? Don't you think Carl has a right to know that his son's in trouble?'

I can see, from the look on her face, that I've struck a chord.

Next morning, as soon as the children had dispersed to their usual Saturday morning activities, Julia determined to set about rectifying the omission Evie had highlighted the previous day. She confronted Carl.

'Josh?' Carl snapped. 'Hauled before the Head? And you went to see him alone? Why didn't you tell me?'

Face contorted with fury, he leapt to his feet, crossed the lounge floor and, despite its being only mid-morning, poured himself a Scotch. Seated in her usual place beside the hearth, in which a log fire blazed, Julia winced. She was tempted to retort, in the same hard tone of voice he'd adopted, 'because you're never here'. Instead, chastened by the memory of Evie's statement about a father's right to know what his son is up to, she spoke quietly and penitently.

'I'm sorry. I should have done. I didn't want to worry you when you have so much on.'

Carl drank deeply from the cut-glass tumbler, refilled it and turned to face her. It was the first weekend in December, and outside a heavy mist pressed against the French windows, obliterating the usual view across manicured lawns to the herbaceous borders and summer house beyond. On this occasion, Julia had chosen the timing of her revelation carefully, allowing Carl the respite of a night's sleep following his return from what must, surely, have been a gruelling week in the Welsh factory.

'So who is this boy my son is alleged to have beaten up?' Carl put his drink on a side table then threw himself down onto the sofa.

His use of the possessive noun was not lost upon Julia, but in a way, she thought it positive. 'It was Steve's son, Mike,' she said.

'Mike Hammond? Our butcher's son? He's in the sixth form with Josh? What on earth's he doing there?'

Carl's voice was full of incredulity. Julia crossed her legs. Was he making too much of the idea that a butcher's boy might have enough about him to attend sixth form, and ignoring the fact that a businessman's son, his own flesh and blood, had descended into the vulgarity of brawling?

'Why shouldn't he be there? He's a bright boy.'

'He's hardly the equal of a lad like Josh. And how the heck can a butcher afford the fees?'

'He's a scholarship boy, as you well know.' A sharpness crept into Julia's voice which she instantly regretted. 'And I don't know why you should be looking down your nose at him; you've had his father over for a meal from time to time.'

Carl laughed.

'I like Steve, but it's his fillet steak I really like. It's expedient to have him over occasionally for the odd barbecue. But what's this got to do with Josh?'

'Exactly!' Julia rose, selected a log from a basket on the far side of the hearth, threw it into the glowing embers in the grate and seated herself again. 'I've tried to get to the bottom of it, and so has the Head. He was of the opinion that,' Julia hesitated, before doctoring the facts 'that drugs might be involved. Smoking pot. I think I managed to talk him out of that idea. But neither he nor I could get anything out of Josh. You do realise he's been threatened with suspension and told to write a formal apology.'

Carl turned his head in a series of jerky movements, his features screwed tight against his skull.

'Drugs? I don't know who I feel more angry with. The Head for suggesting that my son would have anything to do with illegal substances. Josh for beating this boy up and letting down the side. Mike, for whatever it is he's done to upset my boy. Or you for failing to tell me. I know, I know. You didn't want to bother me. And for that reason I'll let it go.'

Julia rose again from the chair in which she was seated and went to sit beside Carl on the sofa.

'It's no good getting yourself so uptight about it,' she said, reaching out to lay her hand on his arm. 'You've got enough on your plate. I know that. But go easy on Josh. He's really missed you this summer while you've been away so much.'

Carl put his hand briefly on top of Julia's then stood.

'You're right, of course.' He looked down at her. 'There's a scramble on this afternoon. Nathan's staying over at his mate's, right? Might be the ideal opportunity for me to take Josh out have a quiet word with him afterwards?'

Julia nodded her agreement, then looked down at where her hand had fallen from Carl's arm to the sofa. She straightened herself up. He was probably right to take Josh out for some fun before tackling the more serious stuff. But where did that leave her and Abi? Yet again without husband and father. He was away so much these days. Sometimes, she wondered if things would ever get back to normal. Whatever normal was.

Carl knocked on the door to Josh's room before going in to tell him the good news. The boy was still in his pjs, lying on his bed playing some computer game or other on his cell phone, and he seemed strangely lethargic. Hardly surprising, Carl supposed, given the state of the room - a stinking fug of yesterday's dirty clothes and magazines spread across every surface. But thankfully, no evidence of a cannabis aroma. Still, time Julia did her stuff and ventured in here with the vacuum cleaner and a bottle of disinfectant, he thought.

The silent reproof was quickly followed by an image of the regimented precision of his own adolescent bedroom. No one with a modicum of normality would wish that upon a son. He wiped the memory from his mind; replaced it with a more acceptable impression. Josh was simply a twenty-first century teenager. The possibility of his being on drugs didn't bear thinking about, nor was it worth raising it at this point. To Carl's way of thinking, it was essential that he earn positive pal points with his son before delving any further.

'You okay, mate?' he asked, standing at the door and feeling, to his surprise, somewhat stiff and uncomfortable.

Memories of his own childhood flooded, again, into his mind, like icy waters swirling, stirring, sweeping his present-day comfort out of reach. He slammed the door on them.

'Thought we might have some chum time together this morning; take your bike to a scramble. What d'you think?'

Thumbs still twitching, Josh lifted his gaze, briefly, from the screen in his hands.

'Okay.'

'Have to get a move on, mate. There's an off-road skills academy starting at noon. Thought you might like to take part.'

Again to his surprise, Josh suddenly threw down his tablet and scrambled out of bed.

'Thanks, Dad. You're ace.'

With Josh's bike stowed in the back of the four-by-four, Carl drove down the A38, veered off to pass through Dartington Arts & Craft centre and the ancient town of Totnes, and arrived at the off-road centre, once a farm, in plenty of time for the skills academy.

It was a not a cheap event. Taking out his Mastercard, Carl passed comment, a jovial reference to his expectations of impoverishment by the time he'd raised two sons and a daughter. The cost, explained the instructor, took into account that the academy was conducted on the centre's own bikes, with riding kit and safety equipment provided to ensure the highest standards.

'And at the end, your son will have a certificate to say he's completed the course, and a photograph to prove it.'

Initially disappointed that he would not be riding his own bike, Josh soon came round when he was escorted to the locker room, entering into the spirit of the thing and taking his place among the other young people, despite some of them being kids of primary school age.

Watching his son perform in the indoor arena set in the heart of the South Hams, Carl glanced round at the other families present and felt a surge of pride. Here, among the affluent second-home owners down from London and the Home Counties for the weekend, he could hold his own. This was his territory!

When Josh's session was over, Carl took him to the coffee bar for a Coke. Seating himself opposite his son in the converted barn, he grinned across the table.

'Enjoy that?'

'It was great Dad!' Josh's face was flushed with pleasure. 'Thanks. Can we come again?'

'Course we can. Once you get the hang of it, you'll be able to get outside. I was looking at the aerial shots.' He indicated a series of framed photographs on the wall. 'There's an MX track all round the lanes and through the fields. Imagine that. Might even be tempted to join you.'

Josh grinned. 'Nath's gonna be green when he hears.'

Carl glanced down at his Americano.

'He's not the only one, I don't suppose. What's this I hear about you having a fight at school?'

When he looked up, Josh's face was scarlet.

'She told you!' he shouted. 'Mum. I flaming well told her not to.'

Carl felt, rather than saw, heads turn at his son's raised voice.

'She had to tell me, Josh,' he said, evenly. 'I'm your dad. She may not have understood - mums don't, on the whole. But you can tell me. What's it all about? Some girl jilted you? Not worth it. There'll be plenty more in the offing in my experience.'

Josh gyrated the large tetra-cup before him, watching the dark, swirling liquid within.

'It wasn't - it wasn't a girl, Dad.'

'Then what was it? You're not in trouble with - It's nothing - illegal, is it? Please tell me you haven't got involved with -'

'Oh, for heck's sake! It wasn't me, Dad. It was you.'

Josh's hand jerked, sloshing some of the Coke onto the table. He attempted to wipe it with his fingers, succeeding only in spreading the puddle across the table.

Carl picked up a paper napkin from the drinks' tray and wiped it clean.

'Me?' he said, tight-lipped. 'How come it's always me, Josh, whenever things go wrong?'

'It was you, Dad.' The look Josh gave was full of fury. 'At least - that's what Mike said.'

'Mike Hammond? The butcher's son? So what could he possibly have to say that would make you beat the living daylights out of him?'

'I didn't believe him. Of course I didn't. That's why I hit him. To shut him up.'

'So what did he say?' Carl persisted; and as he heard the words fall from his mouth, the great yawning truth of the matter opened up in his belly.

The pain on Josh's face was all-too evident. For a moment he looked as though he would remain silent. Then, like a broken mains water pipe that could no longer be contained, he burst forth.

'He said - he said you owed his dad thousands. That you never paid your flaming bills. That he wasn't the only one you owed. That you were too busy spending your money on that slut you work with.'

Speechless, Carl glugged down the remainder of his coffee. And as the scalding liquid hit his stomach and nausea rose in his gullet, he wished he hadn't.

CHAPTER NINE

JULIA LOCKED HER purchases in the car boot, in sight of Exeter Cathedral, then walked up the incline and through Southernhay West. With its Georgian houses, winter-flowering communal gardens and leafless trees, it presented a pleasing appearance. Arriving at a gap in the city wall, still standing, miraculously, after two thousand years of ancient sieges and assaults, and more modern bombings and demolition, she emerged into Cathedral Close on her way to see Evie.

Sometimes she felt as if she, herself, were under siege; as if life were a game of snakes and ladders in which every move forward and upward resulted, inevitably, in a downward slide back from whence she'd come. Now December, it was more than six months since her first session of counselling, but even allowing for a break in the summer, she began to wonder if she would ever know the freedom from guilt - the wholeness - that Evie advocated.

Hilary had said something similar the previous week, not to her directly, but to a friend who'd shared with them both some of the details of her difficult marriage and her sense of failure.

'You've been set free of all that!' Hilary said, filling aid boxes to send overseas. 'You have to accept the truth of that. Don't let your emotions tell you otherwise. We're told, as believers, that we have to stand firm. Not to let ourselves be burdened again by a yoke of slavery.'

Intuitively, Julia had understood that 'slavery' could be defined as an obligation always to show gratitude; guilt if one failed to do so; an inability ever to stand up for oneself. Taking all that on board, plus what Evie had worked through with her, she felt, at times, that she *had* made progress; that she was free. After all, she'd stood firm and told Carl how detrimental it was to the children's development for them to have to see him put her down, as he had in the past.

'It's just not on,' she'd said.

And he appeared to have made amends. At least, she thought he had. Perhaps it was merely that he was at home so infrequently nowadays that the occasion simply didn't arise?

Nevertheless, she was convinced there had been positives. Ladders up included having the courage to speak to Carl about Josh's fight and threatened suspension from sixth form. Despite his initial anger when he learned that she'd kept the meeting with the Head to herself, she'd maintained her calm, explained herself to him in a reasoned, mature manner, and he'd eventually accepted it.

'I behaved as an adult,' she'd told Evie the following week, 'despite what I think you would have described as a thwarted authorative parent reaction in Carl. Or even a child.'

She'd felt pleased with herself. What's more it had worked. Carl had initiated an outing with Josh and - she assumed, though he'd never said - had spoken of their disappointment, their concern with their son's behaviour. The evidence of an improved relationship between father and son was certainly there, and Julia felt she had good reason to feel satisfied.

If only that were it. But it wasn't.

Snakes down had followed, and included a number of unexplained bills, plus the phone call she'd received that morning, after breakfast. All of which she intended to discuss with Evie that afternoon. Arriving in Cathedral Yard, she made her way up the dusty wooden stairs to the counselling room.

'It was so embarrassing,' she confessed to Evie when both were seated. 'I went to see our butcher this morning to order the Christmas turkey, and he asked me to go into his office. He was so apologetic you'd think he was the one at fault.'

Evie's eyebrows rose, and her pen was poised to take notes. Julia continued, leaning forward to convey her concern.

'He told me Carl had not paid him for - I don't know how long. The bill was huge. I was shocked. He explained that he couldn't supply us any more until it was paid.'

'How awful for you.' Evie's pen tapped against the side of the notepad on her lap. 'Has this happened before?'

'Never.'

'So what did you do?'

'Fortunately,' Julia relaxed against the back of her chair, 'because Carl gives me a small personal allowance and I hadn't spent anything for a while, I had enough in my bank account to pay a little of it off. Though not much. But I felt so ashamed. I couldn't get out of there fast enough.'

She twisted her hands in her lap, reliving her discomfort.

'And have you managed to speak to Carl about it?' Evie asked, full of sympathy. 'To ask him for an explanation?'

She was so kind, thought Julia; such a good listener, and so full of helpful advice.

'I knew you'd ask me that!' She smiled. 'I could hear your voice in my head. So I tried ringing the office, immediately. But I couldn't get him. Not even on his mobile.'

'Did his secretary - Lucy? - say when he'd be back?'

'I got through to one of the other girls. She wasn't sure where he was.'

Evie scribbled a few words in her notebook, and Julia was shocked to see a hint of grey in the hair on top of her head.

Evie looked up.

'Perhaps it's just a one-off this unpaid bill? An oversight?'

Julia grimaced.

'I wish it were. When I left the butchers', I went into John Lewis for a coffee. And then I tried on a gorgeous red lace dress I thought would do for the Christmas ball at the Golf Club. Only to discover that the account hasn't been paid for months, and I was over the limit.'

'So! No new dress?' Evie asked; and noting her drab appearance, Julia felt suddenly ashamed. She shrugged.

'I don't really need one. It's just that Carl doesn't like me to wear last year's. He says it doesn't do his street cred any good.'

A shaft of winter sunlight again picked out the streak of grey in Evie's hair.

'So what are you planning to do about the outstanding accounts?' she asked.

Julia put her hand on the arm of the chair in which she was seated. There was a tiny rip in the leather and, without thinking, she put her nail into it, retracting it immediately as she realised the potential damage she might inflict.

'Oh, I'm sure there must be some good reason for it,' she said, her voice sounding terse to her own ears. 'I know Carl's stretched to his limit at the moment. I don't mean financially but time-wise. He's had to spend a lot of time in Wales, ironing out the problems I guess you get with any new business.'

'But you *will* raise the matter with him?' Evie persisted.

Julia hesitated. 'Might I have a glass of water please?'

'Of course!'

Evie disappeared to the kitchen, and Julia got up from her chair and walked across to the window. A Christmas tree, dressed with coloured lights, had been erected in front of the cathedral. Passing on the other side of the building on her way to Evie's, she'd not noticed it earlier. She looked from side to side. Around the perimeter of The Green, the boutiques and restaurants showed similar adornment. There was something rather ironic about it, she thought, the juxtaposition of the cathedral and its symbolism, and the pagan festival celebrated by the secular edifices that surrounded it.

Evie reappeared and, thanking her for the water, Julia took her seat again. She drank, and remained silent for a while, staring into space, and only coming to when Evie spoke.

'You seemed a little hesitant when I asked if you were going to raise the matter of the unpaid bills?'

Julia sighed. 'Outstanding bills are not the only problem,' she said, nursing the water glass and rubbing her thumb against the film of condensation that clouded the outside. 'I had a phone call before I left home this morning. To begin with, I thought it was the receptionist at the hotel where Carl and I stayed when he threw the party to launch the opening of the Welsh factory in October. But that was more than six weeks ago, and eventually I realised it couldn't possibly be there.'

She sipped the glass of water again, and unable to meet Evie's gaze, fixed her eyes on the single bar electric fire that burned in the black leaded hearth.

'It was very odd,' she said, frowning at the recollection. 'She began by asking me if I was Mrs Worth. Naturally, I was a bit wary. You can never be too sure with all these scams around.'

'No, indeed!'

'Then she told me who they were. The name of the hotel. And she asked if I'd left my earrings in the drawer beside the bed.'

She fell silent again, fighting the inference this raised in her mind.

'And had you?' Evie asked.

Julia looked across at her. 'Well, that's just the thing. I was so confused I had to ask the name of the hotel again. It was The Leek & Lion. I guess Carl must put up there when he goes to the factory. He always rings me from the office or on his mobile when he's in Wales, so I wouldn't really know where he stays. But the thing is why would they think I'd left my earrings? I'd never heard of the place before, let alone stayed there.'

On the other side of the hearth Evie said nothing. But the way in which she locked her gaze on her face felt unnerving. Julia shuddered. Was Evie thinking the unthinkable; what she, herself, didn't want to think? As if to confirm it, Evie looked away. Outside, a sudden gust of wind rattled the windows. Julia shuddered again.

When I've said goodbye to Julia, I set about tidying my papers away and locking the filing cabinet. She is my last appointment today, and as this is the evening I'm to dine at the Sampsons and meet with Nancy's nephew, Scott, I'm glad of the time to nip home for a shower and change of clothing. Thank goodness, also, that I've now managed to scrape together enough money to resurrect my car from the garage repair depot, before it's deemed fit only for the scrap yard.

'Think this will do, Pumpkin?' I ask, donning a hip-skimming twirly-bottomed floral skirt I bought from the charity shop a year ago, and delighting in the idea of how shocking it would sound to an outsider to hear me consulting my cat. The skirt, completely at odds with my usual austere taste and style, has never been worn before. Well it has, of course, being second hand! But not by me. I apply some make-up - nothing as florid as the skirt, but certainly more than I normally wear, which could almost be said to be nothing.

Driving over to Topsham, my mind is taken up with the events of the afternoon, and what Julia had to say. Plus, of course, what she didn't say. The unpaid butcher's bill and John Lewis account could be explained away, I guess. Never having had much in the way of money, myself, I can't begin to imagine the sums that Carl must have had to raise to set up his business in Wales. But I'd have thought they must be pretty humungous. By stretching my sympathy glands to the nth degree I could just about excuse him for overlooking what, in contrast, must be paltry amounts. If, indeed, he has overlooked them. And therein lies the rub.

What I can't fathom, is why in this day and age any woman should be deemed incapable of paying the bills herself? I mean with online banking, it's hardly the prerogative of a financial whizz-kid. I manage my own finances, for goodness sake. The more I think about it, the greater my conviction. Julia would be more than capable. And as for her being on the receiving end of a 'small personal allowance' - well! That smacks of being a kept woman, to my mind.

I change gear and negotiate the busy roundabout at Countess Wear. Throttling away on the other side, I resume my analysis of the situation. If the financial aspect were the only consideration in Julia's muddled life, I think there might be less cause for concern. Her husband might, for instance, have a legitimate reason for his impecuniosity. He might, perhaps, have a short-term cash flow problem. He might, even, have a genuine long-term problem, brought on by circumstances beyond his control. But it's seeing the financial issues through the prism of other matters that worries me.

The road I'm on passes under the M5, still thundering, even at this hour, with east-west bound traffic. In a few moments I shall be at my destination. Thundering in my mind, meanwhile, is the image of the girl I saw with Julia's husband at the Golf Club. But even that, too, I think might be explained away if it were an isolated incident.

It's the combination of all these factors that makes my assumptions about Julia's husband so unavoidable. I list them in my mind: his frequent absence; his need of lodgings in Wales; the appearance of personal items of jewellery in an hotel in which Julia has never stayed; the fact that they were thought to belong to a Mrs Worth; and finally both Carl's and the PA's absence when Julia rang the office.

Parking the car outside Guy and Nancy's cottage I can draw only one conclusion. And it doesn't look good!

Guy's wife, Nancy, is as amazing as ever when I arrive on the dot of seven per her invitation. She greets me at the door in her wheelchair, and hangs my coat on a hook within her reach. I know from previous conversations with her that she and Guy bought the cottage in Topsham many years earlier, when they married, and were determined, following her accident, to stay put. The changes they've made to accommodate her disabilities never cease to astonish me. They've been accomplished in such keeping with the age of the property as to be almost unobtrusive.

Nevertheless it is tiny, with ceilings and doors clearly not built to accommodate someone of Scott Bingham's height and presence. His head seems only inches below the black ceiling beams, and he has to duck when moving from room to room. The hand in which he takes mine feels huge, with long, bony fingers, and it's no surprise when, having introduced us, Nancy tells me that he's a pianist.

My initial enthusiasm about meeting an attractive, unattached man plummets. With little to boast of in the way of musical appreciation, my contribution to any conversation might be limited. Clearly sensing my hesitation, he steers us in a different direction.

'I understand you're gonna be my guide?' he says, as we're ushered into the dining room. 'Kind of you to give up your time.'

'Not at all! Guy and Nancy have been very good to me. It's the least I can do. Besides, I'm more than a little fanatical about our lovely city and countryside.'

Scott holds the back of my chair while I take my place, then seats himself opposite.

'I'm particularly lookin' forward to seeing the cathedral,' he says, when we're all seated and served. 'I believe it has the longest nave in the world? And that it houses an astronomical clock?'

His face lights up and I wonder why any woman would part company with such a good-looking guy.

'Plus a wonderful seventeenth century organ,' I reply, 'which I had the pleasure of hearing in the summer. I never thought of myself as having a musical gene in my body. But it was a great evening. So inspiring!'

At the other end of the table, diminutive in her wheelchair, but exuding largesse as a hostess, Nancy speaks up.

'Actually, I think there's a Christmas Carols event on Wednesday evening. I'm sure Guy could rustle up some tickets if the two of you were interested in going?'

If I correctly interpret the glance of conspiracy that passes between Guy and Nancy, I'm not for saying. A second opportunity to attend a musical event in the grandeur of the cathedral, and in the company of a charming companion, is not one to be missed.

'Well, if you and Guy are unable to go,' I say, disingenuously, 'I'd love to accompany Scott. Unless he has something better to do, of course?'

'What better than to escort a delightful young lady to a musical event?' he says across the table. And even though I know this is not for real, that it's just a sophisticated game of role play, I feel a warm sense of pleasure begin in the pit of my stomach and spread to my cheeks.

Tucking into roast pork and all the trimmings, we arrange to meet on the morrow with all the enthusiasm of a couple of teenagers. Silently, I congratulate myself. I'm so glad Pumpkin had the foresight to advise me to wear the twirly floral skirt, and to put on a little make-up.

Carl put the car in the garage and entered the house via the interconnecting door. Following a gruelling meeting at the bank with Miller, he'd arrived home much later than usual. Consequently, it was no surprise to him to find the kitchen unlit and unoccupied. What was surprising, startling in fact, was to enter his study with the intention of depositing his briefcase, and find Julia there.

'What the ... Thought you'd have been in bed long ago.'

She was seated on the sofa bed, her knees drawn up under her chin, and only the desk lamp on for illumination.

'I've been waiting for you,' she said, the chill in her voice suggesting that a row was imminent. He sighed, put his briefcase down beside his desk, and glanced at her.

'Look, whatever this is, could it wait until the morning, please? I've had a long day.'

That was a euphemism if ever there was one, he thought. He rubbed his hand over his chin, and felt the stubble rasp against his skin.

Julia swivelled on the sofa; put her feet to the floor.

'Me, too,' she said.

And then he saw that she'd been looking through a photograph album - a recent one, if he wasn't mistaken. A sense of relief flooded through him. That at least explained her presence in his study, though not her icy demeanour.

'No, I don't think it can wait until tomorrow,' she continued. 'We can't keep pretending that everything's alright, can we Carl? Don't you think it's time we behaved as two adults and brought a degree of transparency to our relationship?'

'Well! That was psycho-babble and a half!' said Carl

It took all his will-power to restrain himself from snorting aloud. He advanced into the room, but remained standing, looking down at his wife, noting her air of dishevelment, deploring her bare feet and lack of grooming.

'I don't know what's got into you these days,' he said. 'Doesn't your allowance cover a trip to the hairdressers these days?'

She looked up at him, meeting his eyes with a coolness he'd not seen before.

'Oh, no Carl! You're not going to put me off with your usual tricks. I have things to say, and I intend to say them. First off is the fact that you omitted to tell me the reason for our son's fight with the butcher's boy.'

Carl nodded. So that was it. She was getting good, his wife. Impressive! Full marks for her skill in attacking rather than retreating in defence. He especially liked the use of 'our son' instead of Josh's name. He softened his voice.

'I didn't want to worry you.'

'You didn't want to enlighten me.'

Boy, she was not going to give in. He'd never seen her like this. Was this the result of all the time she was spending with Hilary Bankster and her mob? The thought of it irritated him no end.

'I take it you're referring to the unpaid bill?'

'Bills plural,' said Julia. 'For a staggering amount. Steve showed me what we owe for meat. And then there's the John Lewis account, plus, of course, a number of others.'

Carl sat down hard at his desk and switched into sympathy-appeal mode.

'For heaven's sake, Julia. Can't a man expect a little compassion from his wife? You know damned well how busy I've been with the new factory. Everything I do is for you and the kids. If I've overlooked one or two bills - so what?'

Julia appeared unperturbed. Certainly unrepentant.

'But that's not all, is it?' Her voice was quiet and even, quite different to what he might usually expect from her.

'You mean the garage bill?'

She raised her eyebrows and he kicked himself for admitting to something she evidently hadn't known about.

'I mean the hotel in Wales. The one that rang me this morning and asked if I was Mrs Worth. The one that told me I'd left my earrings in the bedroom. Beside the bed. A bedroom I've never been in. A bed I've never...'

'Okay! Okay! I get the picture.'

Actually, he didn't. He felt genuinely puzzled. What was the woman on about? He tried to get his head around what she was saying. Nothing came to him.

'So? Why would they think I'd left my earrings there?' Julia persisted.

'How the heck should I know?'

'But you do know, don't you Carl? Because they're not my earrings.'

Carl leapt to his feet again. 'Well in that case, what is this all about?'

Julia looked at him impassively. Clearly, she thought he was shamming.

'Look,' he said, tiredness creeping up on him, 'I don't know what you're talking about.'

'Then I'll tell you,' Julia said in measured tones. 'They're not my earrings. They're hers.'

With that, she spun the photograph album round on her lap so that it was visible to him. It took him a moment or two to comprehend. And then he saw. And understood where she was coming from. Because before him was a series of photographs of the party he'd thrown to launch the Welsh factory. And there, beneath Julia's pointing, accusing finger, was an image of Lucy. Lucy wearing a pair of earrings. A particularly distinctive, sparkling pair of earrings.

CHAPTER TEN

THE GREAT THING about Exeter city centre, one of the many virtues I extol, is that it's so compact. I've arranged to meet Scott Bingham at St David's railway station as he'll be travelling in from Topsham by train. From there, we can either walk or take a short bus ride over to the quay, a popular and historic tourist resort. I'm looking forward to our sightseeing together while Guy and Nancy are visiting her consultant, and although I'm wearing practical corduroy trousers and trainers for the day, I have taken a little more care than usual with my face.

I hope it's not my imagination, but Scott's eyes appear to light up as he steps off the train and sees me. It's been a long time since anyone of the opposite sex has shown any interest in me. And though I'm not entertaining any notion of romance in the air, it's a good feeling. A cloudless blue sky and crisp winter air add to my sense of wellbeing.

'All set for a day steeped in history?' I ask, aware of his penchant for all things ancient.

'I know we Yanks are notorious,' he responds with a smile that reveals the gleaming white teeth you'd expect of a nationality known for its orthodontic perfection. 'Can't get enough of it because we've so little of our own.'

'I've never been to America so I wouldn't know. But you'll find plenty to interest you here. There's been a quayside in Exeter since Roman times.'

Aware of my every need - his hand at my back to steady me on the bus, a gallant ushering into my seat - Scott succeeds, nevertheless, in looking utterly relaxed and debonair. He's a head-turner, that's for sure. And though I can't imagine who endowed him with such height and stature, given Nancy's tiny frame and that she's a blood relative, I can, and do, bask in his presence.

We alight from the bus and make our way to the visitor centre and ticket office. Scott insists on paying our admission fees, which I'm more than happy to permit, and we walk in until we're standing at the water's edge where the River Exe and the Exeter Shipping Canal converge to become the Canal Basin.

'Whoa!' Scott is clearly impressed.

A jumble of ancient buildings, boats and taverns surrounds us, plus a few tourists - and the smell of fish pervades the air.

'So what sort of trade would the locals have been involved in?' Scott asks, turning this way and that to take it all in.

'Wool,' I reply. 'Or more precisely, woollen cloth. Down at Cricklepit Mill. We can walk there later.'

'And was it a money-spinner?' Scott laughs. 'Excuse the pun.'

I grin, happy to know that today is going to be fun.

'Very much so. In fact St Nicholas Priory, which I hope to take you to just up the hill, was the home of one of Exeter's most successful wool merchants.'

'And the canal was the means of shipping it out to the world?'

'It was eventually. In the early days, the river was navigable as far as Exeter. But I think round about the 13th or 14th century there was a bit of trouble between rival merchants. The quay became redundant for a while when some of them built weirs further down to prevent cargoes getting up or down from here.'

'Trade wars. Somewhat contentious!'

A hint of nostalgia in Scott's voice makes me wonder if he's still mourning the demise of his marriage. However, as he's not mentioned it, and I have only the scantest of detail from Guy, I can hardly ask. I turn to him, cheerfully.

'Well, as they say, where there's a will there's a way. That's why the canal was built, to get round the obstacles.'

'Sounds like a plan.' Scott grins down at me and we stand in silence for a moment until a thought occurs to me.

'Except that they then built the Customs' House to ensure that they all paid their dues. Party poopers!'

For some ridiculous reason, this strikes us both as hilarious. We break into spontaneous and companionable hoots of laughter before setting off to walk down the tow-path to the locks.

Julia walked up the steps to Evie's counselling room. There was little laughter in her household these days, she reflected. With less than a week to go until Christmas, she felt, as she and the children put up the decorations and dressed the tree, that she was on a roller coaster.

'Sometimes I feel I'm getting somewhere,' she explained to Evie on what was to be their final meeting before the holiday. 'And the next moment I'm plunged into despair again. I think it's beginning to affect the children.'

'I'm afraid that's how it goes,' said Evie, her voice conveying the sympathy she obviously felt. 'So what happened about the John Lewis account? Is that what's made you despair?'

Julia shivered, with cold as much as with the memory. The usual single bar electric fire burned in the grate and, looking at Evie clad in a thick fleece and woollen socks visible beneath her trousers, she wondered how on earth she coped through the winter.

'Surprisingly, that was one of the ups,' she said. 'You'd have been proud of me. I thought through what I wanted to say first, then tackled Carl in a very calm and adult way.'

'Well done!' Evie beamed with what Julia took to be satisfaction.

'Trouble is,' she continued, 'it turned out that it's not just the John Lewis account that's outstanding, but the butcher, the baker and the candlestick maker. That was the down.'

Evie grimaced. 'Don't let the negatives take hold. You've done well. Now stay positive. Every step you take on this journey takes you closer to your destination.'

Unused to praise, Julia felt suddenly shy.

'I have found what you've taught me enormously helpful,' she said.

'Good!' Evie scribbled in her note book. 'Now all you have to keep in mind is that every time you behave in a *considered* manner, rather than a pre-programmed emotional way, you're one step nearer to being the person you're meant to be.'

Julia pulled the sleeves of her jackets over her wrists in an effort to keep warm. It was embarrassing, given that Evie seemed oblivious to the temperature.

'Yes, I can see that. I still remember that first session with you, when I told you I felt like a puppet with Carl's hand up my back manipulating my every move.'

'And now, little by little, you're becoming a free agent.'

A warming surge of fulfilment coursed through Julia's veins. What Evie was saying tied in so neatly with what she understood was the prerogative of every human being. She was beginning to realise, more and more, that being the person you were meant to be was not, as some people seemed to think, to bind you to rules and 'thou shalt nots'. Nor was it about God becoming the puppeteer, with his hand up your back manipulating you. It was about being set free. Free of guilt; of trying to conform to other people's expectations; of shame when you failed.

Evie interrupted her reverie.

'So what are you going to do about the unpaid bills?'

Julia put her head on one side, considering the matter.

'I'm not sure there's much I can do,' she said at last. 'I know for a fact that Carl wouldn't let me pay them. He's always insisted that we have separate accounts, and my allowance wouldn't cover them. I suppose I just have to trust that having brought them to his attention, he'll settle them.'

A cold wind rattled the windows. Julia shivered again.

'But that's not the only thing that's happened,' she said, injecting enthusiasm into her voice, determined to be positive as Evie had urged her. 'I think I deserve an A+ for my homework this week.'

Evie, seemingly oblivious to the cold draughts and the discussion they'd had in their previous session, raised an eyebrow.

'Oh? What's that, then?'

'You remember, last week, I told you about the phone call I had saying I'd left my earrings in an hotel in Wales? Well, I brought that up with Carl, too.'

Evie seemed a little distracted, Julia thought, as if she had other things on her mind. Not surprising, she supposed, with Christmas so close.

'I have to say, even though you appeared to dismiss it, I thought the worst,' Julia continued. 'So when I got home, I rang the hotel and got them to describe them to me. Then I went into Carl's study and looked through the photo albums. I was sure I'd seen something that matched that description. And lo and behold, I had. Lucy - Carl's PA - was wearing them at the party we put on to launch the Welsh factory.'

Evie settled back in her chair, now apparently, all ears.

'I did wonder if there had been a mistake,' she said in even tones. 'So what did you do?'

'Carl found me in his study, and once we'd dealt with the bills, I confronted him with that, too.' Julia relaxed, pleased with herself, and waited for Evie's reaction.

'To begin with he denied any knowledge of the earrings or the hotel,' she continued, when Evie gave an encouraging incline of her head. 'And then I showed him the photograph album.'

She paused for dramatic effect.

'And?' said Evie.

'Well, to begin with, I thought he was going to hit me. He was furious. Swore, called me all sorts of names which I won't repeat, and accused me of undermining his endeavours to earn us a decent living because of my constant suspicions. Then he blamed Hilary's influence - the 'do-gooders'. I suspect if he'd known about my visits to you, he'd have blamed you, too.'

She smiled.

'Judging by your demeanour,' Evie said, 'I'd say this episode had a happy ending?'

'It did,' Julia admitted. 'Once he'd calmed down, Carl told me that he'd bought the earrings for Lucy in lieu of a Christmas bonus.'

'But I thought you said she was wearing them at the party. That was in the autumn, wasn't it?'

Julia nodded. 'That's what I said, too. But Carl said he also wanted to thank her for her part in helping to set up the Welsh factory. He thought it would be a nice thing to do, rather than give her a cash bonus; especially seeing that her long-term relationship had broken up and she's on her own. He gave them to her at the hotel because he didn't want other members of the staff to know and think it was favouritism.'

Evie's eyes were bright and penetrating and, for a moment, Julia felt unnerved, as if her soul were exposed for all to see. Evie shifted on her seat.

'So you've established that Carl gave the earrings to - Lucy, is it? And you've been told that it was for legitimate reasons. But that doesn't explain why the hotel thought they belonged to you. Nor why it was a different hotel to the one you went to in October.'

Julia nodded.

'That's what I thought, too. Carl said the only explanation was that he now stays at a less expensive hotel, to save money, and he must have dropped the bill on one of his visits, the chambermaid came across it, saw his name on it, put two and two together and made five.'

Julia stopped. She found herself leaning forward toward the meagre heat of the fire. Putting her tension down to the cold, she forced herself upright, sat back and looked across at Evie. Her face was in shadow, but Julia thought she looked unconvinced.

She swallowed hard. She knew the questions that would be lurking in Evie's mind because they'd plagued hers, too. Until she'd applied herself to her new resolve. Determined now, she refused to think the worst. Carl had accused her of undermining him with her suspicions. He was her husband. The least she could do was to give him the benefit of the doubt. She shivered. Then pulled her jacket closer across her chest.

There are times when I feel like banging my head against the proverbial brick wall and this is one of them. Everything in me screams, *Julia Beware*! Bidding her goodbye that Friday afternoon I have, of course, to abide by the ethics of my profession which, rightly, would frown upon such rash behaviour.

There is no evidence to confirm what my heart and head tell me, namely that Carl Worth has embarked, or is about to embark, upon a full-scale affair with his PA, Lucy. Yet all the markers appear to have been laid down.

'Don't you just wish you could shake some sense into your clients sometimes,' I ask Guy, rhetorically, as we depart for our respective homes.

'Tell me about it!' he says, not as an invitation for me to spill the beans, but as affirmation.

Speaking of invitations, I remember, as I arrive home, that I'm due next door for a small pre-Christmas, belated wet-the-baby's head drink with my neighbours. As soon as I've fed Pumpkin, washed and changed, I head off up my garden path and down theirs.

I suppose it must be about five years since Sharon and Ben moved into No. 5 and, apart from the Economy Seven washing machine scenario and the odd shouting match, their lives have scarcely impinged upon mine. In their mid-to-late-thirties, I'd say, she is a dinner-lady at the local school, while he, like my ex, is in the police force.

'Hi Jason.' I greet the seven-year old who opens the door to me, and whose wobbly bike-riding lessons caused me such concern in the summer. 'How are you, and how's the new baby?'

Jason gives me a cheeky grin. 'Noisy and messy,' he says, ignoring the first part of my question. 'But she'll do.'

From the look on his face, I'd say she'd more than just 'do'. With unexpected composure for such a small boy, he shows me into the sitting room, a mirror image of my own, though furnished rather more flamboyantly.

'Evie!'

Sharon greets me warmly and proceeds to introduce me to the half-dozen or so guests who crowd into the tiny space between florid stylised paper on the walls, huge modern sofas and an equally huge flat screen TV. Ben, having first asked my preference, produces a glass of red wine of tolerable distinction. Then I spend the next half hour conversing on what is clearly of great import to the other women present, but I consider to be the most vacuous elements of Christmas. Tinsel, tree and turkey monopolise.

Suddenly, all heads turn as Sharon appears at the door with the baby. Despite the advancing evening and a mere seven or eight-month tenure on life, she's dressed like a little princess with pink tights, pom-pom bootees, a beribboned full-skirted frock and decorated headband. Plain and simple being my style, I find myself deploring this adulation of designer adornment, and have to chastise myself for my judgemental attitude. To my surprise, Sharon passes the baby to me, depositing her in my arms before I have time to protest.

I stand there, awkwardly, while the women in the room cluck and fuss and the men obediently raise their glasses to drink a toast. Having no experience of babies, I feel stupid, conspicuous, an object of ridicule. Then Lily-Rose-Marie - yes, really - turns her chubby pink face to mine and gives me a toothless smile of such endearing quality it would melt a heart of steel. I'm aware that, like Babaji's tiger, I am now nothing more than a pool of ghee.

Would that this baby were mine. How I should have loved her. Adored her. Shopped for her. Dressed her in ridiculously expensive pom-pom bootees and designer frocks. Yes, and the pink tights. But not the Alice band restricting her tiny head. No never that. And never the mutilation of pierced ears and gold studs with which Lily-Rose is adorned. Nor the bracelets that bite into her chubby wrists.

I could go on. But as if on cue, Lily-Rose grasps my little finger. And with it my heart.

So when, later, with the baby back in bed and most of the guests departed, Sharon tackles me in the kitchen and asks me if I would be the child's Godmother, I am sold, a slave to the idea of having a part to play in this baby's life.

'We'd love you to be Lily-Rose's Godmum, Ben and me,' Sharon says, easing her plump figure past me. Up to the elbows in soap suds and wine glasses, I rein in my natural response.

'Wouldn't you be better having someone in the family,' I ask. 'Perhaps your sister, or Ben's brother?'

Sharon shakes her head, ruffling the glassy surface of her hair like ripples on a pond.

'Me and my sister haven't talked for years, Evie. And Ben's brother lives down under. We was so hoping you'd do it?'

I rinse a wine glass under the tap to wash away the suds, thinking, as I do so, of the symbolism of a christening.

'Thing is, Sharon, I'm not a believer. Well, it's not that I disbelieve in any active sense. Just that I have an absence of faith in my life. I'm not sure I could make those promises and mean them.'

Sharon takes a tea towel from a hook on the wall and begins to dry the glasses.

'Oh, we don't mind that,' she breathes, dismissing my concerns as irrelevant. 'We just want someone who will give Lily-Rose some good tips on life. Be there for her. I think they call it a guide-mother instead of Godmother. You'd be just right. Please say yes.'

How can I resist the big blue eyes and pleading face that confronts me when I turn from the sink? I swallow hard in an effort to do so. And fail.

'Okay,' I say weakly. 'I'll think about it. Promise.'

As if one social event were not enough for me to cope with, the party next door is swiftly followed, next day, by a date with Scott Bingham to attend Carols at the Cathedral, due to start at one o'clock. He arrives shortly before midday, this time at Central Station, and tells me, no ifs and buts, that he's taking me for lunch.

'We're going to the Rougemont Hotel if that's okay with you. My aunt tells me it's just over the road right opposite the station. But if you don't mind, I'd love to take a quick look around before we go in. I've been reading up on the history of the area.'

Looking every inch the American tourist, Scott takes his 4G iPad - yes, I do know about such things - from the bag he has slung over his shoulder, and brings up the information he's found on Google. I confirm that I'm more than happy to amble before we eat.

'You probably know more about the history of the place than I do,' I say, as we turn away from the hotel into Rougemont Gardens. 'All I know is that it's a volcanic outcrop and is renowned as a place of national archaeological interest. I believe the name is taken from the red sandstone.'

Scott consults his more reliable electronic source.

'It says here that Rougemont Castle was built soon after the city's rebellion against William the Conqueror. And that it gets a mention in Shakespeare's *Richard III*.'

We walk through the gardens, now in their winter dereliction, to the castle and courthouse - site of England's last execution for witchcraft, so Scott tells me - until we reach the old city wall, where we turn back.

'So what brings you to Britain,' I ask, 'other than to see your aunt?'

'Gee, I was afraid you were going to ask me that,' Scott replies, replacing his tablet in his bag.

I'm intrigued.

'Sorry. Am I being nosy? Comes with the job. Endless questions.'

Scott grins.

'Not at all. It's just that I haven't yet told Guy and Nancy the real reason for my visit, so I'd be grateful if you didn't mention anything to them.'

I nod to confirm my acceptance of his condition.

'I expect you know that my marriage came to an end rather abruptly,' he continues. 'Long story. I'll tell you sometime. Anyway, I got the offer of a job just north of London, subject to interview of course, and thought it might be an appropriate new start.'

I touch his arm in a show of affirmation.

'That's great! And is it? A new start?'

'Hope so. Just heard this morning when I was on the train. An informal email confirmation that I've got the post, to be followed in due course by a formal letter.'

'That's brilliant! But you haven't said who you'll be working for, or what the job entails,' I finish.

Aware that the thrill of enthusiasm that rushed through her veins was not entirely altruistic, Evie grasped Scott's arm in hers and squeezed. Grinning with pleasure, he gave her a peck on the cheek.

'I'll be working for The Boss,' Scott grins and points heavenward, 'though it will be the college that pays me. And I'll be lecturing in the music faculty. So as of now, you better address me as sir.'

I click my heels and ape a military-style salute.

By the time I've expressed my pleasure and congratulations, we've retraced our steps and are back at the hotel. Before going into the bar to order a snack lunch, we part company briefly, to visit what Scott calls 'the bathroom'. And it's in the Ladies' Room that I come across Julia.

'We must stop meeting like this!' I joke, inserting my hands into the dryer and recalling the previous occasion at the Golf Club. 'What brings you into town on a Saturday?'

'The children are all involved in various activities,' she explains, standing by the exit ready to depart, 'so I thought I'd have a quick lunch and then go across to take part in Carols at the Cathedral.'

No mention of Carl, I note.

'What a coincidence. We're doing exactly the same. Would you like to join us if you're alone?'

Dismissing her protestations of not wanting to impose herself on us, I lead the way into the bar and introduce her to Scott.

'A friend from Exeter,' I say, indicating Julia. 'And one from America.'

I stand there for a good half minute while they grasp one another's hands and murmur their greetings. One look from one to the other, and I realise I might as well not be there. It's not that they are so rude as to ignore me but, as the evening progresses, I swear, even if I were not a counsellor trained to pick up on the nuances of human behaviour, I could not have missed the intense interest that passes between this man and this woman. Do I feel jealous? Yes, if I'm honest.

CHAPTER ELEVEN

WITH LESS THAN twenty four hours to go to Christmas Day, Julia stood in the middle of the kitchen, ticking things off in her mind, determined that all would be ready for lunch next day with the minimum of fuss. She'd filled the turkey cavity with homemade sweet chestnut, pork and apricot stuffing; prepared the sprouts; the potatoes were peeled and cut all set to par-boil and roast; two puddings, laced with brandy, stood at the ready; and - blow! - she'd forgotten the white sauce and brandy butter.

She took a bowl, whisk and sieve from the cupboard, and a bottle of cognac from the sideboard. Standing the mixing bowl in a pan of hot water, she unwrapped the butter she'd taken from the fridge, cut off a slab and put it in the bowl to soften. When she'd finished assembling all the other ingredients, she called across the hall to the children.

'Boys, have you brought plenty of logs in for the fire in the sitting room? You know Granny likes to be warm.'

A chorus of 'Yes Mum,' drifted down from upstairs. In the face of chores to be done, they'd evidently retreated to their rooms.

'I hope you're telling me the truth.' Julia injected a note of warning into her voice.

'Yes Mum. Honest.'

'And how are you getting on with laying the dining room table, Abi? Don't forget to use the best silver cutlery. And somewhere there should be a box of silver crackers.'

'All done, except for these.' Abi appeared at the dining room door with a box of red candles in her hand.

'Good! I want us to be able to go to the service at the cathedral tonight, knowing that everything's ready for tomorrow.'

Julia returned to the kitchen and began weighing and measuring. She'd hardly dared hope that things would fall into place so well. The boys had grumbled when she'd first suggested the idea of going to the midnight service.

'How's Father Christmas going to know where to deliver my x-box if I'm not in my bed?' asked Nathan.

'It's Christmas Eve, Mum!' said Josh.

Neither believed in Father Christmas, but it was clear that they didn't want anything to interfere with their idea of what the festival was about. To her surprise, though, Carl had gone along with her request.

'Precisely!' he said. 'It's Christmas Eve. And it's a tradition. It's what people of our ilk should be seen to be doing.'

It might not be for the right reasons, Julia thought, but he did seem to be more amenable to the idea. In recent weeks, there had also been fewer snide remarks about 'men in frocks and believers in need of props', her friendship with Hilary, or the 'do-gooders' with whom she associated. Plus, she'd received the occasional gift of a bunch of flowers! One might almost think that the reality of marriage enrichment had rubbed off on him, Julia reflected, given his acceptance of her right to a life, and the improvement it appeared to have made to their relationship. Not to mention his acquiescence of her desire to celebrate the real meaning of Christmas *en famille*.

The boys had continued to object to the idea of going to the cathedral. But Carl had then followed with a lecture which, to Julia's mind, was bordering on racism, about the necessity of keeping 'British values' alive in the face of 'foreign interlopers' and their religions. She'd tried to intervene but had to concede, eventually, that some of what he'd said made sense, though not the tone.

He should have been a politician, she thought now, beating brandy and icing sugar into the softened butter. He could always be relied upon to put together a cleverly constructed argument, no matter what the subject; nor whether he was for or against it. But at least it had gone in her favour on this occasion. And even Granny, persuaded by the concept of a traditional elitism, would be accompanying the family.

'Please,' she whispered, pouring in more spirit from the bottle, 'let my family - Carl, Granny and the children - discover the wonder, the real meaning, of Christmas.'

Her thoughts returned to the previous week when she'd been invited to join Evie and her friend, Scott, for a bar snack before the Carol Service at the cathedral. It was strange how instantly she and the American had enjoyed a rapport she would once have thought reserved for friends of long standing. Or even family! Perhaps it had something to do with their shared beliefs?

It certainly hadn't taken long to establish the link. A charming man, a true gentleman, he'd chatted quite openly and naturally. Julia had found herself marvelling at his freedom of speech. It was so unlike anything she'd heard before, outside church. Heart-warming, but at the same time almost embarrassing. Almost, but not quite. Because she'd realised then that this unfamiliarity, this - this departmentalisation that was so prevalent in the British, was a problem. God was kept in a box. With the lid firmly on.

She'd heard a sermon on that once. And she'd come to understand, in her own life and experience, that though he might be 'up there' in some people's opinion, if he was truly who he said he was, then he must be 'down here' as well. Wasn't that the real message of Christmas, in fact? Emmanuel. God with us.

Switching off the beater, Julia scraped the brandy butter down from the sides of the bowl, rinsed her hands and searched out a lidded container in which to put it. As she straightened up, Abi appeared at the kitchen door with a bunch of envelopes in her hand. They were clearly late Christmas cards.

'Postman's been. Do you want me to open them for you?'

Julia put the brandy butter in the fridge and began to gather up the dirty utensils to put in the dishwasher.

'Please. They're probably from neighbours.'

'I don't think so. They'd have hand delivered them.' Abi examined the postage stamps. 'This one's been redirected. Looks like it's from - France, I think.'

'Probably one of Daddy's business contacts, then. Better leave him to open them.'

Abi put the cards down next to the kettle.

'When's he going to be back, Mum?' she asked. 'I don't see why he had to work on Christmas Eve.'

Good question, thought Julia. Nor me.

'Not long,' she said aloud, with a conviction she didn't feel. 'I'm sure he'll be here in time for lunch.'

Squashing the feelings of disappointment that filled her, she determined to make this Christmas the best ever.

I've decided to part with tradition and swap an evening in the pub for the Christmas Eve service at the cathedral. As I don my furry boots and muffle up in sweaters and scarves in preparation for the bike ride into town, I jokingly reflect on how worrying this is. My third trip there in the last six months! Am I getting hooked on religion? Or is this, as I hope, simply a belated discovery that I enjoy good music? Set this new passion for music in conjunction with a long-held love of ancient history and architecture, and I think I can safely say I've found the answer.

I'd put my hypothesis to Scott the previous week when we bumped into Julia at the Rougement, and he was telling her about our trip to the quay, and how beautiful the city and surrounding countryside appeared to a stranger.

'Makes you wonder how anyone can *not* believe in God as the author of creation,' he said, clearly unaware that I might be one of them. Or perhaps, quite possibly, to provoke me into deeper thought and discussion.

'I know plenty of people who are passionate about nature and the arts but don't hold with a belief in God.' I countered, mildly.

We were seated at a table in the bar, Scott with a large baguette in his hand, and Julia and I each with a prawn salad before us.

'But an appreciation of beauty and majesty comes from being made in God's image,' Scott protested.

'Says who?' I asked. 'That means nothing to someone who doesn't believe.'

Julia sipped her apple juice, and we all fell silent for a moment. Then Scott sat back in his seat.

'Yeah, I think you're right,' he conceded. 'But the absence of belief doesn't negate the existence of God.'

Julia and I both looked up, frowns on our faces.

'That's a complex sentence,' I said. 'Have to think about that one for a moment.'

Julia put her fork down on her plate, tipped her head on one side and looked thoughtful.

'I think what Scott means,' she said, surprising me with her sagacity, 'is that you can neither prove nor disprove God. We were talking about this one evening at Hilary's a few weeks ago, and someone said it's like trying to prove the existence of electricity to someone who lives in the jungle. You can talk about it to them *ad nauseam* and they'll never understand. It's only if they're transported to another country, another place, and see the effect of a light switched on that they'll ever begin to see the truth for themselves.'

'That's brilliant,' said Scott, slapping his thigh.

Julia blushed. I sat there bemused, looking from one to the other.

Nevertheless, despite the fact that the metaphorical light has never been switched on for me, a week later I admit to being captivated by thoughts of the evening ahead. Will this, like the Christmas Carols event last week, be an evening of religious music intended to inspire? Or will it be simply a moving and uplifting experience intended to counter the darkest period of the year? I suppose, once again, it depends who you are.

The air is crisp and clear as I set off through the lamp lit streets on my way to the city centre, but I arrive at my destination glowing and, I imagine, rosy. It's just as well I've given myself plenty of time. The West Door is crowded with people piling in to listen, to sing, to be inspired.

We filter in and take our seats beneath the extravagant fan-vaulted ceiling held aloft on huge fluted pillars. And as the evening unfolds and the music swells, engulfing the gold bosses, the gargoyles, the richly painted choir screen, the stained glass windows, the depiction of Christ on the cross, I am inspired. Transported. In a way that I was not when in the company of Scott and Julia the previous week.

O come, o come Emmanuel, and ransom captive Israel... Rejoice! Rejoice!

Can this be heaven on earth, I ask myself? A sharp, ecstatic tingle runs the length of my spine, lifts the hair on the back of my neck. I am lost in wonder. Love. And praise.

Carl got to his feet and looked about him as the Christmas Eve service at the cathedral drew to a close. He felt high with a sense of achievement. The whole purpose of attending an event like this was to see and be seen. Networking. Hobnobbing with the big-wigs; impressing the wannabes.

Naturally, there were also people to be avoided. Julia's new friend, Hilary Bankster, for one. He hadn't seen her in decades, but in a city as small as Exeter - locals thought of it as no more than a big village - he supposed it was inevitable that their paths would cross one day. Even so, it was a shock when he came face to face with her across the main aisle. Despite the considerable time lapse since he'd seen her last, he'd recognised her instantly.

It was clear that she, too, had made the connection. She'd nodded, cursorily, in his direction when Julia had spoken with her before the service and, returning the salutation, he'd felt a familiar tightening of his chest.

'I didn't realise you knew Hilary,' Julia whispered when they took their seats. 'She says she was Matron at your school. She must have been very young.'

'She was. Far too young!' Deliberately turning his back on further questions from Julia, Carl had made a show of giving his undivided attention to his mother.

Now, at the end of the service, he was intent upon avoiding any further encounter with the woman. Particularly, with his mother in tow! Ushering her and the rest of his entourage from the building, he led the way back to the multi-story car park, unlocked the Porsche and helped his mother, a tiny, white-haired woman, into the front seat. When Julia and the children were installed in the back, he started the engine and drew away.

'Not a bad evening,' he proclaimed, 'if a little long.'

'Boring, boring,' Josh said under his breath. Nathan sniggered.

'I liked the singing,' Abi protested. 'It was just the reading bits that were -'

'- boring, boring,' finished Nathan.

'Now, now,' Carl cautioned them. 'Mummy and Granny enjoyed it. And it doesn't do you two heathens any harm to have a bit of culture. Besides, I was able to chat with several people who were previously unaware of our expansion into Wales. So that was useful.'

'I thought I saw you talking to the mayor.' Behind him, Julia leaned forward. 'And was that the editor of the Exeter Express? He seemed interested in what you had to say.'

Before Carl could answer, his mother turned in her seat to address Julia over her shoulder.

'Wasn't that the woman who works with Guy Sampson, I saw you with Julia? A psychiatrist, or something. How do you know her?'

'Counsellor. She's not a psychiatrist.'

'That's right! I met her once at Nancy's. Nancy and I were at school together. I didn't know you were friendly with them?'

Carl glanced in his rear-view mirror. By the light of the street lamps he could see that Julia was sitting back in her seat, staring out of the side window. If he had to hazard a guess, he'd have said she looked uncomfortable. As if she had something to hide. Now what! She'd never made much of a pretence when it came to liking his mother. He looked back at the road.

'I don't know who you mean,' Julia said, in what sounded, to anyone with a modicum of intelligence, like a belated cover-up.

'The woman you were talking to at the end,' Carl's mother persisted. 'The one who was so overdressed in scarves and coats she looked as if she was to set off across the Antarctic. I'm sure she's a colleague of Guy's. Eve? Yes, Eve something.'

'Evie Adams,' Julia said. 'Carl, could you turn the heating down please. It's very hot back here.'

'Mum!' screeched Abi. 'I'm frozen.'

Carl studied Julia again in his rear mirror. She was still staring out of the window. What on earth was going on? He'd been too immersed in his own conversations after the service to register what Julia was doing. But now Mother had brought it up, he realised he had seen his wife talking to some woman he'd never seen before. A psychiatrist? No. A counsellor, she'd said. Why on earth would Julia be meeting up with someone like that? As if Hilary and her barmy do-gooder friends were not enough to contend with . . .

'Dad!'

'Carl!'

A chorus assailed him. And almost too late he realised he'd strayed into the path of an oncoming car. Wrenching the wheel round, he narrowly missed a collision. It was not, however, enough to shake him from his resolve to delve further.

Julia felt rigid with tension. Back at home, once Granny had been deposited at her retirement apartment on the other side of town, she went straight to the cloakroom. Fancy Carl's mother knowing Evie! Just her luck that among all the crowds at the cathedral, she should have been seen talking to her. All they'd done was to exchange civilities about the evening. Then Julia had grabbed Evie's arm and begged for the possibility of an earlier appointment in the New Year.

'Carl came back from Wales earlier today reeking of perfume,' she whispered to Evie. 'And it wasn't mine.'

'Give me a ring and I'll see what I can do,' Evie had said. And then they'd parted company.

Trust beady-eyes Granny to have picked up on a private conversation conducted by her daughter-in-law, but to have had no nose for the sickening fragrance that had emanated from her son. So much for the 'best Christmas ever' resolve she'd made earlier.

Anyway, Julia hung her coat in the cloakroom cupboard, there was nothing for it but to maintain the status quo until after the festivities were over. It was no good picking a fight with Carl and spoiling the celebrations for everyone. Besides, there might be a perfectly rational explanation for the perfume. Perhaps he'd been buying some as a gift for herself or Abi and had sprayed some on his handkerchief to try it out? Or perhaps it was for his mother, who would be coming over tomorrow for Christmas day?

Julia emerged from the cloakroom feeling calmer.

'Anyone want a snack before bedtime?' she called.

She could hear from the rumpus upstairs that the children had dispersed to their rooms, and only Abi responded with a negative. She crossed the hall to Carl's study and put her head around the door. He was sprawled on the office chair with his feet on the desk, speaking to someone on his mobile. He looked up as she made a T-sign with her forefingers, swung his feet back down to the floor, nodded and put his thumb up to indicate a yes. Then he pointed at the phone, grimaced, and spread his hand in the air to show he'd be only five minutes longer.

Julia retreated to the kitchen. It was still too early to go to bed. She flicked the switch on the TV to catch the end of the news, then went to fill the kettle to make a pot of tea. There, forgotten on the worktop where Abi had laid them earlier in the day, was a handful of Christmas cards. Julia picked them up.

The first three were addressed to Carl and herself. She ripped them open, read the messages inside, stood the cards on the dresser and discarded the envelopes in the bin. The newsreader on the TV finished speaking of the devastation a recent storm had wreaked in some far-flung country of the world, and moved on to the power shortages that were expected to hit the South West of England overnight and next day.

Julia turned the fourth envelope over in her hand. This must be the one that Abi had told her about earlier; the one from France, which she said had been redirected. Redirected from where, Julia wondered?

She turned off the TV. And as the kettle came to the boil, dropped two teabags into the teapot, poured water onto them and left it to brew. Then she took another look at the envelope in her hand. The stamps were definitely French. A plain label, redirecting the item to their Exeter home in handwriting that looked familiar, had been stuck over the original address. It bore the moniker Worth, but it was difficult to see whether it was plain Mr. or Mr. and Mrs.

Something stirred in Julia's chest, a tightening of her airways, a missed beat of her heart. An inexplicable fear gripped her. The scent of suspicion hung in the air.

Scent! That was it. She sniffed. The scent on the envelope was, unmistakably, identical to that which had lingered on Carl's clothes. Cautiously, she peeled back the redirection label to reveal the address beneath. Flat 2, it read, followed by the name of a block of apartments somewhere in Monmouthshire, South Wales. Clearly typed above the address was *M. et Mme. Worth.*

Julia didn't hesitate. She was Madame Worth, so had every right. Ripping open the envelope, she pulled out a large and expensive Christmas card. *Bon Noel*, it stated in flowing script. With trembling fingers, she looked inside. *Mes chers amis, Carl et Lucie...* Julia let out a little cry. Clamped her hand to her mouth. Dropped the card.

'What's up?' Carl entered the room, wandered over to the dresser, picked up the cards she'd put there earlier, and began to read them. 'Did you say there was a cuppa going?'

Julia retrieved the card at her feet which he'd evidently not seen. She felt faint. Breathless. In need of a seat before her legs gave way. She had just enough presence of mind to open the card again. *Mes chers amis, Carl et Lucie* she read, *Merci encore pour votre hospitalité...* Her vision blurred. She grasped the edge of the worktop.

'Hey! Are you okay?' Carl appeared at her side. Wordlessly, she passed him the card.

He took it, read it, his face paled.

'Oh, It's from Pierre. A thank you for the launch party in Wales.'
'*Mes chers amis, Carl et Lucie...?*'

'I think Lucy helped him with something - his accommodation?'

Carl moved away, further into the kitchen. Still gripping the worktop on which she'd discarded the envelope, Julia turned to face him.

'It's taken him rather a long time to write and thank you, hasn't it?

Don't you find that odd?'

She didn't recognise her voice, punctuated as it was with steel bullets, as if shot from a gun. But neither did she recognise Carl's face, purple, etched with white.

'That's the French for you.' He turned away, head down, his back to her.

'He's writing to thank you for an event that took place at the end of October. And it's now December? Two months later?'

'Must have got lost in the post. Can't be anything else. I haven't seen him since.'

Julia watched and waited. On the oak dresser on the far side of the room, the clock struck midnight, the sound reverberating around the silent room.

'Then why does this Pierre go on to say what a charming place you have?' she asked when, at last, Carl turned, looked up.

'Does he? My French is obviously not as good as yours. Must mean the factory, I suppose.'

His voice was stilted. Still Julia persisted.

'So why didn't he address his card to the factory?'

Carl blanched, visibly.

'Didn't he?' He turned the card in his hand. 'There's no envelope here.'

'No. I have it here.'

'For heaven's sake, Julia. What's this all about? You've been reading too many thrillers. Cheap paperbacks.'

Julia ignored him.

'Would you like to know what it says on the envelope,' she asked, her voice saccharine. She held it before her as if she'd not seen it before. 'Oh, it's addressed to *Monsieur et Madame Worth*.'

'So? Isn't it natural that he'd address us both?'

'Even though inside it's Lucy who is his *chère amie?*'

Carl strode toward the door.

'I've had enough of this. If some Frenchman I barely know is stupid enough to muddle the names of my wife and my PA, I hardly think it's grounds for a Christmas Eve drama of this magnitude.'

Julia stopped him as he reached the door.

'Don't take me for a fool, Carl.' She spoke quietly, evenly. 'The perfume on the envelope, and your suit, is Lucy's. The name on the card is Lucy's. The handwriting on the label is Lucy's. And the address it was originally sent to - Flat 2 - is where, precisely?'

As she thought he might, Carl caved in.

CHAPTER TWELVE

CARL WOKE WITH a crick in his neck. He rolled his head, looked around him, disoriented. Why was he on the sofa? In the study? He tried to swallow but couldn't. His tongue felt like a swollen lump of putrid flesh blocking his airway. His head felt thick, his vision blurred. He sat up, leaned forward, rubbed his eyes with the heel of his hands. Opened them again. Immediately, the events of the previous evening exploded on his mind. Yesterday, Christmas Eve, he'd had a wife, a family, a home. Today, Christmas Day, he had none. What had he done?

He'd drunk a skinful of whisky, that's what he'd done. What a fool.

He got to his feet. Staggered. Righted himself, crossed the room to the window and peered through a slit in the blinds. It was still dark outside. But that didn't mean he had time on his hands. Today was Christmas Day. The kids would be up soon. The one day of the year they could be guaranteed not to sleep in. They mustn't find him like this. He'd promised Julia, sobbing like a baby while she stood there invincible, that he'd see this day through. That he wouldn't spoil it for them.

Spoil it? It was already spoiled.

He sniffed. The room stank of booze. He opened the fanlight.

Overhead in the night sky, the moon hung like a segment of dried citrus fruit. He turned, caught sight of himself in the mirror. Red eyed, unshaven, unkempt. He couldn't be seen like this. He opened the door, stealthy, fearful, looked towards the stairs, then tip-toed across the hall to the cloakroom. He was pretty sure Julia kept a stack of clean towels in the cupboard. He rummaged around, found one and undressed.

The boys sometimes used this shower when the bathroom was occupied and, sure enough, a bottle of cheap, evil-smelling gel stood on the rack. He stepped inside and gasped as the cold water hit his head and naked body. Oh, the irony of the cold shower! He soaped himself, then stood there beneath the relentless onslaught.

In a rare moment of philosophical analysis, he pondered certain truths, and the mystery of why they'd previously eluded him. In the self-sustaining process of life there had to be cause and effect, didn't there? Circumstances that provoked action that resulted in consequences? So how come he'd never considered what might have been triggered by his actions? Was there some mechanism released by the circumstances of falling in love that erased any sense of responsibility, common sense, or even the possibility that there might be a cost? Was it true, what they said, that love is blind?

The thought triggered another.

'Do you love her?' Julia had asked of him last night.

He'd blustered. Hadn't answered, because he couldn't. Did he love her? Lucy? Or had it simply been opportunism? She'd been there for him. When Julia had not. When Julia had betrayed him by allowing herself to be influenced by - that woman! Hilary Bankster. The Matron who had utterly failed those in her charge. Not only prior to Spud's death. But in the aftermath. Standing there in the witness box, on oath, and lying through her teeth. Or at very least allowing the accuracy of her memory to be contorted. Unforgivable!

And now? Here she was, just like his father, a so-called pillar of society. Hilary Bankster the do-gooder. Was Julia blind? Could she not see through the sham?

And who was this woman his mother had seen Julia talking to? As if Hilary Bankster were not enough to contend with, why was she now involved with a psychiatrist? A counsellor? *What are you thinking of Julia?*

Julia! She would be down soon. He must be gone before she put in an appearance. Shivering with cold, he turned off the shower, stepped out onto the cold hard surface of the shower room, towelled himself dry. Dressing in the clothes he'd worn yesterday was an unfamiliar and highly unpleasant experience. But there was no way he was going to go upstairs and risk being seen. No matter what he'd promised Julia about seeing it through for the sake of the children, he wanted out. And he wanted it now.

With the utmost caution, he peered around the door, emerged from the cloakroom, paused in the middle of the hall. Was that a whisper he heard upstairs? He sped forward. Once back in the study, he shut the door, took a sheet of paper from the desk drawer and scribbled a note for Julia and the kids. Humiliatingly, he found himself consumed with self-pity. Vision blurred, he pinched the inner corners of his eyes between thumb and forefinger to stem the threat of tears. As soon as he'd finished, he folded the paper, put it in an envelope, sealed and addressed it, then propped it against the pen holder on the desk.

He glanced at his watch. It was coming up to six o'clock. The kids would be up soon, knocking on his bedroom door, wondering where he was, questioning why his side of the bed was unslept in. Grabbing his mobile, he rang Lucy in Wales, watching the door, poised to ring off if anyone came in. Lucy answered in the confused manner of someone woken from a deep sleep.

'It's over,' he said. 'She knows.'

'How? What happened?'

He imagined Lucy in bed, sleepy eyed, pulling herself into a sitting position. He hesitated.

A floorboard creaked overhead. Carl looked up.

'Have to go. Speak later.'

He rang off.

Steeling himself, he retrieved his jacket, crumpled from where it lay on the floor. Then, briefcase and car keys in hand, he took a last look around him. His chest felt tight. His head pounded. He opened the door, paused, listened, shut it softly behind him. By the time he'd crossed the hall there were definite sounds of life from upstairs. Exiting quickly and quietly from the kitchen into the garage, he pressed the remote control to open the garage door, threw his briefcase onto the passenger seat of the car, started the engine and drove away without a backward glance.

It was done. No turning back. No room for regret. He cleared his mind, wiped it clean. No memories. There was only now.

He turned the corner at the end of the road, stopped, for what seemed an age, at the traffic lights. He'd had no breakfast and his stomach crawled.

It was not until he reached the roundabout on the main road into the city that it dawned on him: Lucy, in Wales, was at least two hours away; he was drink-driving over the limit; the fuel tank in the car was almost empty; it was Christmas Day; and he had nowhere to go.

Julia lay on her back staring at the ceiling, as she had done for most of the night. She felt as if the heavy weight that pinned her to the bed might prove immovable. At the same time, she knew it must be anything but. The moment one of the children knocked on the door to share the contents of their Christmas stockings, she would have to exert herself; draw herself up on her pillow; smile; pretend nothing untoward had occurred; that Daddy's having fallen asleep downstairs was of no consequence; give the appearance that this Christmas Day, like all others, would pass in an orgy of bounty and harmony.

She thought of the stuffed turkey in the fridge, the glittering Christmas tree in the sitting room, the wrapped gifts beneath. Symbols of - what precisely? What was it all for? The hype? The extravagance? What was the point?

She couldn't do this. How could Carl expect her to behave as if nothing had happened? She felt like a piece of wrapping paper, torn, crumpled, thin and useless. The gift of love it had contained, discarded by the person to whom it had been given; the one who had ripped her apart.

There were those who spoke of God's gift of love. But where was he, now, at Christmas, on what was supposed to be a celebration of the birth of his son? How could he abandon her and the children on this day above all others? Did he not care? Hadn't she followed him? Obeyed him? Worshipped and adored him? And for what?

God was supposed to be the Way, the Truth and the Life. But when confronted with the *truth* last night, Carl had taken the *way* of least resistance and put an end to their *life* together. He'd retreated to the study in search of whisky. She'd followed close behind.

'Oh, no you don't,' she'd cried. 'You're not shutting me out with any more lies. I want to know what's going on.'

She'd closed the door behind her, mindful of the children in their bedrooms. The overhead light was bleak and remorseless. Bottle and glass in hand, Carl threw himself down onto the swivel chair behind the desk. With what seemed to her to be a touch of arrogance, he leaned back, his legs stretched out on the floor in front of him so that his body formed a perfect straight line.

'You're making something out of nothing,' he said, his eyes glittering, grey and cold. 'I bought the flat because it was the obvious thing to do. You know yourself how much time I'm having to spend in Wales, setting everything up.'

There was a whine in his voice. It reminded Julia of the children when they were pleading innocence for some misdemeanour; something for which they were blatantly and knowingly at fault.

'Last I knew, you were staying in an hotel,' she began. And even as she said it, the penny dropped: the earrings that had been left next to the bed, the phone call from the hotel, the assumption that they belonged to Mrs Worth. Her self-deception was manifest. She despised herself for her weakness. How could she have allowed herself to be taken in by Carl's explanation? He must have been passing his PA off as his wife even then. He and Lucy had been living together for - how long?

'Staying in hotels is hardly an option in the long term,' Carl continued, and again she was struck with the similarity to the boys' dissembling. 'Dead money. At least this way we have an asset at the end of it.'

'We?' Julia's knees felt weak. She advanced into the room and sat on the sofa. 'You mean the flat's in my name as well as yours?'

Even to her own ears, her voice sounded full of bitterness.

Carl swung himself upright, poured himself another drink.

'I shall ignore that. You live here, don't you? Enjoy the privilege of -'

'Stop it!' she'd yelled. And he had. It was as if his inflated belief in his power to prevaricate had been punctured. He physically shrank into himself. They sat for a while in silence. Julia felt no emotion, no tears, only an unbridled need to know.

'How long?' she persisted, watching him.

He swirled the whisky in his glass, his eyes following it. His face looked grim, lines she'd not noticed before now clearly etched into his cheeks, his jaw.

'Don't know, exactly.'

'Before the launch?'

'Probably. Possibly.'

'You mean, even when I was with you in Wales?'

'No. No. Must have been after that.'

'But it might have been before?'

'I don't know. These things just happen.' Carl rose to his feet. For a moment, Julia thought he was about to leave the room. But without a glance in her direction, he stood aimlessly, hand in his pocket.

She felt faint. 'These things? You mean there've been others?'

He remained standing. Reached for the whisky decanter.

'Not for a long time.'

Pain ripped into Julia's chest. Unable to catch her breath, she lapsed into silence again. The heating was off and the chill bit into her flesh and bones. She leaned back on the sofa, tucked her feet beneath her skirt, drew her knees up under her chin and hugged them to her as if they were the only tangible reality in life at that moment.

'What started it?' she asked in a whisper.

Suddenly, Carl dropped his defence. The hard lines on his face crumpled.

'I don't know,' he said, his voice low. 'That's what I keep asking myself. You seemed to be tied up with the kids.'

She looked up, sharply. He raised a hand.

'No. I take that back. It wasn't you. I honestly don't know. Lucy -'

Julia flinched at the sound of her name.

'- she was,' Carl shrugged, 'just there.'

Julia couldn't bring herself to look at him. Lucy, the girl she'd admired, praised, taken under her wing, had been there! There for the business. There for Carl. There for his wife? Bile rose in her throat.

And where had she been, Julia Worth? Hadn't she been *there* too? Making a home for Carl and their children? Hosting the launch of his new business venture? Making excuses for the hours he spent in the office? His neglect of the children? His scorn for anything she did for herself?

'So what now?' she asked, her voice flat.

Carl was still standing.

'I'll go. Now. That would be easiest for you and the kids.'

From the corner of her eye, Julia saw him move.

'No,' she rasped, jumping to her feet. 'You can't. You have to stay for their sake. You're their Daddy. What are they going to do if you're not here on Christmas Day?'

Carl crumpled before her, his eyes welling with tears, his shoulders shaking, until he was sobbing uncontrollably; until she couldn't help herself; until she reached out and put her hand on his arm in a gesture of comfort, his pain added to hers more than she could bear.

Immediately, she regretted her weakness. He grabbed her, pinned her in his arms.

'I'm sorry,' he blubbed. 'I'm so sorry.'

He pressed his lips to hers. His breath was rancid. He fumbled with her clothing. Did he think she was his to have? Had he left Lucy's bed thinking he could come straight to hers? Julia struggled free, engulfed in a sense of revulsion. She slapped his face and ran from the room.

She took the stairs two at a time. Locking the bedroom door behind her, she threw herself onto the bed, wept until every last ounce of emotion was spent. At some point she must have undressed, turned on her back, covered herself with the quilt, and lay staring at the ceiling till morning.

Early, long before it was light, she heard the sound of the water tank refilling in the loft, overhead. Through the numbness, a vague understanding of what was taking place downstairs filtered into her thinking. A short time later, it was confirmed. Almost with relief she heard the mechanical whirring of the overhead garage door opening, the sound of the car starting up, the crunch of tyres on shingle as it sped away down the drive. She shivered, pulled herself into a sitting position and wrapped her dressing gown around her. The sickening memories of the previous night receded. Only to be replaced, as she heard the whispered voices of Abi, Josh and Nathan outside her bedroom door, by the terrifying spectacle of the day ahead.

Preparing to go to my next door neighbours on Christmas morning, I can't help wondering how Julia is faring. Did she really believe the earrings her husband's PA had left at the hotel were a Christmas bonus? Somehow, I doubt it. Yet she was so determinedly positive when we met last week, blinding herself to reality by replacing it with some far-fetched story he had spun. Amazing how adroit the human brain can be when grappling with unsavoury truths. What do we do? Why, we rewrite the script in our heads until it more nearly conforms with what is acceptable to us.

I shrug on my coat, step outside and close my front door. It's all of four steps up my front path, eight along the pavement and a further four down the adjoining garden path until I arrive at my neighbours. Juggling the gifts, bottles, and boxes of chocolates that I'm clutching to my chest, I find I can hardly reach their door bell. It appears, though, that my arrival has been noted.

'Hello Auntie Evie. Mummy says to come in.'

Once again, it's Jason who opens my neighbours' door to me, an earnest little chap with close-cropped hair and a maturity that belies his seven years. Knowing I'm alone, his parents, Ben and Sharon, have been kind enough to invite me to join them for Christmas lunch. I have to admit, it beats sitting on your own with nothing more than a turkey leg joint to tuck into, followed by the Queen's Speech. Besides, I'm looking forward no end to seeing baby Lily-Rose-Marie. And Jason, of course.

'Hi, buddy.' I make to ruffle his hair as I step inside, but he ducks.

'I got Daddy's hair gel on,' he says, by way of explanation. 'Mummy says you got to look good for Christmas.'

'Absolutely!' I grin, apologetically. 'Silly me. And boy do you look good in your red shirt and black velvet waistcoat.'

Suitably mollified, Jason closes the door behind me.

'And I've put my best dress on,' I continue, 'red silk, like your shirt. We look like holly berries.'

With childish innocence, he reaches out to rub the silky fabric of my dress between his fingers and comments on the 'funny noise' it makes.

'So how's that baby of yours?' I ask as he leads me into the kitchen where Sharon, hot and flustered, is basting the turkey.

'A pain,' he announces with gusto. 'She keeps me awake at night.'

'Oh, sorry,' red-faced, Sharon turns from her task. 'I didn't hear the door bell. Take Auntie Evie's coat, Jason, and put it in the living room. I'll hang it up in a moment.'

I deposit my goodies on the worktop in the tiny kitchen that's a modernised mirror-image of my own, and remove my outer coat.

'No need to stand on ceremony,' I say. 'I'll put it over the bannister, shall I?'

Three hours later, replete with good food and more than enough alcohol, there's certainly no standing on ceremony as we slump on the sofa in the lounge. Jason is happily deployed playing with the remote control dumper truck I've given him. And I've had the pleasure of feeding Lily-Rose-Marie her liquefied turkey and sprouts - lots of curled upper lip as the distasteful mixture is inserted in her mouth - and my holly-berry red dress has been duly christened! Naturally, I suppose, conversation turns to the baby's naming ceremony.

'We was wondering, Ben and me, if you've thought anymore about being Lily-Rose's Godmum?' Sharon asks. 'Thing is, we want to book the church and everythink for Easter, when Ben's bruv will be over from Oz. But they won't let us do that until we can put down who the Godparents are going to be.'

Ben offers to pour me another Tia Maria which I decline.

'It's going to be at the same church as our other Lily-Rose,' he says, assuming a knowledge I don't possess.

I frown and shake my head.

'What Ben means is the church where our other baby's buried,' Sharon explains. 'Not where she was christened. That was in the hospital chapel.'

My chest tightens.

'I had no idea...'

Teary-eyed, Sharon shrugs.

'Well you wouldn't, would you? We hadn't moved here then. We was in a rented flat when she - passed away. We just couldn't stay there, no more, so we decided to scrape together a mortgage and move here.'

'So - what happened?' I hardly dare ask.

'Meningitis. She wasn't even one. Same age as this Lily-Rose. She's so special to us; that's why we want to name her after her sister.'

'But,' I'm hesitant, 'might this Lily-Rose not feel that she's just a replacement?'

'Oh, no! Never.' Sharon shakes her straight blonde hair. 'The first Lily-Rose didn't have Marie added. We made sure this one had something special all to herself.'

I nod my understanding. Who am I to argue? This little family has been through tragedy, heartache and loss, similar to my own, though they know nothing of that. And here they are, welcoming another baby into the world, and honouring me with an invitation to be involved in her life. How can I refuse? Why would I want to?

'The chaplain at the hospital spoke to us about having our first Lily-Rose christened,' Sharon goes on. 'He said she'd be in heaven and that we'd be able to see her again. That's why we want this Lily-Rose christened too. So that one day we'll all be together.'

I'm not at all sure that this is quite the interpretation others would put on it, but I now know, with unshakable certainty, that I shall be Lily-Rose-Marie's Godmother. I also know, without a shadow of doubt, that, although I can't promise to endow her with a faith I don't possess, I shall do everything in my power to see that she is brought up with a set of morals I feel sure even God, himself, would be proud of. I lift my nearly empty liqueur glass to propose a toast.

'To Lily-Rose-Marie, whose Godmother I shall be proud to be.'

We all raise our glasses to our lips. Then Ben says,

'And you're sure you're okay about Pete being her Godfather? No problem about him being your ex, and all?'

The Tia Maria hits the back of my throat and nearly chokes me. Coughing and spluttering, I'm glad of the diversion when Jason climbs onto the sofa next to me and begins thumping me on the back. My earlier thoughts about rewriting the script in our heads until it more nearly conforms with what is acceptable to us return to me. Isn't that exactly what I've done?

CHAPTER THIRTEEN

JULIA RANG EVIE from her bedroom. It was only two days after Christmas and she knew she had no hope of contacting her at work until after the New Year. But she simply had to talk to someone and Evie was the obvious choice, even if her message was only going to answer phone. Doubled over and perched on the edge of her bed, she kept her voice low so the children wouldn't hear.

'Evie, I know you won't be there. And I'm sorry for bothering you. But,' her voice faltered, 'things have taken a turn for the worse.'

Well, that was an understatement! She rocked back and forth, struggling to stem the tears that fell freely now. Around her the unmade bed, discarded clothes and dirty coffee cups spoke of her wretchedness, her despair. With her free arm wrapped around her abdomen, she hugged herself tight.

'Carl's left,' she gasped, 'and the children -'

'Julia!' Evie's voice came down the line.

Julia's heart hammered. The phone nearly dropped from her hand. She clutched at it and expelled the breath she'd been holding.

'Is that you, Evie? I was just leaving a message. I didn't expect you to be there.'

With her eyes closed, she could see Evie's counselling room, the phone on her desk at the window, Evie seated there, or perhaps standing, looking down at The Green below.

'I shouldn't be. I just popped in to pick up my diary. What's happened?'

Julia turned towards the bedroom door. She could hear the sound of muffled crying outside on the landing. Then it moved away.

'I was just trying to leave a message,' she repeated. 'Oh, Evie . . .'

At the other end of the line, she heard Evie draw breath and repeat, 'What's happened?'

Unable to stem the anguish of the last few days now that she had someone on whom to unleash it, Julia found herself uttering meaningless, incoherent words.

'Are you alone?' Evie asked

'Just the children,' Julia sobbed.

'Carl's gone?'

'Yes.'

'I can come over now, if you'd like me to?'

'Oh, yes please. But I don't like to bother you.'

'No bother. Fortunately, I brought the car down. Remind me of your address and how to get to you.'

Within twenty minutes, during which Julia had washed her face and done her best to disguise the ravages of her distress, she heard Evie's car on the drive below. The children, fortunately or not, she wasn't sure, had retreated to their bedrooms. Julia hastened down the stairs, opened the front door and threw herself into Evie's arms.

Prizing my boots off at the front door, once Julia has let go of me, I take in the scene before me. This is a client's home, I remind myself. It wouldn't do to walk mud onto the chequered parquet flooring in the hall, nor the immaculate pale carpets that are visible in the entrance to every room.

One look at Julia's pallid, but less than immaculate state, convinces me that I've made the right decision to come over. Responding to a client's distressed phone call with an immediate home visit might break with convention and professional etiquette, but I can see no other appropriate, or humane, response. With no obvious friend or confidante in Julia's life - other than the Hilary woman, whose presence seems, ironically and inexplicably, to be the root of the problem - I appear to be her lifeline. I'm really only here in a listening capacity, and to convey the appropriate signs of empathy, but I hope that will be enough to encourage her to pour it all out.

Julia shows me into a room off the hall on the right, where it's immediately apparent that my initial perception of perfection is in error. The hearth is full of cold ash and half-burned logs that spill out onto the carpet. Christmas wrapping paper litters the floor, plus several days' worth of dirty mugs and plates, by my estimation.

'I'm so sorry,' she says, attempting to gather things up, and it's obvious that until my arrival she must have been oblivious to the mess.

'Don't worry.' I plonk myself down on one of those oh-so-popular-and-I-don't-know-why leather swivel chairs that always remind me of the dentist's surgery. 'You should see my place. And I don't have teenagers to blame.'

As I hoped she would, Julia smiles and relaxes. She hasn't a trace of make-up on, her big brown eyes are red-rimmed, her hair doesn't look as if it's been brushed in days, and her feet are bare.

When we've dispensed with the offer of coffee, which I decline because I can see she's not up to making it, I ask Julia, again, what's happened? She sits herself on a futon, opposite me, and wraps her arms around her midriff, then launches into an account of the row between her and Carl on Christmas Eve. I can't let on to her, but I acknowledge to myself, that this is exactly what I had anticipated.

'So when did he leave?' I ask.

'On Christmas morning. Very early before the children were up. I'd begged him, the night before, to stay. For their sakes. I just couldn't face the thought of them waking up on Christmas morning to find their father gone.'

She lapses into silence, flicking one of the buttons on her cardigan aimlessly back and forth with one finger.

'But he didn't stay?' I prompt her.

She refocuses on me with an air of surprise, as if she hadn't expected to see me there

'I heard him go into the shower room downstairs, when it was still dark. I suppose I could have gone down. Tried to stop him.'

'But you didn't?'

She shakes her head.

'Why not?'

'I don't know.'

Again, she looks surprised, but I take it that this time it's more to do with her inaction than my presence.

'When I heard the garage door go up a bit later, and heard him drive away, it was - well, to be honest, it was a relief.'

I nod to indicate my understanding.

'You decided it would be easier without him?'

'Well, yes. I just didn't think I could keep up the pretence of normality all day. But -'

'So you weren't planning to tell the children?'

I'm genuinely surprised.

Face down, Julia shakes her head, her hair hanging lank and lifeless about her.

'I know! It was stupid,' she says, her voice rising. 'I just didn't think it through at all. But of course, once Carl had gone, there was no possibility of normality.'

I'm trying to establish a train of events, but it's proving difficult.

'So the first the children knew about their father's departure was, when?' I ask.

'Josh's bedroom's over the garage.' The anguish in Julia's eyes is unmistakable. 'He heard the door mechanism and saw the car leave. He thought there must be something wrong with his grandmother. Carl's mother. She was supposed to be coming over to us for the day.'

'Right! So he thought his grandmother was ill. And then what?'

'He came running in to me. It was terrible. Just terrible. And then they all came in. And I had to tell them. Tell them their father had left.'

Julia is weeping. I cross the room and crouch beside her, patting her hand, offering her a tissue, murmuring inane words of comfort.

'So did you tell them why? Or where he'd gone?' I ask, rising stiffly to return to my chair, at last.

'That's just it!' Julia jumps to her feet and begins pacing the floor. 'Abi seemed to know. And so did Josh. It didn't appear to come as any surprise to them.'

I raise my eyebrows. Julia stops pacing and looks down at me.

'I've just realised. Do you remember all that business I told you about with Abi before the launch of Carl's new business? I kept telling her what a great girl her daddy's assistant was; what a help she was with the factory in Wales; how we should support her and encourage her because she'd just split up with her boyfriend, and she was all alone.'

From where I'm seated, I watch as recognition dawns on Julia's face. Then she turns away.

'What a fool I've been! Abi would have none of it. She didn't seem to like Lucy.' Julia spat the name out. 'I couldn't understand it then. But now it makes sense. She must have known something was going on; or at least had an inkling.'

Julia collapses onto the futon again.

'And did Carl have no contact with any of you after he left?' I ask.

'He left a note. In the study. Nathan found it. It was addressed to us all. It just said that he was sorry. Sorry! He hoped they'd understand. He couldn't help it. He'd fallen in love. It wasn't something he'd looked for or wanted. He still loved the kids. And he hoped to see them once things were settled.

'It made me mad! He'd told me the previous evening that it was all down to Hilary. That if she'd remained in Canada - hadn't re-appeared and insinuated herself in my life - none of this would have happened.'

There is a note of sarcasm bordering on bitterness, in Julia's voice which distresses me. I don't want this to be the legacy of her split with Carl. I make a mental note that this is something we'll have to work on in future counselling sessions.

'She lived in Canada? Hilary? And Carl knew that? But - you don't know what he meant?'

'No idea! His explanation sounded just like one of the children to me, pointing his finger and saying -' Julia's voice took on a note of sarcasm and derision, ' - *it's not me, it's all her fault.*'

I shake my head. I can only agree.

'So how - where, did you spend Christmas Day?' I ask.

'Here. On our own. No one wanted turkey and all the trimmings. We brought the duvets down. I made a big fire,' she indicates the grate, 'and we just vegged out, watched TV, and ate whatever. Whenever.'

'And Carl?'

Julia's lip curls.

'We'd been expecting his mother to come to us for the day, but it seems he went to her flat, instead. Spent the day there and presumably the night. She rang to let us know.'

'So he didn't go to Wales, then?'

Julia looks scornful.

'He'd never have made it! He'd had far too much to drink on Christmas Eve. I imagine he's there now, though.'

We both fall silent. The house is quiet as a morgue, with no evidence of its being inhabited by three teenagers. Then Julia, who has evidently been brewing up to this, bursts out,

'I can't believe I could have been so stupid! How could I not have known? You must think me completely insane. I mean, there was all that business with the earrings. It was plain as can be that Carl must have bought them for *her*. But it never occurred to me. And even then, I was more than willing to believe him when he said they were a Christmas bonus. How stupid can you be? Everyone must be looking at me and wondering why Carl bothered to stay with me for so long. An intelligent man like him with a bimbo like me!'

She leans forward, breathless, hugging herself.

I shake my head. In common with more clients than I care to recall, it's clear that failing to see calamity coming is as painful to Julia as the event itself.

'You? Stupid? It's certainly not my opinion of you. And I'm sure it isn't what others think.'

She continues as if I've said nothing; as if I'm not there.

'And then there was the fact that the hotel rang me. They obviously thought I was *her*. Or she was me. Why didn't I put two and two together then? I can't believe I could be so dumb.'

With her feet curled up beneath her in a semi-foetal position, Julia stares into space, a frown between her eyes, her mouth turned down, and her whole demeanour one of abject self-loathing.

'Don't beat yourself up,' I say, in an attempt to soothe her ruffled self-esteem. 'You'd no reason to think differently. Anyone could have made the same mistake.'

I pull my scarf from my neck, aware of how much warmer this room is than the temperature at which I can afford to heat my own home.

'When you love someone,' I continue, 'you're going to put your trust in them. There's nothing stupid about that. It's only natural.'

Julia throws her head back and fixes her gaze on me.

'Yes, but you're talking about Carl, aren't you? But what about God? I put my trust in him. And he let me down. Big time.'

I pause, aware that I'm the last person Julia should be addressing with such questions.

'What does your friend, Hilary, have to say about that?' I ask, but it's clear from the look Julia gives me that she hasn't discussed it with her.

Sighing, I run my scarf through my hands. For someone like Julia, someone of faith, what has occurred is a double whammy. I can see that. But what can I say that won't make matters worse?

We sit in silence, opposite one another. I think it's probably best if I steer Julia into talking through her current feelings for Carl and how she wants to proceed for the future, and then leave her to mull over her options. It'll be New Year in a couple of days. Perhaps, by then, she'll have begun to see things differently, I hope.

Carl looked around the lounge-dining room of the apartment in Wales, groaned and held his head in his hands as if it were an eggshell about to shatter. It was mid-morning on New Year's Day, and here he was nursing a hangover of humungous proportions.

Actually, there was nothing new about it. He'd been drinking far too much lately, and New Year's Eve, last night, had topped it off. And why? Drowning your sorrows was the explanation usually given. But what if the so-called sorrows were what you'd once thought of as the desires of your heart? The very thing that, intentionally or inadvertently, you'd been aiming at all along? What anyone with a modicum of common sense must have seen coming?

He shook his head, his deliberations confused and bewildering. If his mother had been surprised at the change of plan when he'd arrived at her flat on Christmas morning, she'd hidden it well. It was only to be expected, he supposed; their relationship was strained at the best of times.

'Need to get to Wales first thing tomorrow,' he'd said. 'Any chance of a bed for the night?'

Without further explanation, she'd appeared to accept the status quo. She'd made up a bed for him and, thankfully, had refrained from any comment along the lines of 'like father like son'. You could almost be forgiven for thinking that leaving your wife and kids on Christmas morning was an everyday occurrence, he'd concluded.

And Lucy, when he'd finally managed to speak to her on the phone, had seemed to take a similar stance.

'At least you don't have to worry about her finding out any more,' she'd said. 'That must be a relief.'

As if! She'd meant well, of course, but then she'd never been married. What could she possibly know of the torment of tearing yourself apart from your family? The wrench of leaving the woman with whom you'd shared everything for the past seventeen years or more. Then betrayed. The kids you'd fathered, fed and - yes, neglected at times.

He'd expected, if he'd thought about it at all, to feel elated. This sense of dejection, of culpability, was unforeseen. But then, had he ever really thought it through it at all? His thoughts twisted this way and that. If the end of the old year was to be epitomised by the demise of his marriage, then the start of the New Year would be defined by the pain of that loss. He couldn't help but feel that it didn't augur well for what was to come. He closed his eyes and nursed his head in his hands.

'Hey, come on, honey!' Lucy came into the room. 'We've got a party to go to.'

He opened one eye and peered through his fingers at her. She wore a scarlet polka-dot dress with a short, full skirt plus black tights and spiky heeled black boots. It was reminiscent of something Abi might have worn, he thought. Her hair, milky blonde, hung about her shoulders like glass. Her mouth was puckered, red and full.

He ought, he supposed, to feel flattered to have the attention of such a doll. And so he did! But the energy levels required by such a relationship... He sighed. It wasn't so much that they eluded him. Just that they were hard to sustain.

'Do we have to?' he asked, flopping back on the elegant oyster coloured sofa Lucy had chosen from the John Lewis range.

He'd allowed her to select all the furnishings for the apartment, confident that her style and panache would be innovative; contemporary. And so it was. A delight. She'd purchased their King-sized divan bed, curtains and quilt covers scattered with huge stylistic blue roses for the bedroom; sofa, chairs, a futuristic black ash and smokey glass coffee table, pictures and mirrors, rugs and cushions for the lounge. The store account, when it came through the post, had shocked him to the core. But how could he complain? He'd given her carte blanche. And she'd done nothing more than provide him with a home from home.

'Come on,' she urged him now in seductive tones, sliding onto his lap and pressing her face against his so close that her long dark eyelashes brushed against his cheek, and her perfume made his senses reel. 'Don't want me to think I've ended up with an old man, do you?'

He winced. Then something bright caught his eye. He drew his head back to look.

'Are those the earrings I bought you?' he asked.

Lucy moved her head briskly from side to side so that the gemstones swung from her ears, glittering in the light from the window.

'They match the bracelet you gave me for Christmas,' she said.

'But are they ones I gave you at the launch party?' Carl persisted.

Lucy drew away, looked at him suspiciously.

'Well, you haven't bought me any others - yet. Not regretting it are you?'

Carl struggled beneath her, easing himself out, forcing her to stand. 'What was that all about?' he asked. 'Leaving them at the hotel?'

Lucy looked down at him.

'Yes. That was a bit of a *faux pas*. Sorry about that.'

She walked across the room and peered into the mirror on the wall, pulling her eyelid up as if looking for a speck in her eye.

'Caused me no end of trouble with Julia,' said Carl, faintly irritated with her air of complacency.

'Sorry.'

'And the bill from the jeweller? What were you doing with that?'

Lucy swivelled on her heel.

'What is this? The inquisition? For goodness sake, honey. It's all in the past, now, isn't it.'

'But why did you have the bill? Seems somewhat strange, doesn't it?'

'Not really! You must have left it in the bag with the earrings. Guess the hotel just put two and two together and made five. Now come on, or we'll be late for the party.'

Lucy left the room in search of her coat. Staring after her, Carl couldn't help feeling that there was something more to this than she was letting on. He'd yet to tackle her about why she'd redirected the Christmas card that had alerted Julia to the existence of the flat and brought about the end of his marriage. His irritation grew. And with it the pain in his head.

It's New Year's Day and I've grappled, for the past week, with the bombshell my neighbours dropped on Christmas Day, when they told me that Pete was to be Lily-Rose-Marie's Godfather. Bad enough that Pete's my ex. Worse still that we lost our own baby. And incredibly distressing when I now know that he's expecting a baby with his new lady friend.

How can we possibly be joint Godparents with all that history? Not to mention what's to come. There will be birthday parties to attend, school sports' days, and all sorts of future events. Pete and Barbara will be in my hair for evermore. And so will their offspring.

'How am I going to cope?' I ask Pumpkin, before ringing my mentor, Grace.

'Ben and Sharon, the baby's parents, are lovely neighbours,' I tell her, 'but they're not the brightest buttons in the box.'

Seated on the sofa in the front room, I suppose that the same could be said of me.

'Didn't you know before you accepted the role?' Grace asks.

'Nope! But I suppose I should have guessed. Ben's in the police force with Pete. They're mates.'

Like Julia, a few days ago, I could kick myself. Why didn't it occur to me that Pete might be asked to be Lily's God dad?

'So what are you going to do?' Grace asks.

I raise my shoulder and pick at the frayed cording on the sofa.

'They obviously think that, being a counsellor, I can shrug it off.'

'And can you?'

'I shall have to! Or at least I'll have to give the appearance of doing so.'

I can't tell Grace, but there's no way I'm having Bosomy Barbara muscling in and giving me the heave-ho for a second time.

The christening is set for Easter week, and the reason I was in my counselling room when Julia rang a few days earlier was to check my diary. Coincidentally, I've also accepted an invitation that week from Scott Bingham to do some more sightseeing together.

'I start work at the college in the New Year,' he told me on the phone, 'but I'm planning to be in Devon again when we shut down for the Easter vacation. Any chance we could meet up?'

Naturally, I agreed. And fortunately, there was no clash of dates.

My meeting with Julia, however, has revealed a clash of integrity on my part. It's one I feel I need to resolve, and who better to talk it through with than Guy? I tackle him the moment he arrives on our first day back at work.

'I thought I'd come to terms with the fact that I shall be making promises I can't keep,' I say, when I've explained about my having been asked to be a Godmother. 'But now I'm not so sure.'

Guy clears a load of papers from one of the client chairs in his room so that I can sit down.

'Why don't you start by telling me your rationale for having accepted this role?' he asks, taking up residence opposite me, his elbows on the chair arms, his hands clasped beneath his chin.

Good question, I think.

'Well, I honestly believe I can have a positive influence in this baby's life,' I respond, tipping my head on one side as I consider it. 'I believe I have a good work ethic, moral code, and a sense of loyalty and affection.'

'So what's put the cat among the pigeons?' Guy asks.

Looking around at the clutter on Guy's desk and his shambolic personal appearance, it looks as if there's been a cat among the pigeons here. I hide a smile and remind myself that though it's sometimes hard to believe he's so good at his job, his kindness and compassion shine through loud and clear.

'Remember the client I told you about sometime ago?' I begin. 'The one whose husband was putting her down because she'd taken up fund-raising with some woman he disapproves of? Well he's since started an affair, their marriage has broken down, he's left the matrimonial home, and she appears to have lost her faith.'

'And how, exactly, does that affect your decision?' Guy asks, pointing his forefingers above his clasped hands and wafting them back and forth beneath his beard.

I stand up and cross the room to the window. The view from here is almost identical to that from my own, and even this early in the day I can see people scurrying back and forth across the Cathedral Green, presumably on their way to work, including some of the cathedral clergy, clad in black cassocks and white surplices. I turn and face Guy, leaning back against the dark oak panels on the wall.

Well - I'm going to have to promise to bring this child up *in the faith* and I don't have one,' I venture. 'And that means I'll be short-changing her.'

Guy looks thoughtful.

'Forgive me. But I still don't see what this has to do with your client?'

I push myself off from the wall and walk back to my chair.

'It's just that, having attended a convent school, Julia found faith for herself as an adult. In other words, that experience in childhood must have laid the groundwork of her belief. But my Godchild - if I took on the role - would be at an immediate disadvantage. What does that say about me? My integrity?'

Guy removes his elbows from the arms of his chair and leans forward.

'Evie! I think the very fact that you're worrying about this says barrow loads about your integrity.'

He waits until I look him in the eye and nod a tacit agreement to his statement, then continues.

'And did you listen to yourself when I asked you to give me your rationale for having accepted the role of Godparent in the first place? You started with your honesty, your belief that you could be a positive influence; your belief in a moral code, your belief in the loyalty and love that you could impart to this child, not to mention your work ethic. That's a lot of belief in there.'

I give him the smirk I think his answer deserves.

'Yes, but belief isn't the same as faith in God, is it?'

'No, it's not!' he agrees. 'Even the devil believes in God. But what I'm saying is that you can have faith in the qualities you'll bring to this child. *And*, although I'm not an Anglican so I can't be certain, I believe that you may be able to make the promises required of you without compromising your integrity.'

'How come? The fact remains that I'm not a believer.'

'You're not married, either. But you counsel people regularly, who are.' Guy sits back and stretches his legs in front of him.

I look beyond him, considering. His observation has merit, I think.

'You mean I could still encourage Lily-Rose-Marie to go to Sunday School? Perhaps even attend church with her in due course?'

He sits up again, animatedly.

'Yes. But you're missing the point, Evie,' he says. 'It's not you who will bring this child to faith. It's God. And I believe he will work in you and through you. Especially as others pray for you both.'

I must still look doubtful because, without any explanation as to who these 'others' are, nor why, or what they would be praying for on my behalf, Guy adds,

'I think you should talk to the vicar who's going to conduct the christening. But in the meantime, have a think about what the alternative is to your being the baby's Godmother. Who else will take it on?'

He looks across the room at me, waiting for me to give him an answer.

'Oh, quite probably someone who would cross their fingers behind their back when they make their promises, and think that all that's required of them is to buy Lily frivolous presents for birthdays and Christmas,' I reply, with a picture of the alternative in my mind.

And quietly, thoughtfully, I admit to myself that the point Guy has made might have some validity, and that perhaps I should have a chat with the vicar.

Chapter Fourteen

WITH CHRISTMAS AND New Year well and truly over, Julia tells me, at her next appointment, that she's been to see a solicitor.

'I feel I have to do something. See where we stand. If only for the children's security,' she says, facing me, as usual, in my counselling room.

I nod to convey my understanding.

'How've they been, the children? I'd be happy to see them. Hear their grievances, if that would help?'

Julia shakes her head, a look of despair on her face.

'Mostly, they just shut themselves in their rooms and play loud music. When they do have to appear, for meals and so on, they're monosyllabic. Occasionally, there's a shouting match.'

The wind rattles the lattice window behind me and, despite the warmth from my electric fire, Julia shivers.

'Did you manage to get to the bottom of Abi's dislike of Lucy?' I ask, recalling one of Julia's post-Christmas observations. 'You seemed to think she might have known what was going on between her and her father?'

Again, Julia shakes her head. It strikes me that she appears remarkably constrained considering the distress she manifested when I visited her at home. A second glance refutes my earlier thought. Beneath the deceptively calm exterior, the cracks are beginning to show. She takes a deep breath.

'I tried asking Abi but she just flew at me. I felt almost,' Julia looks down at her hands, 'almost as if she blamed me. As if I should have known what was happening and,' she lifts her shoulders in a gesture of helplessness, 'somehow, put a stop to it.'

I can see she's struggling. When she fails to look up, I lean forward in my chair and urge her to do so.

'Julia! Look at me. This is not of your doing. You need to take that on board.'

I continue to hold her gaze until she accepts the truth with a barely discernible nod, and only then do I carry on with what I was saying.

'We don't know whether it was Carl who seduced Lucy or she him. Either way, both are adult; neither is feeble-minded; each made a free choice. That choice was theirs. It was not yours.'

Again, still leaning towards her, I wait until I can see that she acknowledges the truth of my statement.

'But this is not a blame game -' I begin.

'You mean I should forgive them?' Julia bursts out. 'That's what Hilary and her friends say. All very well for them, but they should try it.'

I relax back in my chair. I've achieved the breakthrough I'd hoped for. The cracks in Julia's cool facade have split to reveal a super-charged passion of feeling beneath. Better for it be exposed and dealt with than buried and fester. I'll need to work with Julia until she can see for herself that forgiveness is as much about letting go of bitterness as anything else. Only then will she reach a place of wholeness.

'Julia,' I continue. 'When I said it's not a blame game, I didn't mean to imply that your hurt and anger are misplaced or irrelevant. They are not to be trivialised. On the contrary! You've been wronged. And your emotions are a natural human response.'

Julia remains tight-lipped. 'So what did you mean, then?'

'We've acknowledged that Carl and Lucy made choices that were selfish, immoral, and without any thought for the hurt they would inflict on you and the children. Haven't we?'

She nods, stiffly.

'I hope, too, that I've persuaded you to let go of the guilt you were so obviously harbouring? The feeling that you should have known what was going on and done something about it?'

'Doesn't much matter what I feel about it,' Julia says, dejectedly. 'It's pretty clear that that's what Abi thinks.'

Ah! So this is what it's all about.

'And that makes you feel...?' I ask, deliberately leaving a gap for her to fill.

Tears well in Julia's eyes.

'Sad. Hurt. And yes - guilty.'

'Can you explain that to me?'

She looks at me as if I should know the answer, which I do, of course, but I want her to voice it.

'I'm her mother,' she says. 'It's only natural that I should be able - that she should expect me to be able to -'

She lapses into silence.

'Is that how you felt about your own mother?' I ask, gently.

Julia's head snaps up.

'She was an incredible woman. Nothing fazed her. She was wonderful. She did everything. Everything she could for me.'

Her defensiveness - an attack on what I deduce she's perceived as criticism of her mother - reminds me of the way she defended Carl in the early days of our counselling sessions, when she imagined I was putting him down. There's clearly some underlying issue here that needs to be examined. But not now.

'I still don't understand why Abi had a go at me,' Julia bursts out. 'Why me? Why not her father?'

'Because you were there and he wasn't?'

'But why? I don't understand! Why lash out at me at all?'

I draw a deep breath to indicate the depth of my concern.

'It's what you do. What we all do unless we learn to be rational. When you're hurt and angry, you lash out at others. Usually your nearest and dearest. From what you've said, Abi evidently suspected that something was going on. So in addition to the hurt she's experienced from her father's infidelity, she's probably feeling guilty, too. Perhaps she thinks she should have done something to put a stop to the affair?'

Julia looks at me in amazement. It's clear that the thought has never crossed her mind.

'What on earth could she have done?'

'Exactly! There's nothing *either* of you could have done.'

I scribble some notes in my client file to give Julia time to digest what, to her, is evidently an entirely new concept. She sits for a while in silence before quizzing me on the matter.

'So what you're saying is that I should stop blaming myself, and spend the time I've been wallowing in self-pity in trying to help Abi to see that she's not to blame, either?'

I smile, encouragingly. Julia's statement is, understandably, somewhat garbled, but she's an intelligent woman and has arrived at the conclusion I'd been hoping for. She sits again, in silence, looking past me as if deep in thought.

'It's a bit like being a child again, isn't it,' she says at last, fixing me with a sheepish grin. 'The blame game, I mean.'

'It is indeed,' I tell her. 'We'll talk about it on your next visit.'

All the way home in the car, Julia thought about what Evie had said. She was right! It was futile to keep blaming herself. Not only futile, but unfair. Had she been at fault? No! Thinking it through, rationally, she could see that there was nothing with which she could reproach herself. She'd never stopped loving Carl; never stopped supporting his business ventures; and never stopped looking after his home and family. All had remained unchanged as far as she was concerned. No one, least of all Carl, could accuse her of having driven him into the arms of another woman.

Neither, when she thought about it, was there anything she could have done to stop the affair. That would have required prior knowledge and, again, Evie was right. The signs might have been there - the earrings, Abi's inexplicable dislike of Lucy, the re-addressed Christmas card - but unless you had reason to look for them, and she had had none, they were easily passed over.

What mattered now, she thought as she parked the car in the drive, was to talk to the children - Abi in particular - and ensure that they were not suffering similar self-recrimination. Their pain was obvious, and she'd done all she could to mitigate their suffering. But it simply hadn't occurred to her, until Evie had pointed it out, that, however irrationally, they might be doing what she had done: blaming themselves for their father's departure.

Deep in thought, Julia pulled on the handbrake. Evie had asked, also, if she'd been in touch with Hilary. And that, she decided impulsively, was something she could rectify right here and now. In the car. Where there was no chance of the children overhearing. Taking her mobile from her handbag, she rang Hilary's number.

'It's me,' she said, when she got through. But instead of telling Hilary that Carl had left home and was living with his PA, or, indeed, about her sense of God having let her down, she found herself asking some abrupt and telling questions.

'Why did Carl have such a poor relationship with his father when you were Matron at his school?'

She heard Hilary's intake of air as if it were a warning. Had there been some dispute between the two of them she wondered? It was hardly the sort of thing one could ask over the phone. Anymore than she could disclose Carl's dislike for Hilary, herself.

'I know he had no time for him,' she continued. 'But I can't quite fathom why.'

A lengthy pause ensued.

'Hilary? Are you there?' Julia asked.

'Yes. I'm just thinking about your question.'

'I take it you knew Carl's parents?'

'Of course. Though I knew his father better than his mother. He was one of the alumni of the school.'

'So what sort of man was he?'

Hilary sighed. Julia could imagine her screwing up her face in an effort to respond accurately.

'Not easy,' she said, at last. 'There were times when - how shall I put it - he could be quite dominant. Wanted his own way. And would do anything to get it.'

Julia frowned. Had he been abusive to Hilary? The older man with a younger woman?

'What does that mean?' she asked, uncomfortable with the way her thoughts were leading her.

'What has Carl had to say about the situation?' Hilary countered.

Julia shook her head.

'He won't talk about him,' she said, impatience making her voice sound clipped. 'That's the problem. I just wondered if you knew something I don't.'

'Look. It's none of my business, but has something happened?'

Glancing up at the house, Julia thought she saw one of the children peering from an upstairs window.

'Hilary - I'm sorry - I shouldn't have bothered you. I'm going to have to go. Speak soon. Bye.'

Frustrated with the lack of answers, she rang off, gathered up her handbag, got out of the car and walked towards the front door. She'd learned nothing new about her father-in-law from Hilary, and probably never would. But at least, she thought, she might be of some help to her children. Abi in particular. The new school term didn't start until Tuesday of the following week. That left plenty of time to get together with them over the weekend.

She unlocked the door and stood, for a moment in the hall, listening. A ghostly silence hung over the house, as if it were uninhabited. Yet again, she thought, they must all be in their rooms, playing with x-boxes and i-pods, perhaps communicating in abbreviated text messages with friends. Or perhaps not; too embarrassed to admit to their father's frailties.

She'd told them, before heading off to see Evie, that she had an appointment in Exeter, and had suggested that they accompany her, visit the shops, meet with friends.

'We could go to Tea On The Green, afterwards,' she said, naming a well-known tea-room. 'Perhaps even go to the cinema if there's a film you'd like to see?'

Her suggestion had met with a blank stare from Abi, and a mumbled response with no eye contact at all from the boys. Thinking about it now, she wasn't sure which was worse: the violent outbreak of emotion they'd displayed in the immediate aftermath of their father's departure, or the complete apathy that had followed? She hung her coat in the cloakroom and made her way to the kitchen. Perhaps a family tea with scones and cake might tempt them down?

The telephone in the kitchen was flashing, indicating that someone had phoned and left a message. There was nothing unusual about the fact that the children had not picked it up. They had their own means of communication with friends, and besides, they'd made it quite clear that they didn't want to risk talking to their father. Julia picked up the handset and pressed the relevant buttons to retrieve the message.

'This is a message for Mr Worth,' said a disembodied female voice. 'Mr Carl Worth.'

Julia's heart skipped a beat at the mere mention of Carl's name. Curious about the nature of the message, she continued to listen. The caller's name was indistinct, as was the reason for the call. In fact, thinking about it, there was something guarded in the way it was conveyed. What was clear, however, was that the call had been made on behalf of the boys' school, that it was urgent, and that Mr Worth was asked, in no uncertain terms, to respond immediately.

Julia picked up the phone and dialled the number for the school.

Twenty minutes later, she was on to Carl.

'What on earth is going on?'

Julia kept her voice low so that the children wouldn't hear. She'd phoned the school from the kitchen and just caught the Headmaster before he left for the weekend. Explaining that she was responding to an urgent message, and that Carl was 'away', she'd listened, with increasing alarm, as he outlined the situation. During the conversation, it became clear that the reason for the lack of clarity in the telephone message was to protect the children.

As soon as she'd concluded the call with the school, she'd shut herself away in Carl's study and, heart racing, dialled his mobile number.

'Are you alone?' she asked, now.

'Can be,' he replied, and other than vague sounds of movement in the background, the line went silent.

Standing at the uncurtained window, Julia stared into the gathering gloom outside, across to the tennis court. It was getting on for five-thirty on Friday afternoon, but she had no idea whether she'd reached Carl at work or back at the apartment. Having been only once to the factory and never to the flat, she found it hard to picture him and his surroundings. Was Lucy close at hand? In the office or elsewhere? Had Carl taken himself off somewhere more private?

'What's happened? Are the kids okay?' he asked now, the note of alarm in his voice all-too evident.

Julia ignored him, his concern for the children entirely too late by her reckoning.

'I've just been speaking to Mr Roberts. The boys' Headmaster. His secretary left an urgent message for you this afternoon, and as you're not here I rang back.'

At the other end of the line, Carl's expelled breath was clearly audible.

'Thank God! I thought you were going to tell me one of them had had an accident or something.'

'*Something* just about sums it up,' Julia said, surprising herself with the unfamiliar tone of sarcasm in her voice. 'Don't get too complacent just because they're not in hospital.'

'What do you mean?'

Julia paused, rearranged some paper clips on Carl's desk, and realised, to her shame, that she was enjoying her moment of triumph. It was quickly replaced by her concern for the children.

'Mr Roberts tells me that the school fees have not been paid.'

'Oh!' She heard Carl suck in a breath.

'He says this is not the first time.'

'I was late paying them last term. Understandably, I think you'd agree, in view of the new factory.'

'And now?'

'Naturally, I'll get them paid as soon as.'

'Good. Because Mr Roberts made it clear that no fees, no school. I'm sure you wouldn't want to add to the children's trauma?'

The conversation was forced and unnatural. Was this how it was to be from now on, Julia wondered, terse sentences loaded with hidden meaning and dripping sarcasm, aimed, fired and shot from artillery lodged in venomous hearts? It was unfamiliar territory, a battlefield that obliterated truth, then delivered sudden and startling views of a dangerous and unexpected terrain, and a sense of being lost and alone.

'It won't come to that,' Carl replied, briskly. Then his voice softened. 'How are you?'

Julia's eyes welled with tears. Angry and afraid of her vulnerability, she braced herself, answered in steely tones, 'How do you think?'

'I'm truly sorry.' Carl's voice faltered. 'This was never meant to happen.'

'I've been to see a solicitor.'

'A solicitor? Why?'

Full of scorn, Julia laughed out loud.

'Why do you think?'

'You're - you're not planning on getting a divorce, are you?'

The solicitor had asked that self-same question, though not in quite the same terms. It was ironic, really. Sitting there in the solicitor's office, Julia had to admit that she preferred not to have to think of such things. It was easier, somehow, pretending that nothing had happened.

'I had to be sure that the children and I are secure,' she replied, evading the question. 'I needed to know our Rights. Our financial situation. I believe he'll be writing to you shortly.'

Carl's manner changed abruptly, became cold and distant.

'Well you can tell him I shall be paying the school fees without delay. Was there anything further? I have work to attend to.'

He rang off. Alone in the study, with the house like a morgue, Julia felt ever more vulnerable.

* * *

Carl slammed his mobile phone down and remained seated at his desk. The call from Julia had done more than raise the alarm in financial terms. The sound of her voice, brisk and business-like, had thrown him completely. Never greatly in touch with his emotions, he'd nevertheless recognised the mix that churned within: the anger, admiration, and yearning for what once had been but now was lost; together with the disappointment and self-pity for what now faced him. It had all-but engulfed him. Volatile and unstable, it was not a good blend. In fact, since he'd left on Christmas Day - was it only a fortnight ago - he'd felt like something the cat might have brought in. Odd how something illicit, once so thrilling and pleasurable beyond compare, could turn so soon to dust.

He turned his mind back to the present. What the heck was going on with the school fees? They should have been paid by Direct Debit from his account. He picked up his mobile phone again and rang the direct line to his bank in Exeter.

'Mr Miller, please,' he said when he got through, knowing that, despite their friendship, a short identification and security procedure would be inevitable.

'What's going on, Miller?' he asked, the moment the connection was made. 'Roberts has been in touch from St Cuthbert's. Says the boys' fees haven't been paid.'

'And a Happy New Year to you, too, Worth,' Miller said, jovially. 'Right. Let's have a look. Just take a minute to get your account up on the screen. Did you have a good Christmas, you and Julia?'

Oh, no! Miller hadn't heard! Well how would he have? Carl dropped his head down onto his free hand.

'Right here we are,' Miller continued. He then fell ominously silent.

Carl waited, impatiently. His office at the Welsh factory was no more than a Portakabin erected in a corner of the factory. Filled with filing cabinets and other paraphernalia, and lit by the cold hard glare of neon strip lights, there was little comfort. It was merely a designated space within a space, in which the clanging of steel and hiss of machinery on the shop floor reverberated, unnaturally.

Miller cleared his throat.

'Looks like there's a block on your account. Know anything about it?'

Carl jumped to his feet.

'How on earth would I know? You're the bank manager, for goodness sake.'

'Doesn't mean a lot these days,' said Miller, maintaining a noticeably affable tone despite the threat in Carl's own voice. 'Everything's controlled centrally now.'

'Sorry old chap,' Carl apologised, pushing his fingers through his hair. 'So what's the score?'

Again, there was silence, during which Carl imagined Miller studying the figures on the screen. Then Miller spoke in grave tones.

'I'm afraid the account looks as if it might have been hacked. You're way over the agreed overdraft figure.'

Hacked? Carl wasn't sure whether that was good news or bad. It sounded dreadful. But hacked at least meant he hadn't overstretched himself. Hacked also meant that neither Lucy nor Julia had been plundering his funds. Hacked surely meant that there should be some sort of guarantee in force whereby the bank would refund him. Perhaps it wasn't so bad after all?

'Can you tell where the funds have gone?' he asked.

At the other end of the line, Miller cleared his throat again.

'On second thoughts, it looks more as if you've been on a bit of a spending spree, old boy. Gone a bit over the top with the Christmas celebrations, perhaps? There seem to have been some serious purchases made here. That probably explains the block that's been put on there. But you should have had a letter warning you.'

Carl broke out in a sweat as Miller told him the figures.

'So what's to be done?' he asked, wiping his face with his hand.

'I'm afraid you're going to have to come in to the branch so we can go over this together.' Miller's voice took on a less jovial tone, part sympathy for a friend, part bank manager to an errant client.

'And the school fees? You can release those, surely?'

'Afraid there's not a lot I can do about that,' Miller replied. 'The block will remain in force until we can get this sorted.'

Carl banged his fist on his desk.

'So why wasn't I told?' he demanded.

'As I said, a letter will have been sent to you from central office.'

'Where? My Exeter office? I certainly haven't received it here, in Wales.'

'As this is your personal account, it will have gone to your home,' said Miller. 'Might have been held up over Christmas and New Year. But it should have reached you by now, I'd have thought.'

Carl bade Miller goodbye. He felt sick to the core. If the letter had gone home, would Julia send it on or open it? And if the latter . . . The outcome didn't bear thinking about. First there was all that business with the unpaid butcher's bill and Josh having a fight with his son. Now this.

'You look like thunder,' said Lucy, coming into the office. 'Who was the phone call from, earlier?'

'My wife!' Carl spat out.

Only she wasn't going to be his wife anymore, was she? Not for long, if she was seeking a divorce.

CHAPTER FIFTEEN

'ARE YOU AND Dad going to get divorced?' Abi asked, leaning back on the purple heart scatter cushions that were propped against her bedhead, her legs stretched out before her.

Seated next to her, in a similar position, Julia put her hand on her daughter's denim-clad knee, in a gesture of comfort.

'I don't know, darling. Daddy's -' she was going to say 'chosen to live with Lucy' but thought it sounded too harsh, as if he'd deliberately chosen *not* to live with his family.

'I can't think how you didn't see for yourself what that Lucy was like,' Abi said, accusingly.

Julia's eyes swept around Abi's bedroom. It was two days before the January school term was due to start, and the floor was a midden of half-worn jeans, mini-skirts, smock-tops and sweaters, exercise books, pencil cases and girly magazines. If anything was more indicative of the mess their lives were in, it would be hard to find, she thought. She swung her arm around Abi's shoulders.

'I'm sorry you're hurting so much, darling. And that you feel I let you down. But when you love someone, as I did Daddy, you put your trust in them. You're not looking for signs of infidelity, of being let down. What did you see that I missed?'

Abi had the grace to look ashamed. She bit her lip. Julia squeezed her shoulder, bare beneath the strappy top she had on, despite the winter weather outside.

'We're both hurting, sweetie,' Julia continued. 'Let's not add to that hurt.'

Abi dropped her head onto Julia's shoulder.

'I'm sorry, Mum. It's just - something someone said at school. When Josh had that fight last term.'

Delighted to have healed the breach between them, Julia stroked Abi's hair.

'Something about Daddy?' she asked. 'And the unpaid butcher's bill?'

'No. It was about Lucy. Mike, the butcher's son, heard his dad telling his mum that she was nothing but a slut. A leech, he called her. Said she targets men with shed-loads of money and sucks them dry. Dad's not the first.'

Julia's heart raced and the room swam before her.

'So that's why Josh beat him up!'

Abi pulled away.

'Don't tell Josh I told you. He said it couldn't be true. Not our dad. He said Mike was a liar.'

Julia felt as if her mind was spooling away from her. Sound-bites and images reeled in and were then snatched away, like a whip in the hand of a circus trainer. Memories spun before her like flaming torches in the hands of a juggler. A drumming in her ears temporarily shut out all other sound. She opened her mouth to speak, but before she could say anything, the telephone rang.

'Better get it,' she said, and taking a deep breath she swung her legs to the floor and hastened across the landing to her own room.

It was Carl. He spoke rapidly, leaving no room for comment.

'Thought you should know, I've spoken to Roberts about the school fees and everything's sorted. No need to unsettle the boys. Better that they start the new term without you saying anything to them. Okay?'

There was a pause, during which Julia tried to assimilate what she'd heard. Carl waited until she conceded, then cleared his throat.

'By the way, I trust I can rely on you to forward my mail? Send it to the Welsh office, addressed for my personal attention.'

He rang off. Heart still pounding, Julia sat down hard on the edge of the bed. There was nothing like being cannon fodder on the receiving end of Carl's quick-fire communication, she thought. As it happened, she'd gathered up a handful of his post with the intention of dropping it into the Exeter factory for the staff there to redirect. But more important, to her mind, was the matter of the boys' schooling.

Did 'sorted' mean the same thing as 'paid'? Was Carl saying that not paying the school fees was merely an oversight which he'd now rectified? Or, as seemed more likely, given what she'd just heard from Abi, that leech-like Lucy had left him without the resources to pay? In which case, she thought, staring at the phone as if for answers, the whole scenario could be repeated next term.

Julia fills me in, the following week, with all that's been going on, and I must say that, despite the harrowing revelation her daughter's made, I'm feeling much more positive about their future as a family. Julia seems to be rising to the challenge and acting upon some of the strategies on which I've advised.

'Well done,' I say encouragingly. 'It must be a huge relief to you to have your daughter back on side again.'

'Absolutely!' A smile hovers on Julia's lips. 'She's confided in me a lot since then. If only I could do the same with Josh and Nathan. Get them to talk, instead of buttoning everything up.'

I screw my face into an expression of empathy, and nod.

'Different ball game altogether, boys. But don't give up. And don't chastise yourself if you can't get them to open up yet. You're not super woman.'

Julia pulls her cashmere cardigan around her. Surprisingly, though her appearance is far less well groomed than when she first came to me, she looks more relaxed than of late.

'I think I'm beginning to realise that,' she says with a grimace. 'In fact, I'm beginning to realise a lot of things.'

'Oh? Such as?'

'Well, I always thought of my mother as super woman. She was incredible. Kept the house spic and span. Cooked wonderful meals. Always looked immaculate, and made sure my sister and I did, too.'

Julia throws her head back and stares at the ceiling for a moment, before looking back at me and returning to her theme.

'I can see now that my father expected it of her. He basked in the limelight, while she put him on a pedestal. It was like a perpetual charade.'

'Do you think that's what you've been doing?' I ask, recalling previous discussions, and the way in which Julia has always idolised both her husband and her mother.

She nods. 'Yes, I think I have. Undoubtedly. My mother's *raison d'etre*, as far as my father was concerned, was to make him feel good about himself. But although she hid it well, I don't think she was happy, inside.'

I settle back in my chair and put my hand to my face, barely able to hide the satisfaction I feel in witnessing Julia's new-found powers of perception. It's clear that she's beginning to see the patterns of behaviour that have emerged, unbidden, from her childhood and streamed into adulthood. Patterns that have dictated lifestyle responses she's accepted without thought. I hardly need ask why her mother was unhappy; Julia launches forth with her interpretation.

'My mother was a wonderful pianist,' she says, her brown eyes full of fond memory. 'Spent a lot of time at the piano. But only when my father was out. The piano - I think it was hers before she married - was tucked away, out of sight in a boxroom. It was almost as if she wasn't allowed to shine. As if anything that put the spotlight on her and not my father was forbidden. Looking back, I think, she would have loved to have had some sort of musical career.'

'I suppose it would have been difficult to combine a family with the demands of a concert pianist?' I venture.

Julia shrugs. 'She could have given lessons, I guess.'

Hardly the same, I think, but I let it pass. What's more important is where this train of thought is leading, as far as Julia is concerned.

'And what about you?' I ask. 'What might you have done had you been given the chance?'

Julia's face lights up.

'Me? I aspired to be a Mary Berry when I was young. Cooking has always been my thing. In fact -'

She pauses. Aware that our time is nearly up and that I do have another Friday afternoon client to see this week, I'm anxious that she finish what she's started. I tip my head on one side and urge her, silently, to continue.

'In fact,' she says, at last, 'I've decided that rather than leave things in Carl's hands, I'm going to try and find a job for myself. Something in the catering trade or similar. For once in my life, I'm going to be my own woman. The Me I was meant to be.'

I can't help but give her a broad grin. In truth, I could clap my hands and cheer at the decisive note in her voice. What Julia has just said so precisely mirrors my own sentiments when I discovered that any hope of motherhood had eluded me. She's well on the way to achieving wholeness.

Julia left Evie's counselling room, walked through the Cathedral Yard and the gap in the Roman city wall, then turned right down the hill. It was only weeks since Carl had left yet already she felt so much stronger. What she had just said to Evie had crystallised thoughts that, she now realised, had been swirling in her subconscious for years.

She didn't want to waste her life away as she perceived her mother to have done. She wanted to use her talents, such as they were. Baking might not be on a par with the intricacies of engineering, the artistic skills of a pianist, nor the intellectual prowess of a barrister, but it had its own merit. As TV programmes like Mary Berry's The Great British Bake Off had shown, it kindled a fundamental warmth and attraction in the human psyche. She brought to mind a conversation she'd had earlier in the week.

'Mmmm! There's something so basic about the smell of new bread,' Hilary had said, sniffing the aroma when Julia gave her a batch of home-baked rolls as a thank you for her support. 'Something that touches the soul. That awakens an awareness of provision and nourishment. That feeds a sense of being the object of someone's love and care.'

Her comments had made Julia smile, and she smiled again, now, at the recollection.

'That's a bit of poetic hyperbole if ever I heard it,' she'd teased somewhat shyly. But she'd had to acknowledge that Hilary's appreciation had affirmed a sense of worth in her, and in her achievements. And that that sense of worth had fed into her dreams.

We all need dreams, she thought now. What she hadn't told Evie, or the children, was that the possibility of fulfilling her dream looked as if it might be opening up for her.

After an early dinner, that evening, Julia told the children she had to go out for a couple of hours. She drove back into town, parked the car and walked down the hill, towards the river, away from the cathedral. She was on her way to a meeting. Despite her outburst a few weeks ago, and the persistent feeling that God had let her down, she'd found herself unable to turn her back on him.

He's the same yesterday, today and forever, she'd read, somewhere; and when Hilary had told her *'he will never fail you or abandon you'*, she'd found that slowly, little by little, it was beginning to dawn on her that there might be some truth in that, after all.

It was almost, she thought, as if he were telling her that although she was battling her way through a maze of trees and thickets and couldn't find the way out - a simile she'd shared with Evie a few months ago - he was high above it all, looking down, able to see everything from beginning to end, and he knew exactly which path she needed to take. It was all a matter of trust. And as she'd said to Abi when they'd had their heart to heart, when you love someone, you put your trust in them.

Which was why she had told the children that she would not be home until later that evening, and why she was now taking her place with a number of other people in the hall attached to the church Hilary attended, where a special meeting had been convened.

The minister stood on a platform at the front, and beside him sat Hilary and one or two of the people Julia had met at her house. Taking stock, Julia slipped into a spare seat on the back row.

'As you will know from the information pack that was circulated recently,' the minister announced, 'Hilary Bankster was left a generous legacy last year by one of her relatives, which included some real estate. As a result, she is now the owner of a commercial property just off the High Street.'

He went on to describe the building, a place with which Julia was already familiar, before continuing.

'After much prayer and consideration, Hilary has very generously decided that she wants to put the property at our disposal, hence the proposal before you this evening.'

On the back row, Julia unfolded the papers she'd taken from her bag and scanned the notes that had been typed by one of the volunteers who worked in the church office.

'This means,' the minister continued, 'that we would be able to use the ground-floor as a commercial enterprise to raise revenue for our funds. Obviously, Hilary has steered the way in which we should proceed, and a proposal has been put forward that we should turn these premises into a coffee shop and craft centre.'

He paused to look at the audience and Julia felt her cheeks burning. She kept her head down as the scheme was elaborated upon.

'Naturally, we've cleared the project with the Charity Commissioners. We've also spoken to our legal and financial advisers as well as the city council, and they have all conveyed their approval of the project.'

There was a rustle of papers as the audience turned to the next page.

'The anticipated returns would cover a manager's salary,' the minister continued, 'as well as adding a considerable sum to our annual fundraising for overseas aid. But more than that, it would provide us with a focal point in the city centre.'

Even without looking up, it was clear to Julia that there was a buzz in the room, a sense of excitement and anticipation. The minister continued.

'Hilary has identified the person she believes would be best to take this project forward, and the way in which it could be done. And so it is with great pleasure that I hand you over to Hilary who will be able to give you further details in this respect.'

Julia felt her cheeks burn hotter still. She kept her head down as Hilary gave a broad outline of the as yet unnamed person, the reasons for her recommendation, the friendship they'd established over the past year. Then it was time for her to be introduced.

In a daze, Julia heard her name, got to her feet, and took her place on the platform at the front. All eyes were upon her. She knew some of the faces by sight, some by name, but she'd had little chance, to date, to develop any meaningful friendships. What would they make of her?

She cleared her throat, made a conscious effort to adopt an adult to adult approach as Evie would have advocated, and suddenly the nervousness that had all but engulfed her fell away. With increasing boldness, she told the gathering of her credentials, the catering course she'd taken after leaving school, the passion she felt for this local project, for what the minister had spoken of as 'taking the good news outside into the market place'.

She blushed, furiously, as she finished her prepared speech and was applauded. For half an hour or more she took questions as a discussion got underway. Then she was asked to leave while a vote was taken. Having previously told the minister that she would have to return home to the children, she left the building and made her way back to the car park.

'Thank you,' she breathed as she took her place behind the steering wheel.

She could hardly believe how well it had all gone. The congregation had been told that the manager's role - hers, if they agreed to it - would be a paid job, funded commercially by the sales of coffee, cakes and crafts - confectionery created by her hand. The part time staff would be volunteers; an opportunity for service for those who had time and energy to spare.

'The premises,' the minister had added, 'will, of course, need a complete make over. Hilary has indicated that limited funds will be available from the legacy, but these will have to be augmented. If we're to take this project forward, we'll have to be prepared to muck in and help.'

The mood had been more than positive when Julia had left. She'd said nothing to Hilary or the minister as yet about the further part she intended to play. But once she and Carl were divorced, she planned to raise equity on her share of the house. Whatever sum was needed to turn the old fashioned shop into a smart new café-craft outlet, she would be more than willing to make a contribution.

Of course, it would never have been possible had she and Carl still been together. His support would have been impossible to enlist. Yet given how generous Hilary had been - not only in making her legacy available to the charity, but also in selecting Julia as manager of the project - his persistent hostility towards her was all the more incomprehensible. A hypocrite, he'd called her friend, sneering at her passion for helping the vulnerable, questioning the integrity of her fund-raising projects. In the darkness of the car, Julia shook her head in disbelief.

She turned to the passenger seat on which lay a bundle of letters addressed to Carl. He'd asked her to forward them to the Welsh factory, but she saw no reason why she should have to readdress each and every one. If she drove home via the industrial estate, she could drop them into the Exeter factory without incurring the embarrassment of bumping into any of the staff, and either they could forward them, or Carl could pick them up from there. Reaching above her, she switched on the interior light, then lifted the pile to check through them. One, in particular, caught her eye. It was from the bank. A statement?

In the gloomy anonymity of the car park, Julia hesitated. Never, throughout her marriage, had she ever opened a letter addressed to Carl. Now, however, in view of the school fees fiasco, she felt she had the right to know that they'd been settled. Didn't she?

She ripped open the envelope. Inside was a letter, together with a statement. It was dated well over a fortnight ago. *Dear Mr Worth*, it began. Swiftly, she scanned the content. And as she did so, her blood ran cold.

CHAPTER SIXTEEN

IT WAS MONDAY evening and Carl sat at his desk in his make-do Portakabin office in the corner of the factory floor, aware that even in here the sound of rain drumming on the outer roof was deafening. It was also incessant. For weeks now, in the hills and valleys of South Wales, they'd endured leaden skies and starless nights; until it seemed that the gloom pressing upon him had ironed out all hope, and left him feeling flat and two-dimensional.

He glanced sideways. The ghostly outline of silent, stationary machinery loomed grey and foreboding outside the Portakabin window. Inside, a desk lamp cast a solitary pool of light. Lucy had already left work to return to the Monmouth flat, saying she felt unwell, and eliciting a promise from him that he would not be late. Ostensibly, he was to look into some hiccup with Customs and Excise on the next shipment to France; in reality he needed peace and quiet to think through his personal affairs.

He pulled his wallet from his pocket and extracted a photograph. A copy of one taken at the motorcycle skills academy back in November, it showed Josh, all geared up, sitting astride his bike looking as if all his

Christmases had come at once. Did Josh still have the original, Carl wondered? Was it even now pinned to his bedroom wall in all its glory? Had he retained the same sense of oneness father and son had enjoyed that day?

Somehow, Carl doubted it.

He slumped back on his office chair, turning a pen top aimlessly back and forth in his fingers. He'd heard nothing from Julia for what seemed like an eternity. Nothing, in fact, from the kids since he'd left home.

Home? Where was that?

He'd left on Christmas Day and it was now well into the new school term. Four, five weeks of silence? Was that normal? He tossed the pen top back on the desk. What did he mean by that? There was nothing normal about the entire situation. What gave him the right to expect anything of his kids? His wife? Relentlessly he flagellated. And the pain of separation bit deep.

He jumped to his feet; spun his chair; walked around the perimeter of the small space; pulled open filing cabinet drawers and slammed them shut. If you'd asked him where his kids figured a year ago, he'd have said high on the agenda. But it would have been a lie, wouldn't it? The reality, he now realised, was rather different. He'd exercised a complacency about their lives, their potential, their relationship with him, that was shameful in its shallowness. Just as he had about Julia. He missed her. Dammit! He missed them all.

He grabbed his coat. Locked up. Made for the car.

Lucy was curled up on the sofa by the time he arrived back at the flat and put his head round the living room door. She'd scooped her hair off her face into a ponytail, and had on a pair of blue denim jeans and a fluffy pink sweater. Her fresh, juvenile appearance struck Carl as at odds with the churning morass in his head.

'I'm back,' he said, unnecessarily, and divesting himself of his outer apparel, he went into the kitchen to deposit his car keys.

A boxed pizza lay on the worktop, together with a bag of frozen peas. Memories of the succulent scents of Julia's version of dinner assailed his senses, and he swallowed hard.

'Shall we go out to eat?' he asked, unable to face an evening awash with nostalgia, shut in, in front of the telly.

'On a Monday?' Lucy retorted, without looking up from her magazine. 'Besides, that wife of yours has called. More than once!'

Carl jumped as alarm bells jangled his shredded nerves.

'Julia?'

Lucy flicked through the magazine.

'Last time I thought about it she was called Julia.'

Her sarcasm was stinging.

'She rang here? How? We've no landline in the flat.'

Lucy tossed Carl's mobile phone onto the sofa beside her.

'You left this behind when you went off this morning.'

Carl picked it up; stared at the screen. He could have sworn he'd pocketed the phone when he'd left for work that morning. When had he ever not? He and it were conjoined.

'So how do you know it was Julia?' he asked, unwilling to cause controversy, reluctant to admit to the obvious.

Lucy looked up, a scathing expression on her pretty face.

'I listened, didn't I stoopid!'

'You listened to my messages?'

'Of course! It might have been you, trying to find your phone.'

Carl forced himself to relax. He was becoming paranoid. Given that he'd mislaid his phone, naturally Lucy would answer it.

'So what did she want?'

As soon as the words were out of his mouth he kicked himself. It was not only morally wrong to embroil Lucy in his relationship with Julia, he thought, but he found it an affront to Julia, herself.

'Dunno.' Lucy shrugged, indifferently. 'But she sounded pretty irate, if you ask me. *Will you kindly pick up,* she said first time. Last time it was more like, *Carl, if you know what's good for you* - or something like that.'

The prongs of the cleft stick on which he found himself stuck uncomfortably in Carl's side. He hated hearing Lucy speak of Julia like this. She was, when all was said and done, only an employee. Well. She had been an employee before she became his - he couldn't finish the thought.

At the same time, he felt a confusion of anger and fear - a *how dare Julia threaten him* versus *what's happened now?* Obviously something pretty terrible, he thought, since it was unlike her to speak thus. His heart raced. He stood, looking down at Lucy, uncertain whether to return the call or not. Knowing that he must. But whether to do so here, or to go out of the room? Out of the flat?

Lucy looked up from her magazine. Watching him watching her, her face softened. Evidently believing that she had punished him enough, she rose from the sofa and put her arms around Carl's neck.

'I can see you're shocked. You shouldn't let her speak to you like that, honey. Not after all you've done for her and the kids.'

Ignoring the irony, Carl fought the tension in his body. Meekly, he allowed himself to be led to the sofa. He sat down.

Skittering on my bike in and out of the usual Friday traffic furore, I know I am going to be late for Julia's appointment. It can't be helped, and I've at least been able to ring Guy to ask him to make my apologies. The fact is, I've been hospital-visiting during my lunch hour.

A phone call from social services, no less, has alerted me to a situation I had thought dealt with. But no! It seems that Daisy, my client from the outskirts of the city, who fled her abusive husband to live with her sister near Sidmouth, returned to her own home and was soundly beaten up by the brute. Lying in her hospital bed, bruised, broken and bandaged, she is in a shocking state and, frankly, I'm surprised she survived. But at least, on this occasion, Daisy has made no pretence of its being an accident, and the husband has been arrested on a charge of GBH.

'I hope they lock him up forever,' I mutter to myself, arriving back at Cathedral Close and hastening upstairs to greet Julia.

She is seated in the waiting area on the landing, and it's clear that Guy has done his stuff and looked after her, even going so far as giving her a cup of his designer coffee. Far from looking relaxed, however, Julia seems to be in a state of considerable agitation. As soon as I've removed my coat and she's seated in her usual leather armchair in my room, her news bursts forth.

'Of course, I expect you'll tell me I should never have opened Carl's bank statement,' she begins, twisting her hands in her lap. 'But as I've been left looking after the children - not that I'd have it any other way - I need to know what's going on. Reading the accompanying letter from the bank made everything suddenly fall into place.'

With difficulty, I drag my mind back from Daisy and try to piece together what Julia has been telling me.

'You mean the problem with the butcher's bill?'

'And the school fees, and who knows what else,' Julia says, clearly indignant with my lack of concentration. 'The letter from the bank made it clear that a complete stop had been put on Carl's account because he was way, way over his agreed overdraft limit.'

Oh, dear! No surprise there then, at least to me, though it's clear that Julia is only now making the connections. And just as I thought things were improving for her! The raucous cry of gulls on my rooftop reverberates in the chimney and pours scorn on my aspirations.

'Of course, I got nothing in the way of information from the bank,' Julia continues. 'This happened last Friday evening, so I knew no one would be available to speak to me on the phone over the weekend.'

'I don't suppose the bank would deal with you anyway,' I surmise. 'Unless, of course, it was a joint account?'

Julia brushes my enquiry away with an angry wave of her hand.

'It's in Carl's sole name,' she continues, 'and you're right, when I got through to them on Monday, it was a complete no-no. Humble apologies, of course, but -' Julia puts on a mocking tone '- *I'm so sorry, Mrs Worth; understand how you must feel Mrs Worth; data protection, Mrs Worth.* I spent all day trying to get someone to speak to me, even went into the Exeter branch to see the manager - he's a friend of Carl's - and got nowhere.'

I make a note in my file.

'You didn't speak to Carl, then?'

'Too right I did! But not until Tuesday. I was in such a state when I went home on Friday evening that I decided I'd have to sit on it over the weekend. I didn't want to upset the children by having a row with Carl on the phone.'

'Wow! That must have been difficult.'

For the first time Julia gives a small smile.

'Yes and no,' she replies. 'I put it out of my mind as far as possible and just got on with normal family life. Well - if anything can be called normal, these days. And I'm glad I did. Because I tried ringing Carl all day on Monday and got nowhere.'

'Oh?' I raise my eyebrows.

'He just didn't pick up. I got angrier and angrier. I'm afraid I said things I wouldn't normally have said.' She smiles, ruefully. 'There I go again. Talking about normality.'

'So what happened next?'

Julia looks down at her hands lying listlessly in her lap.

'Eventually, Lucy answered. Sounded as if butter wouldn't melt - Told me, just as if she were no more than his PA, *I'm afraid Carl's not here at the moment. Can I give him a message?* I'm afraid I really let rip then.'

Hardly surprising, I think, under the circumstances. And because of the circumstances that made me late, I'm now running out of time before my next appointment.

'So did you eventually get hold of Carl?' I ask, having indicated the time to Julia.

'He rang me on Tuesday morning. I don't think he likes speaking to me in front of her.'

'And how did he react?' I ask, thinking this might be germane.

Julia puts her head on one side.

'Well, that's just it. Obviously he was shocked that I'd opened his mail. He made out he knew nothing about the content. But I wonder how much of that was a pretext? I think he *did* know. After all, only a few days earlier he'd made a point of asking me to forward his post.'

'So what did he have to say about it?' I ask, getting to my feet.

Julia gathers up her handbag and gloves and rises with me.

'Well, that's just the thing,' she says, walking towards the door. 'He spent all his time trying to reassure me. It was no more than a blip, he said. Nothing to worry about. I just wish I could believe that was true.'

Julia woke late on Saturday morning, went downstairs in her dressing gown and spent an hour or so pottering about and tidying up. She breakfasted alone then went for her shower. By the time she emerged, dressed, the children were in the kitchen finishing their cereal, and she found she'd missed two phone calls.

'Sorry, Mum, I picked up, the second time it rang,' said Abi, sitting at the table spooning cocoa-pops into her mouth. 'Maeve said she'd ring me this morning and I thought it was going to be her.'

'And who was it?' asked Julia, dropping a kiss on Abi's forehead.

'It was that lady you know, who does the charity thing. Ms - umm - Bankster I think. Yes that's right. She said -'

'She said,' Nathan interrupted, a wicked grin on his face, 'that God wants you to buy me an x-box. Today!'

'Shut up, Nath,' Josh hissed.

Leaving his half-full bowl of cereal, Nathan got up from the table and flounced from the room.

'She said she had news for you about a café or something,' Abi continued, rising from the table and putting her bowl and spoon in the dishwasher. 'She wants you to ring her back.'

She, too, left the kitchen leaving Josh seated alone at the table looking morose, his head down and spoon dangling dangerously from his hand.

'You alright, Josh?' Julia asked, wishing she could get through to her eldest son.

He didn't answer. Julia tried again.

'So who was the other phone call from?'

She kept her voice deliberately light-hearted, in the hope of eliciting some sort of response. Anything. It worked.

'Old man Roberts. Our Head. He left a message on the answer phone. Wanted to speak to Dad. Said it was important. What am I supposed to have done now, that's what I want to know?'

Josh let go of his spoon. It dropped into the bowl with a plop, splashing milk on the table.

Julia stopped in her tracks. Was this something to do with the school fees?

'You didn't speak to Mr Roberts then?'

'Nah! I told you. He left a message.'

Josh's voice was full of aggression, but in the next moment he glanced up, his eyes full of pleading. And for a moment, her heart flipping, Julia was able to glimpse the vulnerable boy hidden behind the usual adolescent façade.

'I haven't done anything Mum,' he said. 'Honest. I don't know what he's on about.'

Julia sat down at the table at right angles to him and lowered her head to make eye contact with him. Dressed in his pyjamas, the hair on the crown of his head sticking up at right angles, he looked anything but the suave young man he liked to present himself as. She put her hand on top of his.

'I don't think it's anything you've done, Josh. If you say you haven't misbehaved, I believe you.'

Unexpectedly, Josh's eyes filled with tears. He brushed them away, clearly angry with himself.

'So what is it Mum? It's Dad again, isn't it? He's messed everything up for us all. I hate him.'

'No you don't. Not really.' Julia spoke softly, her hand still on her son's, the truth of what she was saying sinking into her heart and mind in a moment of recognition. 'You hate what he's *done*. As I do. As we all do.'

Josh's demeanour changed from chagrin to scorn. He snatched his hand from under hers.

'So what's he done now? Whatever it is, it's sure made Old Man Roberts mad.'

Julia hesitated.

'You can tell me, Mum. I'm sixteen for goodness sake. And with Dad living with that . . . I'm the man of the house.'

Julia sighed heavily. Elbows on the table, she leant her chin on the fist she'd made of her hands, as if her head were too great a weight to bear on its own.

'Alright, I'll tell you. But you're not to get upset about it. I'm sure it's just a hiccup.'

Josh frowned.

'So what is it, Mum?' he shouted. 'Tell me!'

Julia looked down at the table. Josh was right. He was sixteen now. Some would call that manhood. You could leave school; find paid employment; have a sexual relationship that might result in another life; even marry or enlist in the armed forces with parental consent. She couldn't protect this son of hers from the realities of the world forever. Still she hesitated to spell out the truth about the situation.

'There's been a bit of a problem with the bank,' she began. 'I spoke to Daddy about it the other day, and he's sorting it out.'

For a moment, Josh stared at her quizzically. Then he thumped the table with his fist so hard that the spoon in the dish before him jumped and rattled against the rim.

'It's the fees, isn't it?' A stream of profanities fell from his lips. 'He doesn't give a damn about us.'

He leapt up from the table and left the kitchen, slamming the door behind him. Julia sat for a while, gazing after him. Then sadly, and in silence, she went upstairs to her room.

Ten minutes later, she heard raised voices followed by footsteps pounding down the stairs, and more slamming doors. Venturing out onto the landing, she found Abi running towards her, her hair flying behind her, her face distraught and awash with tears.

'Mummy, you've got - to stop him,' she sobbed, reverting to childhood.

'Stop who? What's happened?'

'Josh. Please -'

Abi took hold of Julia's hand, dragged her to the top of the stairs.

'Stop him, Mummy. Please - please.'

Julia felt as if her lungs had deflated. She drew a deep breath, turned towards Abi and took her face in her hands.

'What is it, darling? I can't do anything unless you tell me what's happened?'

'He says he's going to kill himself,' she shouted. 'Josh. On his motorbike.'

'What!'

Julia felt the blood drain from her face. Her legs and feet felt leaden. Dragging herself forward, she propelled herself down the stairs. But even as she ran, with Abi close behind her, they heard the mechanical whirring of the garage door as it opened, followed by the roar of the motorbike Carl had given Josh for his birthday.

CHAPTER SEVENTEEN

THE FIRST TO phone me on my mobile on Saturday morning is Scott. Since the start of his new job at a college in the outskirts of London, he seems to be developing a habit of ringing each week; a habit I welcome.

'I hope you don't mind,' he says. 'I haven't had much of a chance to get to know anyone up here yet. It's nice to have someone to chat with.'

How could I possibly mind? We hit all the right notes when we met at his aunt's, and continue to do so during our telephone conversations. I'm flattered that he should want to keep in touch. At the same time, I remind myself that things may well change once he becomes established in his new home on campus.

'I'll be down at Easter,' he says, now, 'staying in Topsham with Nancy and Guy. I'm hoping you might be my guide so we can walk some of the Jurassic Coast?'

'That would be great! It's always more enjoyable when you have someone to share it with.'

'That's what I thought. So I wondered,' Scott pauses, 'if you're willing - whether you'd attend the Easter service at the cathedral with me?'

I laugh out loud. 'I'm willing! No need to be so defensive.'

He laughs with me, and we chat for a further few minutes.

I've no sooner finished the call than my mobile rings again. It's Julia, and she is distraught.

'Evie. I've been trying to get hold of you for ages. Didn't know who else to ring.'

The relief at making contact with me at last causes her to break down into great gulping sobs. Eventually, after much perseverance, I piece together the story she's trying to tell me. A telephone call from the boys' Headmaster has spooked Josh, who then learned from his mother that his father was having financial problems; he's had a shouting match with his sister, Abi; told her that he has nothing to live for and that he's going to kill himself; then gone off on the motorbike he is neither competent, nor legally permitted, to ride on the road; no one knows what direction he's taken, nor whether he is serious about his intention to end it all.

'I take it you've rung the police?' I ask Julia, sharing her concern, while trying to keep her calm.

'Yes. They've got patrol cars out looking for him. And they're scanning the CCTV videos. But there's not much coverage in this area.'

'And what about his father? Carl? Have you spoken to him?'

'Yes. If he hadn't given him the bike, this would never have happened.'

Understandably, she's full of bitterness, but for now I let that go.

'So is he in Wales? Will he be coming back?'

'Yes. But it'll take him a couple of hours. He won't be here till nearly lunchtime.'

I glance at my watch. It's already just turned eleven. Even if he'd set off immediately, I can't believe he'd be with Julia until about half-past one. I do some quick calculations. Julia obviously needs support. But what is it going to do for their broken relationship if Carl turns up while I'm there?

Evidently sensing my professional concerns, Julia begs me to come. How can I refuse?

I arrive, as predicted, within twenty minutes. Julia and the children are huddled together on the sofa in the family room, where I last saw her. It's the first time I've met the children, and despite the all-too-obvious evidence of their distress, I'm impressed. They're good looking kids, polite, and sensible.

'It's going to be awful for Daddy driving all that way,' Abi says to her mother. 'You don't think - You don't think he'll - She won't come, will she?'

Julia looks across the room to me for answers.

'I wouldn't have thought so,' I state, firmly. 'Your dad won't want any distractions.' Actually, I'm not at all certain of that. He might well want the support of his significant other, I think.

'I suppose she might drive him over,' I add. 'But that might be better for your dad. Safer. Because she's not emotionally involved. But I'm quite sure she won't come here.

'Now. Shall I make us all a drink? Abi, could you show me where everything is, please?'

Abi shows me out to the kitchen, a room of palatial proportion compared to my shoebox.

'Do you have any idea where your brother might have gone?' I ask her. 'Any friends he might have called on? Favourite places in town? Or out in the country?'

Abi shakes her head, her eyes welling with tears.

'Hey, come on,' I squeeze her arm. 'I expect he'll burn up the rubber for a while, get it out of his system, and come back here with his tail between his legs.'

Abi nods, compliantly.

Under her direction, I proceed to make a strong black coffee for Julia and myself, and strongly sugared tea for the kids. It's as I'm carrying the tray back across the hall that the telephone rings. Julia's face, as I enter the family room, has a look of unadulterated terror.

She picks up the phone. I set down the tray. She stands in silence. I move towards her. She gasps, grasps her throat, sways on her feet and passes me the phone. I slip an arm around her waist and lower her onto the sofa.

'Hello. This is Evie Adams. I'm a friend of Mrs Worth's. I'm afraid she's too upset to talk. Who am I speaking with? Can you tell me what's happened?'

Julia felt as if all the life had drained from her. She looked around the room, at the children, at Evie on the phone. Everything looked familiar, yet at the same time she felt as if she were in a dream. A nightmare. What had the police officer said? The words fragmented inside her head. She couldn't make sense of them.

'Right!' On the other side of the room, Evie took the phone from her ear, put it down then came and crouched before her.

'Julia, look at me. The police have found Josh. He's had an accident on his bike. They've called an ambulance, and he's being taken into hospital. We need to get there now.'

Julia wanted to ask *is he still alive?* but she found herself unable to form the words. She had hold of Abi's and Nathan's hands, one on each side of her. Abi was squeezing her fingers so hard it hurt. All three of them were crying. Above the noise, Evie spoke again.

'What about the children? Is there a neighbour who could look after them?'

'No, Mum,' Nathan shouted.

'We want to come with you, Mummy,' sobbed Abi.

'Right then,' Evie stood and Julia felt herself being helped to her feet. 'We'll have to go in my car. Get your coats on. We need to leave immediately.'

Julia allowed Evie to guide them out of the front door and into her car. She felt as if she were floating; as if the voices and sounds around her were muted and distant. She stared straight ahead through the windscreen. The trees, hedges, and driveways on either side blurred and merged.

A picture began to form in her head. It was Josh as a newborn. Blood and mucus covered the tiny body. Inert and lifeless, he failed to cry. The medics moved in. Began to rub him. Yet as she watched, the image morphed into the young man who was her son today. Still he lay, silent and lifeless. Blood and mucus covered the limp body and motionless limbs.

'Julia. Julia.' Someone down a tunnel, far off, was calling her name.

'Mummy. We're here. Come on. Let's go and see Josh.'

Obediently, Julia turned. The car door was being held open by a chubby, pink-faced boy she thought she recognised. She swung her legs sideways, lifted herself from the seat, stood, and began to move her feet, one after the other, towards a large building. Ahead lay an entrance with a sign over it, on which the words Emergency Department were spelled out in white letters on a red background. She sensed, rather than saw, that she was not alone. But who were these people? And where was she?

Julia is uppermost in my mind when I fill Guy in on Monday morning with details of my weekend.

'She was in shock. Completely shut down. Poor woman! She's had a lot to deal with. And still has.'

I'm seated in Guy's office as we speak, while he brews us one of his special coffees.

'It was good of you to go over to see her on Saturday morning,' he says, placing two white pottery mugs on a tray and measuring out the grounds into a cafetière.

'Least I could do,' I respond. 'The eldest boy had learned that his dad, who's gone off with his secretary, hasn't paid the school fees. So what does he do? Tells his sister he's going to end it all; grabs the little motorbike his dad bought him for his birthday; and, despite being underage, goes on a rampage through Devon lanes that ends up with him hitting a tree, being thrown in the air, and then rushed to hospital by ambulance.'

'Good heavens!' Guy's face is etched with concern. 'I take it he's okay? Didn't succeed in his intention?'

I stand up and walk to the window to look across to the cathedral. Do people like Guy, who profess a faith in God, ever reflect on where he is at times like this, I wonder?

'He didn't succeed in killing himself,' I tell him, 'but he's certainly not okay. He's in a coma in intensive care. He wasn't wearing a helmet. And he may well have sustained brain damage. Not to mention broken limbs.'

Images of the scene we'd encountered on Saturday flood through my mind. Julia had been advised that only one, or at most two, people could go to the boy's bedside, and that it would not be advisable for Abi and Nathan to see their brother in that state. Torn between Julia's pleas for me to accompany her, and the kids' needs for reassurance, I eventually succumbed to the former when one of the nurses promised to stay with the children.

Julia and I were shown into Josh's room, and the sight that confronted us was truly shocking. Julia cried out, her knees buckled beneath her, and she had to be supported on either side by a nurse and myself. One side of Josh's face, beneath the bandages around his head, was raw and liver-coloured; tubes snaked their way across him; machines bleeped around us.

'It was horrible!' Turning from the window in Guy's office, I take the coffee he's offering me. 'The consultant, evidently a friend of Julia's husband, gave us a run down on the boy's injuries. But I don't think either of us could take it in. Even I found it hard to maintain a sense of equilibrium. And I don't know the lad.'

'And the father?'

'He turned up, eventually. Carl. Julia had rung him initially, when the boy first went off, but the accident hadn't happened at that stage. I guess one of the kids must have texted him when the news came in from the police. I'm sure Julia didn't contact him again. In the trauma of the moment, we forgot all about him.'

'And how was he?' Guy asks.

'He'd driven over from Wales. He looked terrible. Hung, drawn and quartered. I can't begin to imagine how he must have felt. I know from Julia that the motorbike gift was his idea. She was dead against it. I don't suppose he'll ever get over the sense of guilt he must be going through; knowing that you were not only the reason for your son's death-wish, but that you also provided the means.'

Guy seats himself at his desk.

'He's not the first, and I don't suppose he'll be the last. Think of all the school gun shootings in the States. Sadly, it seems that some of us never learn.'

'Well, that's just it. I was beginning to have hopes for this couple, before he went completely off the rails. I don't suppose Julia will ever forgive him now. Bad enough to abandon your wife and family for someone else. Unforgivable to be the reason for your son lying in intensive care.'

Guy swivels in his chair.

'Nothing is unforgivable, Evie,' he chides me, gently. 'Don't give up hope for this family yet. And if you have even a mustard seed of faith, pray for them from time to time.'

He's right, of course. Just wish I could see some evidence of either forgiveness in Julia, or faith from her husband.

Carl sat at the bedside in intensive care looking at his son.

'You can touch him, you know,' the nurse in attendance told him. 'Hold his hand. Speak to him.'

Carl was aware of the so-called therapeutic nature of doing so; it was just that in this instance he thought it would probably be counter-productive. He couldn't tell the nurse that, of course. 'If my son felt my flesh on his, his would crawl,' or 'the sound of my voice would make my son want to let go of his tenuous hold on life,' were thoughts best left unsaid. Even so . . . He couldn't tear himself away from Josh's bedside.

Except when Julia was there!

She'd rung him the morning it had all kicked off. Saturday, wasn't it?

Only three days ago? It felt like months. He'd been breakfasting late in the flat with Lucy when he'd taken the call. He recognised Julia's voice, but though it was immediately obvious that something was wrong, he could hardly make out what she was saying. She was incoherent. With anger? Jealousy? Fear? All three would be justified; he knew that. But strangely, it no longer evoked in him the fury and scorn that would, once, have been his response.

Lucy raised her eyebrows, quizzically. He shrugged, spreading his free hand in the air to signify his own perplexity, then left Lucy at the breakfast bar in the kitchen and went through to the bedroom.

'It's Josh,' Julia said, her voice strangulated. 'He's gone off on his motorbike. He told Abi he'd had enough. Says he's going to end it all.' She broke down.

When he thought about it now, Carl was full of admiration. Julia had attached no blame to him. Not outwardly, at any rate. Yet he'd felt consumed with guilt. He'd given his son what, in Julia's words, was a lethal weapon. And he'd failed, miserably, to ensure that he knew how to use it safely.

'The police are out looking for him now,' Julia continued when she regained control, and Carl felt overwhelmed with fear and self-loathing.

'I'm so sorry,' he said, his voice breaking. 'Forgive me. You were right.'

'What did *she* want?' Lucy asked him, coming into the room the moment the call came to an end.

Bridling at the absence of Julia's name and emphasis on the pronoun, plus the fact that Lucy must have been eavesdropping outside the door, Carl turned abruptly.

'It's my son. Josh. I have to get back to Exeter. Immediately.'

Lucy sat on the edge of the unmade bed.

'Can't she sort it out? His mother?' she asked. 'Are you sure she's not winding you up? Pulling your heart strings?'

Carl had treated her to a withering look and, as he threw a few things in a holdall and gathered together his keys and wallet, a blazing row had ensued. Lucy wanted to come with him. To drive him up to Exeter. Carl had refused the offer. He wanted no distractions when it came to sorting out this mess of his making.

'Besides,' he said, 'you need to be here for work in case I don't get back before Monday.'

Lucy had retaliated with her version of the sort of adolescent tantrums he'd seen in his kids: sulking; shouting; door slamming. She hadn't said goodbye, and he'd left the flat with a sense of relief.

It was while he was en route that he'd received a text. Ignoring legal requirements, he picked up his phone and glanced at the screen. It was from Abi. 'Dad. Cme qck. J in hosp. Not gd,' it read.

His heart skipped a beat. He glanced again at the text, doubting that he'd read it correctly. Josh in hospital? What had happened? Was this an accident? Or the suicide attempt he'd threatened?

The steering wheel jerked in his hand. He was dangerously near the edge of the road; had hit the lip, in fact, where the tarmac gave way to a rocky verge. With difficulty, he wrenched at the wheel, brought the car back to its rightful trajectory; his attention back to the road ahead.

What to do, he thought? He'd have to stop to text Abi back to ask which hospital, and that would mean delay. He wrestled with the options. In what state was Josh? How fast might he deteriorate? Would he be in time? Any other alternative was unthinkable.

In the end, he'd pulled in at the next service station and spoken with Abi. She was tearful; in need of reassurance.

'I'll be there soon,' he'd promised. 'Just short of an hour.'

By the time he'd arrived, Josh was on a life-support system and what greeted Carl was truly shocking. Barely able to suppress his grief, he sank to his knees beside the bed, and only then saw that Julia was seated there with another woman.

'You're here!' She stood and turned towards him. To his surprise, it was relief rather than anger that suffused her face at that moment. The anger had come later.

Intimating that she'd leave them alone together, Julia's friend had left the room. Her identify was unknown to him, but it was immaterial. All that mattered to him was that he was the cause of the wretched situation that lay before him. Anguish tore at his heart.

In the days since then, he and Julia had taken it in turns to sit with Josh. She returned home each evening with the kids while he was on duty; he'd booked into a nearby Premier Inn when she sat with their son. The arrangement was emotionally exhausting, but he was big enough to admit that it must be the more so for Julia who had the added burden of the children's needs.

'Wake up, Josh,' he urged his son in a whisper.

With a start, he became aware of a sudden incessant beeping from one of the machines. Josh was thrashing about on the bed. The nurse in attendance rushed forward.

'Please leave the room, Mr Worth,' she said. 'Now!'

In a daze, his heart pumping fit to burst, Carl went out to the corridor. Instantly, he felt overcome. Gulping air as great sobs racked his body, he sank down onto the floor. Nothing mattered, except Josh.

'Please God, let him live,' he implored. 'Let him be okay.'

'You alright, sir? Come on. Let's go in here.' A hand gripped his elbow, helped him to his feet and led him into a side room.

'It's Mr Worth, isn't it?' the male voice continued. I'm the chaplain, Rev Jones.'

'It should be me in there,' Carl found himself saying through his tears. 'I've made such a ruddy mess of things. How can my wife and kids ever forgive me? How can I forgive myself?'

For twenty minutes or so, Carl poured out his story, while Rev Jones listened, intently.

'I don't even want to be with Lucy,' Carl finished. 'I'm not sure I ever did. In fact, I know it was never a decisive action on my part. It just -' he shrugged '- sort of happened. And that sounds so clichéd, so ruddy inexcusable, it makes me hate myself even more.'

'Would you like me to pray with you?' asked the chaplain. 'And then I'll go and find out if you can see your son again.'

Carl nodded. It felt so good not to have to hold it all together by himself. To have someone else in charge. He closed his eyes and let go.

CHAPTER EIGHTEEN

UNDERSTANDABLY, I'VE SEEN little of Julia in the past few weeks, though she has texted me an occasional progress report on Josh's condition, and expressed profuse thanks for my support when he was admitted to hospital. Now, with the February half-term come and gone, she books in for her usual appointment on a Friday afternoon.

Grabbing a sandwich at lunchtime, I reflect on the situation. I'm not sure what to expect from her visit. If the divorce is proceeding, she will need ongoing support for some time to come. Likewise, if the financial circumstances have come to a head, as seems likely given the school fees fiasco. But in that case, will she be able to afford it? If, on the other hand, the togetherness enforced by Josh's condition has brought about a truce between her and Carl, then who knows?

Julia arrives after lunch, with a bunch of daffodils for me in her hand and a spring in her step. Nevertheless, despite her smile, the harrowing circumstances of the last few weeks and months remain etched in her face.

'I can't tell you how relieved I am,' she says, removing her winter coat and scarf and seating herself in the usual place. 'Josh is out of intensive care on a general ward, and he's sitting up and talking now. He's still bandaged, of course. But there's a chance of his coming home soon.'

'That's brilliant!' I can't help but be enthused by Julia's news.

'It was touch and go for a while,' Julia continues. 'We were told that even if he made it through, he might well have brain damage.'

'And he's okay?' I shake my head in amazement. 'From what I saw, I'd say that was a miracle.'

Julia looks at me, quizzically.

'That's exactly what it was, Evie!'

The tables have been turned. Feeling suitably chastised, I nod my head in agreement.

'So what does Josh have to say about the incident?' I ask. 'I imagine that having his father at his bedside must have made some impact on his frame of mind? But is it positive or negative?'

Julia pushes a strand of hair from her face.

'Well, that's another miracle, of a sort. He's thrilled to see his father. It seems he has no memory of Carl going off; or the business over the school fees; or anything to do with his accident.'

'How strange.'

Julia smiles.

'Not really. The doctors have told us he's suffering from a mild form of amnesia. They think it will only be temporary. That his memory will return little by little. I'm just hoping for the best.'

Again, I shake my head in astonishment. But the possibility of a different outcome has to be faced.

'So in theory, he may have complete recall of the situation?' I ask.

Julia nods, but continues to smile.

'In theory, yes. But I think the more he sees of his father, the more the bad memories will recede. It's as if Carl is - as if we're all - being given a second chance.'

The sun shining through the window illuminates Julia's face so that, despite the ravages of the last months, she looks radiant.

'I haven't explained myself very well, have I?' she continues.

'Do you mean that Carl's affair may be over? That you and he might get back together again?' I ask.

Julia shakes her head.

'The truth is, I don't know. To the best of my knowledge, Lucy is still installed in the Monmouth flat. But again, as far as I'm aware, Carl hasn't been back there since Josh's accident. So who knows?'

This is the third time Julia has spoken of Josh's motorbike crash as an accident. Is she, I wonder, deliberately erasing the real reason for her son's rampage? And if so, why? I make a note in my head that this may be something to be explored in the future.

'And the financial situation?' I ask. 'What's happened about the school fees?'

In an unconscious symbol of covering herself, Julia pulls her pale blue sweater down over her waist and hips.

'Abi's are not a problem,' she says. 'Her paternal grandmother set up a fund for her. As for the boys - I've paid them for this term. Fortunately, between what remained of my personal allowance, plus some premium bonds my mother bought for me when I was a child, I had enough. I felt it was the least I could do to maintain some stability for the children.'

'Well done!' I'm impressed.

Julia shrugs, and smiles ruefully.

'I don't know what will happen in the future, of course. At several thousand pounds each per term, it'll be quite beyond me. We'd need yet another miracle. And I suspect we may have had more than our fair share.'

I return her smile.

'As you say, though, it has bought you some time. And who knows, Carl's Welsh factory may yet take off and yield dividends. Whatever happens between the two of you, I'm sure he'd want the best for the boys.'

Julia looks grim.

'It seems it wasn't only the school fees,' she says. 'Carl had even re-mortgaged our home behind my back. He says it was to finance the Welsh factory, but I suspect that some of it went into the Monmouth flat.'

'Good heavens! So where does that leave you?'

'Exactly!' For once, Julia refrains from rushing to his defence. 'He told me about it recently. He seems to be full of remorse. But who knows?'

'Remorse or not, I guess that doesn't change the fact that you may end up homeless if the bank does foreclose?'

'No. Indeed.' Julia rummages in her handbag, pulls out a leaflet and passes it to me. 'But that may not be the end of the world. It's almost as if we've been provided for. I've recently been appointed by Hilary's church to be the manager of a new café-craft shop in the middle of town. I haven't told the children about it yet. But despite all the trauma and upset -' her eyes fill with tears '- it does mean that I'll have an independent income. I'll at least be able to provide for myself and the children.'

A huge sense of relief courses through my veins - for Julia, and for her children.

'That's great news!' My voice is filled with the enthusiasm I feel.

Though still tearful, Julia's face is wreathed in smiles.

'And here's the really good bit,' she continues, 'there's a large two-story apartment overhead that I can rent.'

I shake my head in amazement and pleasure.

'Someone's certainly been looking after you! What do you think the children will have to say?'

Julia waves her hand in an attempt to dismiss any cause for concern.

'I'm hoping they'll be able to put the past behind them and move on. They're all of an age now where living in town will have a very positive appeal. And I get the impression that they're a bit fed up with having to rely on me for transport, where we are now.'

Despite certain reservations, I can't help but feel enthused.

'That's great news, Julia. So you get to fulfil your dream of going into business in the world of catering. And to re-house yourself and your family into the bargain.'

I sit back in my chair. It may seem a bit glib. A bit premature. And Julia may well have a set back. But at this moment, I think I can say that if I didn't believe in miracles before, I'm close to doing so now. With which thought, a flash of lightening fills the room, and a clap of thunder rattles the windows.

Carl stood in his room at the Premier Inn and stared through the window at the gathering gloom outside. Then he reached up, drew the curtains and extracted his phone from his pocket. Turning back to the room, he punched in the speed dial number for Julia's mobile. He'd made a conscious decision not to ring on the landline because he didn't want to have to speak with Abi and Nathan. He'd seen them, of course, during the weeks that Josh had been in hospital, but he'd continued to live at the hotel and had not returned to the house at all.

Their initial response in the waiting room, on the day of Josh's accident, had been guarded. But when Josh had rallied and they'd been able to visit him on the ward in hospital, their relief and exhilaration appeared to have translated into forgiveness for their dad. At least, that was how Carl had interpreted it, and he couldn't have felt more grateful. Nor more humbled.

Julia answered her phone.

'I - er - I wondered if we could talk?' Carl asked.

There was a pause, during which he imagined her leaving the room to seek a little privacy from the kids.

'You mean now? On the phone?' Julia asked.

'No, I er, I wondered if we could meet; talk face to face.'

There was no response from Julia. Had she not heard him? Or did she not like what she'd heard? He paced around the room, and hastened on.

'I'm not hoping for anything to happen between us,' he said, 'but we do need to iron out a few wrinkles.'

'A few wrinkles?' Julia exploded. 'That's putting it mildly.'

Stopping in front of the mirror on the wall, Carl looked at himself and cringed. She had every reason to be angry. What a crass way to describe their situation. Whatever had possessed him to be so stupid, when he'd always prided himself on having the gift of the gab? Pride? Wasn't that what came before a fall?

'I'm sorry. I'm not going about this very well, am I?' There was a catch in his voice. He cleared his throat. 'What I'm trying to say is that there are things we need to talk through. For the kids' sake.'

To his relief, Julia appeared to relent.

'I agree,' she said. 'But where? You're not talking about coming here, are you? I'm not sure that would be a good idea.'

'No. No. That wasn't in my mind at all. I wondered if you'd - if you'd agree to have a meal with me here, at the Premier Inn. It's pretty basic, but there aren't many residents. The restaurant's quite quiet at this time of year. We wouldn't be disturbed. And it's neutral ground.'

Fearful of her response, he began pacing again. But he needn't have worried.

'Alright,' she said. 'But it'll have to be soon. Josh will be home next week.'

They arranged a date and time, and hung up. Carl sat on the bed; looked down at his hands. They were shaking. Actually shaking! Relief didn't begin to describe his feelings. He'd envisioned Julia refusing to speak to him, hanging up on him without a word. And who could blame her? Not him. He couldn't begin to conceive of how angry and let down she must feel.

And rightly so. The man she'd said 'I do' to all those years ago had turned into a wimp. What had he said about his affair with Lucy to the chaplain at the hospital? *It just sort of happened.* Pathetic! When had anything ever 'just sort of happened' for him before? He'd always prided himself on his decisiveness.

Pride! There it was again. Was that the problem? If he were one of his employees, would he now be admonishing himself to analyse that pride? To ask if it bordered on arrogance? To question whether it blinded him to truth?

The thought prompted a leap of logic. What was truth? His mind went back to his schooldays. Wasn't it the French novelist Gustave Flaubert who had defined perception as truth? And Proust who had pointed out that the voyage of discovery is not in seeking new landscapes, but in having new eyes for current ones?

Carl applied each of the axioms to himself. Was it his own perception of life and love, truth and meaning, that was at fault, he wondered? Had he, in *seeking new landscapes* in his affair with Lucy, failed to *have new eyes* to see the enrichment, comfort and security present in Julia's love? That of his family? And the home that had been his?

Even as the thought lingered, he was reminded of the Rev Jones' prayer for Josh's recovery and for his own enlightenment to see the way ahead and to have the courage to take it.

'Please God, let my meeting with Julia go well next week,' Carl said out loud without thinking, and immediately he felt foolish, casting his eyes about him as if he thought there might be other ears in the room who could hear him.

Julia was late arriving on the appointed evening, and Carl sat alone in the restaurant, his anxiety levels high. The sight of her coming through the door, slim and petite, dressed in slacks and jacket, was enough to make his heart race and his breathing grow shallow. Her hair was a burnished brown with a hint of auburn, her face was a little drawn but her eyes, dark and peaty, were alight with - hope?

Awkwardly, he pulled out her chair and waited until she was seated before he sat down, himself.

'Thank you for coming,' he said.

She looked around her, the surprise on her face plain to see.

'I just wanted somewhere, anywhere,' he said, interpreting her reaction as a judgement on his choice of hotel. 'Somewhere anonymous, to be on my own. To think.'

She nodded, her understanding of what was not being said clearly discernible.

He had, actually, been back to the Monmouth flat and its inhabitant twice since Josh's accident, but he didn't want to mention that to Julia. The first occasion had been traumatic enough, without resurrecting it now. The second more of a relief. Thoughtfully, carefully, he'd planned to spell things out to Lucy, his financial position, Josh's accident, his love for his children. And his wife. As it happened, there had been no need. Lucy had clearly resigned herself to the fact that, however you described their fling, it was now over. Packed and ready to depart, she'd been cool and distant.

The following weekend, with the flat vacated, Carl had instructed the local estate agent.

'The flat has been emptied and is on the market,' he said to Julia when their meal was before them. 'And Frank and his wife are selling-up here and moving to Wales to manage the new factory. I shall take over the Exeter office again.'

Julia listened, impassively, as Carl continued to unburden himself.

'I can't tell you how sorry I am for the stupid things I've done. I don't expect anything from you in the way of forgiveness. But I want to do my best to put things right as far as you will allow me. To pay the school fees. See something of the kids. Find somewhere up here for me to live.'

To begin with, Julia listened, but said nothing. He hardly dared mention the house, hoping against hope that selling it wouldn't be necessary; that the bank would be satisfied with the proceeds from the flat; that they wouldn't foreclose. At the same time, he knew he had only this one occasion in which to be honest. The truth might hurt. But it had to be spoken.

Then Julia broke her silence.

'You might want to put the house on the market as well,' she said before he could say anything about it, and Carl, with a mouthful of food, nearly choked. 'I have a job in town,' she continued, 'managing a café-craft shop. There's a big flat above it, and we're moving in there next month. The children are quite excited.'

Carl looked at her in amazement. So was this how it was to end? The truth was out. The way was mapped out before him. An empty life yawned ahead.

They talked on, Carl put some figures before Julia, and they agreed a sum for maintenance for herself and the kids. Access, too, was discussed. Then it was over.

'I guess our solicitors will sort out the details,' Carl said, and he barely recognised his own voice.

He helped Julia on with her coat, his finger accidentally brushing against the soft, peachy skin of her cheek. He felt a stab of pain.

Was this it? He paid the bill and walked her back to her car. She opened the door and turned towards him.

'We're having a grand opening of the café-craft shop next week,' she said. 'It will include a time of thanksgiving for Josh. So many people prayed for him. They want to thank God for his recovery.'

Carl stood there, listening to the even tone in his wife's voice, the confidence and assurance of her demeanour as she gave him the date and time, and he was filled with admiration.

'Josh won't be home until the following weekend,' she continued. 'I figured it would be too much for him to cope with. But I'm setting up a Skype session with him. It's going to be at the café-craft shop, not at the house. It would be good if you would come too - if it's not too much for you to take on board. I know the children would appreciate it. And I would too. A united front. On neutral ground, like tonight.'

She turned away and sat in the car, pulled the door closed, and started the engine.

'Think about it,' she said through the open window. 'It would mean a lot to Josh.'

Then she closed the window and drove off. Alone in the car park, Carl stared after her, his thoughts churning.

Julia felt pierced with a great sadness as she drove home after her meal with Carl. She was shocked at how gaunt he looked; worried that he wasn't eating properly; concerned about his apparent loss of drive. Clearly, the stuffing had been knocked out of him. Negotiating the roundabout at Countess Weir, she reflected that the contrast between the two of them couldn't be more marked. There he was, languishing on a pile of unfilled dreams with Lucy, and here she was, excited with the challenges of the new job that lay before her.

Not only that, Josh's memory had returned, and with it an understanding about his father's departure. Having made his big emotional and life-threatening statement by crashing his motorbike, he now seemed, with the ongoing support of the hospital chaplain and psyche team, to have calmed down, put it behind him, and moved on with a new maturity. Consequently, when the prospect of moving out of the family home and into the flat above the café-craft shop in town had begun to crystallise, it was Josh she'd turned to for advice.

'How do you think Abi and Nathan would take to the idea?' she'd asked him.

As she'd anticipated, taking him into her confidence had proved to be exactly the right way of going about things. Clearly gratified to have been consulted, he'd responded sensibly, with a maturity beyond his years.

'I think you'd have to make ground rules for us all, Mum. The temptation of hitting the night life might be a big pull for Nath as he gets older. Abi too. But otherwise, I think a new beginning would be great. A good thing all round. And it would give us kids more independence. We wouldn't have to rely on you to ferry us around all the time.'

With that in mind, she'd presented the idea to Abi and Nathan, and met with a similar response. Though without the proviso of ground rules, she reflected with a smile.

Arriving at home and leaving the car on the drive, she went into the house. With Josh's absence and Abi still only fourteen and Nathan twelve, she'd asked Hilary to sit with them until her return. Over the last few weeks she'd found her incredibly supportive. So much so that despite having had to cancel all appointments with Evie, she'd hardly missed their weekly chats.

She found Hilary watching TV on her own in the family room.

'They've gone up to bed,' she said. 'But we've had a great evening together. I think I've even persuaded them to come along to the youth activities I run mid-week. They seem to be up for it, if it's okay with you?'

Julia smiled, broadly.

'I've been trying to get them to go to youth club for months now,' she said, dryly. 'You obviously have something I lack when it comes to the powers of persuasion.'

'Oh, I don't know about that,' Hilary protested. 'I think it was more to do with the fact that we've got a live band coming this week rather than anything I had to say.'

'Of course, thanks to you, it's going to be so much easier for them to get to events like that once we've moved into town,' Julia said, seating herself opposite Hilary. 'Another positive to be chalked up.'

Hilary smiled but said nothing. She looked, thought Julia, as if she had something on her mind.

'Is everything alright?' she asked.

Hilary hesitated. 'Just wondered how the meeting went with Carl.'

Julia stared at her. Was there something odd about the way she'd asked? Something wistful, she wondered? Her heart hammered.

'Do you and Carl have some sort of history?' she asked, not at all sure that she wanted to know the answer.

Hilary blanched, or at least, Julia fancied that she did.

'I told you,' she said, picking up her bag from the floor. 'I was Matron at Carl's school.'

'And what age would he have been then?' Julia asked, a terrible thought vying for supremacy in her head.

'Sixteen. Seventeen, I suppose.'

'And you would have been -?'

'Twenty-five, or thereabouts.'

'You didn't -? You didn't have a - relationship did you?'

Appalled that the thought in her head had made its way out of her mouth, Julia jumped to her feet and began to pace the floor.

'Good heavens no!' The look of dismay on Hilary's face convinced Julia of her error.

'I'm sorry, I'm truly sorry,' she gabbled. 'It's just that - ever since we got to know each other - it seems as if Carl has something against you.'

Hilary's eyes moistened. She took out her handkerchief and, looking down at her, Julia saw lines of anguish on her face that she'd never noticed before.

Hilary sat for a while composing herself. When she spoke, there was a break in her voice.

'Carl's best friend died in my care; while I was Matron. A terrible death. Carl believes I was to blame - at least in part. And he had - has - good reason to do so. He's never forgiven me.'

Julia couldn't believe it. It was too incredible. Carl had some adolescent perspective on his best friend's death? It was probably completely erroneous. And here was Hilary, her beloved friend, who'd done so much for her, taking the rap.

'I don't believe you could possibly be to blame for his death - Spud, or whatever his name was. Carl's got it all wrong. And it's about time he grew up and got over himself, as the children would say. What was it? Measles? Mumps?'

Hilary stood up and walked to the door.

'Nothing as ordinary as that, I'm afraid,' she said, sadly. 'But it would be better if you heard it direct from Carl. And don't pre-judge him. He has good reason to be angry.'

She kissed Julia on the cheek and made her way to her car.

Julia frowned, trying to make sense of what Hilary had said. She recalled the plaque she'd found in Carl's suitcase prior to the launch of the Welsh factory; the reference the Secretary of State had made to 'the story' when he'd cut the ribbon to declare the factory open; and a brief, unfinished, conversation she'd had with Carl's bank manager, Mr Miller. She stared at Hilary's departing car, and felt utterly bewildered.

CHAPTER NINETEEN

THROUGHOUT THE FOLLOWING week, Julia had little opportunity to follow up on what Hilary had said. Everything had happened so quickly since Josh's accident, her appointment as manager of the café-craft shop, the refurbishment that had been necessary, the stock she'd had to order and the decorating she'd had to undertake in the flat, above, before they could move in.

Naturally, she supposed, she'd felt a pang of sadness when departing the house that had been her home for the last ten years of her marriage, but there were painful memories too, and she was glad to leave them behind. It was the children's reaction that she found particularly gratifying. Josh had accepted that he would move straight from the hospital to the apartment, and Abi and Nathan, far from showing any sense of nostalgia, appeared to be enthralled with the prospect of being at the heart of things, geographically, and in respect of the business. They were all, as a family, she thought, ready to move on.

The premises, on a small back lane just off Queen's Street and only a stone's throw from the High Street, backed onto Rougemont Gardens, beyond which lay Northernhay Gardens. With open grassland areas, formal flower beds and, of course, the castle built by William the Conqueror, it offered ample space for Abi and the boys to let off steam. In addition, the city provided diverse facilities, including sports fields, swimming baths and tennis courts, all within easy reach either on foot or by bus.

Behind the shop front lay a large kitchen, newly modernised, and a small office. The living quarters, generously proportioned, were accessible both from the office, with a code and key, and via a private front door onto the lane. From the second-floor bedrooms, the Roman city wall was visible.

The party Julia had planned, and invited Carl to attend, was, in fact, a grand opening, to be held in the large café-craft shop. But it was, also, as she'd said, a thank you to all the faithful friends and medics whose help and support, she had no doubt, had eased and aided the period of Josh's recovery.

On the Saturday morning of the party, they were all up bright and early. Abi and Nathan, along with the volunteer workers - all of whom had been instructed in health and safety procedures - had been briefed in what was expected of them.

Julia, dressed in a smart but casual outfit that comprised a cap-sleeved fitted dress with a black and white floral pattern, topped with a grey linen jacket, took a last look around the public area. Small circular tables and larger rectangular ones filled one half of the large room, while the other half was entirely given over to arts and crafts.

Some of the merchandise she'd purchased was from Traidcraft, a well-established charity set up to fight poverty through trade in developing countries. The remainder was from local artists: sculptors, painters, weavers and jewellery makers. There was also an area where customers could learn a craft, under the tuition of local professionals. Satisfied that she had a good mix and that everything was well presented, she was about to go out to the kitchen, when the shop door opened, and in walked Carl.

He cast a glance around the empty tables and chairs, with an abject look of uncertainty and apprehension on his face.

'Oh, I'm sorry. I'm too early. I'll - I'll come back later.'

He turned to go, but Julia took his arm to prevent him.

'No, please don't go. Forgive me. I deliberately asked you early. There's someone I want you to meet.'

Clearly uncomfortable, he followed Julia to the back of the premises, where she showed him into the office. Carl visibly balked. Seated on a swivel chair at the desk was the person whom Julia now knew as his number two arch enemy, second only to his father.

Carl felt no anger towards Julia for the deception she'd played out in asking him to come earlier, nor towards the person who now faced him. But that was not to say that he felt nothing. The sight of Hilary, seated on a typist's chair in the small office, sent his senses reeling. His chest tightened, his breathing became laboured, the room around him lurched, then steadied.

'You,' he said, his voice tinged with stupor.

He'd met her only the once in the twenty-eight years since Maurice's death, and that was a brief and distant encounter, in the dimly lit confines of the cathedral, before the carol service. He'd registered little of her appearance on that occasion, and found himself shocked, now, to see what the passage of time had wreaked in terms of her face, figure and hair.

She would be - what - mid-fifties, he supposed. But the years had not dealt kindly with her. There was an air of sadness about her down-turned mouth, the pale eyes she turned upon him - and then he saw red!

If she thought she could evoke sympathy in him, she was mistaken. He knew, from Miller, that she'd absconded, soon after the court case. A new life for her in Canada, while his friend lay buried beneath the sods in the cemetery, with nothing but a headstone to mark his time on this earth.

'You!' he said, again, his voice filled with contempt, his fists bunched, his stomach leaching bile, his foot already turning on its heel prepared to leave.

And then, to his horror, his shame, he crumpled. Fell onto the chair opposite her. Doubled over. And wept. Great sobs racking his body. Nausea rising in his throat.

He felt her hand on his arm. Flinched, but didn't flee. He heard her voice, her tears, her remorse. Recoiled, but continued to listen.

By the time he emerged from the office, the café-craft shop was full. Emotionally exhausted by what he'd heard from Hilary, Carl's one intention was to make good his escape. It was not to be. Thwarted by the handshakes and back-claps he received from people he knew, he at last relented and stood at the back of the room as someone unknown to him took the centre floor.

'Ladies and gentlemen,' the speaker began. 'Nelson Mandela who, sadly, is no longer with us, was renowned for his perspicacity on life. I'm reminded, as I invite you to take a look around this wonderful new café-craft project, of a speech he made many years ago. What he said, in effect, was *Who are you not to shine?*'[1]

Carl watched as the man paused and looked around at the men and women gathered before him, as if waiting for an answer.

'Mandela continued by pointing out,' the man read from a laptop that stood before him on a table, 'that *There is nothing enlightened about shrinking so that other people won't feel insecure around you. We are all meant to shine.* He then concluded that as we do so, we *unconsciously give other people permission to do the same.*'

Again he looked around the room as if to ensure that everyone had heard him correctly. Carl felt his heart beat faster. Combined with what Hilary had told him, what this man was saying had the power to make him want to cry again; to sit down and howl his eyes out. To know the cleansing release of tears.

Aware of others eyes upon him, he steeled himself. What on earth had Mandela's observations to do with opening a shop like this, he asked himself? Was this man, whoever he was, about to explain?

'I want to suggest,' the speaker continued, 'that by her generosity in making these premises available for our use, our dear friend Hilary Bankster has let her light shine. And in doing so, she's enabled another dear friend, Julia Worth, to let her light shine, by managing the shop and providing home-baked produce. And she, in turn, through the nourishment and inspiration that these premises will offer, plus the arts and crafts that are on sale, will allow the dreams of others to flourish, will raise funds, and will bring light and hope to the needy.'

Carl shifted, uncomfortably, from one foot to the other.

'The money raised here, in this café-craft shop, will help to support surgeons and medical technicians to mend the broken limbs of children in war-torn countries like Syria, Israel and Palestine, Iraq and Afghanistan, so that they, in turn, might have the opportunity to grow into adulthood, and allow their potential to shine. We'll also be supporting pastoral aid which, we hope, will help them to learn to forgive rather than seek revenge in further war.'

Someone started to clap, and immediately everyone broke into spontaneous applause.

'But that's not all,' the speaker continued as the ovation subsided. 'Some of you here this morning, medics, nursing staff, consultants and technicians, have been allowing your gifts to shine, and were responsible for mending the broken body and mind of a certain young man so that he will be able to shine in future.'

He tapped the keyboard of the laptop on the podium before him and immediately the screen on the wall behind him lit up.

'Ladies and gentlemen,' the speaker finished, as wild cheering broke out, 'I give you Josh Worth.'

And there, for all to see, sitting in his hospital room with a broad grin on his face and waving to everyone was a living, moving Skype image of Josh.

Carl could stand it no longer. Desperate, terrified of making a spectacle of himself, he cast around for a way out. The exit was on the far side of the room. There was no way he could push his way through the crowd of people between himself and the door. Immediately behind him lay the office. It was a no brainer. He turned, barely able to stem the tears that sprang from his eyes, the pain that burst from his chest. Staggering under the crushing weight of his own guilt and pride - yes, that contemptible pride again - he sank down on the swivel chair and gave in to his grief.

It was Abi who found him.

'Come home to us, Daddy,' she said, sliding onto his lap, hugging him, and adding her tears to his own. 'We need you. Mummy needs you.'

'Yes.' He jerked his head up as he heard Julia's voice. 'Come home to us, Carl.'

He felt her hand on the back of his neck and, as Abi quietly let go of him and left the room, he turned to Julia and wept as he'd never wept before.

Julia had told Evie some weeks earlier that this would be the end of her counselling sessions, but they'd agreed to stay in touch. With Josh due home on the Monday, she rang that evening to explain what had taken place at the party.

'How did it all go?' Evie enquired.

'It was brilliant!' Julia enthused, standing at the window of her new bedroom. 'I wish you'd been able to come. Hilary's minister gave a short speech before he announced the café officially opened. What he said epitomised everything you've been telling me for the past ten months. It was amazing.'

'Sounds good,' said Evie. 'Pity I couldn't make it.'

'It was all about being the person you're meant to be. Using the gifts you have. Not being modest or shy about the talents you've been given. Not hiding your light under a bushel, because it's not yours to hide. Because it's only as you use what you have, that other people are freed-up to use their gifts.'

'Well I can't disagree with any of that.' Julia could hear the smile in Evie's voice.

'And then,' she continued, 'he finished by saying that the medics who were there had used their gifts to heal Josh, to give him a chance to shine. Oh, Evie, you should have heard him. And the applause that followed.'

'It certainly sounds as if I missed out,' Evie agreed. 'How did Carl take it?'

'Well. . . Hilary asked me, last week, if she could speak privately with Carl before everyone arrived,' Julia said, 'She didn't tell me what it was about, and I didn't ask, but I sort of guessed that it must be about the death of his friend, when she was Matron at his school. Anyway, by the time she and Carl came out of the office, the chairman had already started with his speech, so I'm not sure how much of it Carl heard.'

She sat down on the edge of her bed.

'I'd set up my laptop beforehand and Skyped Josh in hospital. So when the connection was made, there was Josh on the big screen on the wall, smiling and waving to everyone. I think it was too much for Carl. He disappeared out the back, to the office. He was clearly upset. By the time I managed to get through to see him, he was in a terrible state.'

Julia cast her mind back to the scene that had greeted her in the small, dimly lit office. Abi was sitting on her dad's lap, as if she were still a little girl, and the two of them had their arms wrapped around each other.

'Come home to us, Daddy,' Abi was saying, over and over.

And before she could give it any thought, Julia had found herself echoing her daughter, with the words that were in her own heart, 'Yes, come home to us, Carl.'

Abi had left the room then, and Carl, sobbing and clinging to Julia's hand, had protested, over and over, that he'd made such a terrible mess of things; that he'd hurt so many people; had been wrapped up so much in himself that he'd failed to notice the needs of his family; he'd made their lives a misery; he was so ashamed; so sorry; he deserved only to be cast out, to be left to wallow in his misery; to be punished.

'It isn't about punishment,' Julia had found herself saying, perching on the desk in the tiny office and holding both Carl's hands in hers. 'It's about love. It's about forgiveness. It's about putting the past behind you. It's about starting again. About healing. And wholeness.'

Carl had looked at her in disbelief.

'You heard what that man said,' he whispered. 'Quoting Nelson Mandela. Shine? When have I ever let you shine? All I've ever done was to think about myself. Polishing my own halo. Making sure that my light shone so bright it outshone anyone else's.'

Julia recognised, then, that this was exactly how her father had been with her mother. But there was no revenge in her. No recrimination. Only hope. And encouragement.

'Carl, you gave me three lovely children,' she said, softly. 'Their lives are the best thing you and I have ever created, or ever will. And we did that together.'

As she spoke, the truth of what she was saying seared itself into her thinking.

Carl wiped the back of his hand across his eyes and stared at her.

'That's just the point,' he said. 'I loathed my father, and with good reason. I promised myself I'd never treat my kids as he did me. And look what I did. Let them all down - Josh, Abi, Nathan, and you. That's why it's so unforgivable.'

Julia felt tears pricking her eyes.

'No it's not, darling. Nothing is unforgivable. I don't know what your father or Hilary did to you, but if you could forgive them, let go of the past, you'd be free to move on. As it is, you're shackled to something that happened - what, nearly thirty years ago?'

Carl continued to stare at her for a moment, then he dropped his gaze.

'Hilary said much the same thing,' he said, his voice full of emotion. And then, as they sat there in the office, out came the whole story.

'My father was a bully and a tyrant,' Carl said. 'He was also a hypocrite, because he set himself up as a pillar of society and church. Everyone thought he was this wonderful, amazing man, opening bazaars and fetes, speaking up for the poor and downtrodden.

'But behind closed doors, it was a very different scene. He beat my mother into submission - literally at times! As a result, she lost what would have been my brother. Or sister. And he beat me, too.'

Julia shook her head, too emotional to speak, as Carl went on.

'All he ever wanted from me was a clone of himself. He sent me to boarding school in Wales because that's where he went. It was run by a strict religious order. He was a scholarship boy. His parents were too poor to pay the fees. He owed it to them to make good, he used to say. And he instilled in me the idea that the harsh regime would be the making of me, as it had of him.'

'And so it was!' said Julia, seeking to reassure him. 'You've been highly successful in your chosen field.'

Carl shook his head.

'You don't understand. This was not normal discipline. The sort of punishment meted out by the school beggars belief. The slightest misdemeanour warranted the cane. And for anything more serious . . .'

Julia stared at Carl's face, at the anguish in his eyes, and the penny dropped.

'Is that what happened to your friend, Spud?'

Carl nodded.

'He failed to turn in a history project on time, and was then found to have copied someone else's work. Mine, as it happens. Yes,' he held up his hand, 'I know it was wrong. But what happened to him as a result was - brutal. Inhuman!'

Julia hitched herself into a more comfortable position on the desk.

'What happened?'

Barely able to control his emotion, Carl spoke in halting and broken tones.

'The usual punishment was being made to stand under a cold shower until you were on the point of collapse.'

As he probably had, Julia recalled, before he left on Christmas morning.

'But they wanted to make a point with Spud,' he continued. 'He was made to go on a cross-country run after that. All night Miller and I stayed awake in the dorm, waiting for him to return. But he never came back. The search and rescue helicopter found him, next day, alone on the Welsh mountains. He'd suffered hypothermia, and never regained consciousness.'

Julia clasped her other hand to her mouth, tears springing to her eyes.

'Oh, Carl. How terrible.'

'There was worse to come.' Carl's voice became bitter. 'Much worse.'

Julia couldn't comprehend anything worse. She shook her head in disbelief. Carl tightened his grip on her hand.

'Naturally, there was an Inquest,' he continued. 'And naturally, Spud's parents wanted justice. Equally naturally, my father, a successful barrister and an ex-pupil, was asked to defend the school.'

He paused, the frown on his face deepening, his lip curled in disdain.

'It was a complete cover up. A whitewash. There was no mention of the punishment meted out to Spud. As far as the Coroner, the courts and the public were concerned, he'd taken it upon himself to run away from school. That was the defence my oh-so generous, do-gooder, barrister father put forward. The school was exonerated. And the rest, as they say, is history.'

Julia slid off the desk, crouched before Carl, and put her arms around him.

'So that's why you've been so against what I've been involved in. I understand now.'

She clung to him in the hope that the compassion and understanding that engulfed her would now wrap itself around this man, assuaging his grief, expunging his acrimony.

'But what about Hilary?' she said, pulling away from him at last. 'What part did she play, if any?'

Carl sat in silence for a moment, then he rose to his feet and peered out of the narrow, barred window, that looked out into a tiny dingy courtyard.

'She was Matron at the time, as I've said before,' he began, with his back to Julia. 'I always believed she was party to the regime of punishment and brutality. I hated her for it. I hated you for befriending her.'

Julia sat back on her heels, then stood.

'I did wonder. I couldn't understand why you hated her so much. Why you were so hostile.'

Carl turned, and rubbed the back of his fist across his eyes.

'You commented on how young she was to be a Matron in a boys' school. Well, what I didn't know until she told me this morning, was that my father got her the post. He obviously had clout with the governors, because he was a major financial benefactor of the school. It appears, from what Hilary said, that he expected her to do certain favours - though she says she was too naïve to realise that before she accepted the job.'

Julia could hardly believe what she was hearing. She frowned. What she'd heard put a different slant on her friend. One she didn't like at all.

'But surely - didn't she have anything to say about what was happening in the school? Couldn't she have stopped it?'

'Oh, yeah!'

'Well, at very least she could have spoken the truth at the Inquest. For the boy's parents' sake, if nothing else.'

'That's what I thought, too.' Carl's voice was full of bitterness.

And with increasing anxiety Julia now realised the terrible situation she was in. What she had done! In accepting the post of manager at the café-craft shop, she was now beholden to Hilary. The woman she'd admired; counted a friend. The woman who now controlled her life. Her home. Her work. Her income.

Carl opened his mouth to speak but a knock at the door prevented him from continuing. It was Abi.

'Mum, you need to come,' she said. 'People are beginning to wonder where you are.'

In a trance, Julia rose to her feet. Telling Carl she'd be back as soon as she could, she returned to the café-craft shop. The speeches were over. Tea and cupcakes were being served by the volunteers, people were milling about between the tables, talking animatedly about the shop's future.

Immediately swamped by enthusiastic admirers of what she'd achieved, Julia did her best to respond with a smile. The thought of Carl, however, and all that he'd revealed about the death of his friend, was uppermost in her mind. And with it, a confusion of troubling thoughts about her one-time friend, Hilary.

Endnote:

1. See author's note on p225

CHAPTER TWENTY

'SO WHERE DID your friend, Hilary, fit into this?' Evie asked Julia during their telephone call that evening.

Where indeed? Julia wondered.

With Abi's summons to fulfil her duties as hostess at the café-craft shop launch, there had been no opportunity for Carl to answer the questions that had teemed in her head. But once all the guests had left, the clearing up had been done, and the children had gone upstairs to explore their new home, she'd immediately returned to the office. Not surprisingly she supposed, she'd found it empty. All that remained to indicate Carl's earlier presence was a one-word note: *SORRY!*

All that night, she thrashed her well-worn assumptions with as much diligence as she beat her pillow. The dream she'd thought fulfilled, had turned to nightmare. The sweet taste of success had soured. Her time to shine, to earn her own living by realising her potential as a cook, had dimmed and darkened. Everything she'd thought solid and sterling she now saw as reduced to tinsel.

By early morning, she knew she must confront her fears face to face. Only Hilary - her benefactor, but Carl's arch enemy, the woman who had, herself, admitted that he had good reason to feel hostile - could fill in the gaps; justify her behaviour; explain the reasons for her silence in the face of injustice. Leaving a note for the children, Julia set off in the car for the other side of the city.

Her heart hammered as she rang the doorbell. Was Hilary, with her church connections, her fund-raising events, and her appreciable generosity, actually no better than Carl's father? A charlatan, who hid her misdeeds behind a façade of goodness? A deceiver? A betrayer of friendship?

Hilary was dressed for church when she answered the door. She expressed no surprise at the sight of Julia, but stepped forward to greet her in the usual way, with a kiss.

'I wondered if you'd want to talk,' she said, stepping back to allow Julia access. 'I take it Carl has been filling you in?'

Julia was racked with confusion. Hilary's attitude was hardly one of guilt or shame.

'Not entirely,' she said, uncertainly.

Over coffee, in Hilary's sitting room, she asked the questions that were uppermost in her mind - tentatively to begin with, but over time, with increasing assurance. At last, she picked up her keys, bade Hilary goodbye, and, having rung the children, set off for the Premier Inn.

Carl was about to buy a Sunday newspaper when Julia rang him on her mobile from the car park of the hotel, and asked if they might meet for a coffee in the restaurant. He felt a heady mix of hope and elation, confusion and trepidation.

'I'm sorry I couldn't finish what I began yesterday,' he said, awkwardly, when he met her at the door. 'It was all a bit hectic, wasn't it - though an excellent launch, I thought.'

Pointing out that he could hardly be blamed for Abi's interruption, or the need for her to attend to her guests, Julia waved his apology aside.

'I did have a ghastly night though,' she admitted, seating herself at a corner table near the window of the empty restaurant. 'But I've been to see Hilary this morning.'

'I'm sorry,' he said, again. 'I was in such a state of shock myself after she'd told me about the true state of affairs. I'm afraid I wasn't thinking clearly about the effect it might have on you.'

'So you believe what she had to say, then?' Julia asked.

Carl looked at her, quizzically.

'Yes! Don't you?'

'Of course! I just wasn't sure if you would. I mean it's been a long time hasn't it? Difficult to change one's stance after so long.'

Carl felt some of the tension ease from his body. Julia's face was still taut with anxiety, but it was clear from the way she was speaking that she was open to discussion. He picked up the teaspoon on his saucer and gave his cappuccino a stir.

'Hindsight's a wonderful thing. Looking back, I can see that my ongoing understanding of the situation was coloured by my adolescent perspective on things,' he said, slowly. 'I suppose it's only natural that, as a boy, I thought Hilary was part of the school hierarchy. An advocate of its ethos. I mean, she was a member of the staff. I guess I just assumed that, as Matron, she was responsible for the harsh punishment that was inflicted on us. I now know that wasn't so.'

He looked up to see how Julia would react to his analysis of the situation. Frowning slightly in the low winter sun that streamed through the window, she nodded.

'Hilary told me she was appalled with the brutality at the school. That she took it up with the staff, the monks, but got nowhere.'

Carl replaced his spoon in the saucer.

'That's right. My father threatened to ruin her if she didn't keep quiet.'

Julia shook her head, and seeing her hair gleaming, rippling around her face, Carl found it almost beyond him to refrain from reaching out to stroke it. In an attempt to redirect his thoughts, he glanced down at the plastic topped table at which they were seated. Julia, meanwhile, continued with her thoughts.

'But surely she could have - *should* have - spoken out about what was going on?' she said. 'I mean, if the sexual misconduct between her and your father came out, he would have had more to lose than she would.'

Carl shook his head, sadly.

'From what I understand, there *was* no sexual misconduct because Hilary refused to give in to his demands. But you obviously didn't know my father that well. As I say, he was a tyrant. But he was also a very successful, highly acclaimed barrister. He would have twisted it round so that Hilary, would have appeared to be a sex-mad predator.'

'Even so . . .'

Carl pursed his lips and shook his head.

'It wasn't fear of being maligned that prevented Hilary from doing anything in the beginning. It was because she felt that my father would be believed and she wouldn't. And that would mean she'd lose her job. She reckoned she could do more good inside the establishment, where she might be able to exercise some influence - and comfort, of course - rather than outside as a disgraced ex-employee.'

Julia raised her eyebrows in an attitude of recognition and acceptance of Hilary's reasoning.

'I still can't understand, though, how come your father wielded such influence at the school?' she asked, leaning back in her chair.

'Well, as I told you, he was Chairman of the Board of Governors, and a major financial benefactor. His name gave the school huge prestige. Without that they would, probably, have foundered long ago. Besides, you forget, he was a great believer in the merit of corporal punishment.'

They sat in silence sipping their coffee for a few moments, then Julia rose to her feet, explaining that she'd left the children on their own in the flat and felt she ought to get back.

'Hilary told me that when it came to Spud's punishment, she begged the Abbot to relent,' she continued, when Carl had paid the bill and the two of them walked out to the car. 'She said that when he didn't and the boy died and it became clear that there was going to be a cover-up, she threatened to go the police and was promptly sacked.'

'That's right. And then the Abbot appeared to relent. He said he'd spoken with the parents and everything was okay. He told Hilary she'd have her day in court, and he would accept whatever was coming to him. So when he offered to write a glowing testimonial for a job in Canada, and said the monastery would pay for her fare there, and back for the court case, she accepted, believing that justice would be done.'

'But it wasn't?' Julia's comment was as much a question as a statement.

Carl snorted as she unlocked the car door.

'Depends how you define justice,' he said as a message came through on Julia's mobile.

'Sorry,' she said. 'It's Abi. She can't find anything for breakfast, and the boys are playing up. I'll have to go.'

Carl attempted a smile.

'Nice to know you're needed,' he said. 'Perhaps we could meet up again sometime?'

Catching sight of his reflection in the car window, he realised he must look and sound like an immature teenager, lusting after some girl he hadn't the courage to ask out.

Julia nodded, started the car, waved and drove off. Alone in the empty car park, Carl felt more bereft than ever.

A lot has happened since Christmas and now, at the party following Lily-Rose-Marie's christening on a chilly Easter Sunday morning, I find myself in conversation with my ex. Unlike me, he knows most of the guests, at least those in the police force. I'm intrigued, and I suppose a little flattered, therefore, as to why he's singled me out. I can't help wondering if he ever has second thoughts about our divorce, as I once had? Is he happy in his second marriage? Have I truly come to terms with what happened? Watching him, surreptitiously, I think I can safely say I have. Now the father of a baby boy, he has changed dramatically, and bears little resemblance to the young man with whom I fell in love.

'Makes you think, though doesn't it?' I ask him, unwittingly betraying my thoughts as, drinks in hand, we toast the baby to whom we've both made promises as Godparents.

He looks at me, quizzically, clearly unsure as to my state of mind viz-a-viz marriage and parenthood. I laugh, shake my head, and say, in an attempt to reassure him, 'It would never have worked. I'd probably have murdered you by now. Then you'd have had to arrest me. And I'd have had to counsel you through the trauma of having a criminal for a wife.'

He roars with laughter, the awkwardness of the moment dissipated by the zany humour we once shared.

It appears that Bosomy Barbara - I really must stop calling her that - has chosen to stay at home.

'Morning sickness and other complications,' Pete explains. 'Her mum's got Ryan for the weekend, so she's making the most of it and having a lie in.'

'Morning sickness?' I'm astonished.

'I know! Bit quick off the mark.'

'I'll say! Can't be much fun being pregnant again when you have a - what is he - five month old?'

'It isn't much fun!' Pete agrees, with feeling. 'I'm the one having the sleepless nights while Babs has to keep her feet up, doctor's orders. Anyway, she just wasn't feeling up to partying.'

Although I'd been dreading the encounter with Pete's second wife, I find myself now, strangely, in sympathy. A couple of dozen people squashed into the confines of a small terraced house when you're not feeling your best wouldn't appeal to me either. But I wonder if this is the real reason for her absence? Could it be that she couldn't face seeing me partnered with Pete as Lily-Rose-Marie's Godparents?

'You'd have made a great mum,' Pete says, raising his glass to me. 'Any -?'

'- significant other?' I finish for him.

The tall lean image that had once entranced me is now stocky and unremarkable; his close presence in the crowded room well within my comfort zone.

'Actually, yes!' I say, considerably embellishing my friendship with Scott Bingham which, to date, has resulted only in a couple of outings together, followed by a few telephone calls. Instantly, I feel myself blush.

A plate of sausage rolls, circulating in the hands of what I assume to be one of Ben's or Sharon's relatives, proves the perfect distraction and gob-stopper. We munch away in silence for a few moments, until, empty-mouthed, I ask the obvious question.

'What do you think of all the promises we had to make in church? Is a christening something you'd think about for your baby?'

'Good question,' Pete wipes a few stray pastry crumbs from his mouth with a paper napkin. 'Have to be honest, I had my fingers crossed, at least metaphorically, during the service.'

I conceal a smile. The irony of Pete's 'honesty' is evidently lost upon him.

'But you'd still go ahead and expect people to make similar hollow promises for your kid?' I ask.

Pete looks up at me.

'Hey! That sounds a bit serious. You're not into all the churchy thing are you?'

'Nooo. Not exactly.' I shrug. Even to my own ears I don't sound entirely convincing. 'But it did make me stop and think.'

Pete looks incredulous. Then, clearly bored with the topic, asks, 'Talking of church, didn't I see you with some bloke at the cathedral before Christmas?'

'You were there? At the carol service? Not your scene, I wouldn't have thought.'

'No. But Barbara wanted to go. So come on. Dish the dirt. Is this the new plus one?'

Has there, I ask myself, ever truly been a 'plus one' in the three years since our divorce? I've been out with blokes from time to time, most of them fellow students from the days when I was taking my degree in counselling, but I can't say that there's ever been anything serious. Would admitting to this depict me as some lost cause - the butt of one of Pete's jokes at some point, about the plight of men in the wake of needy blood-sucking single females? Or would he see me as someone strong and individualistic? I decide to duck the issue.

'Scott?' I ask, lightly. 'Oh, we've had a few dates, and more coming up shortly. This week, in fact.'

I refer to Scott's imminent visit to Guy and Nancy's, plus a concert he's invited me to at the college where he lectures next term, but I'm not about to divulge that to Pete. Saved by the bell, I turn to Ben as he arrives on the scene with baby Lily-Rose-Marie in his arms.

'Come on you two. Time to circulate or I'll clap you in irons.'

Taking the baby from her dad, I move away, leaving the two police officers in hoots of esoteric laughter. As for me, I'm feeling all the stronger for having faced up to my demons in the form of Pete and his family, and finding them only to be dwarves.

What's more . . . I think of the conversation I had with Julia when she told me of the way Carl's school had responded at Spud's Inquest. It appears that Hilary had never been recalled to give evidence, as promised. Instead, under Mr Worth's direction, the staff had presented a united front and portrayed the death as an accident. Appeasing Spud's parents with the gift of a free scholarship for the boy's younger brother, they had avoided all culpability. And it didn't seem to have occurred to the parents that they'd been bribed.

'Carl realises there's nothing he can do to change things,' Julia had said. 'And he's beginning to see, now, that Hilary did all she could. He's really putting it behind him, and moving on now.'

'That's excellent news,' I agreed.

'Yes. We've got a long way to go. But I've even managed to convince him that the harsh regime put forward by the school as *religion* has nothing to do with the love and mercy and forgiveness Hilary and I have found in our relationship with God.'

Recalling the occasion on which Julia had imparted her news - the last time we spoke - I can't help but feel a surge of pure pleasure. I glance down at the child in my arms. Lily-Rose-Marie's blue eyes are fixated on mine. For a moment she just stares. Then she smiles. Her little round face is transformed. My heart leaps with joy. My face is wreathed in smiles.

I am no longer childless. I am a Godmother, and this is my Goddaughter. Not only that - I think of the invitation Julia and Carl Worth have sent me.

Your presence would be greatly appreciated by Julia and Carl Worth it reads, *at a ceremony to renew their wedding vows, and a party afterwards at the Café-Craft Shop.* The date is the Sunday before Whitsun.

'So,' I tell Lily-Rose-Marie, continuing my earlier thought, 'not only am I your Guide-mummy, but with a little help from God - oh, okay, a lot of help from God - I am also a marriage mender.'

Watching me, Lily purses then opens her little rosebud mouth in an attempt to formulate a reply. And in my mind's eye, I can see Pumpkin nodding in agreement. At last, my time has come. My time to shine.

THE END

Quotation used in Chapter 19

'We ask ourselves, Who am I to be brilliant, gorgeous, talented, fabulous? Actually, who are you not to be? You are a child of God. Your playing small does not serve the world. There is nothing enlightened about shrinking so that other people won't feel insecure around you. We are all meant to shine, as children do. We were born to make manifest the glory of God that is within us. It's not just in some of us; it's in everyone. And as we let our own light shine, we unconsciously give other people permission to do the same. As we are liberated from our own fear, our presence automatically liberates others.'

Widely accredited to Nelson Mandela, this quotation is actually by Marianne Williamson from her book *A Return To Love* (Published by Thorsons, 2009).

About The Author

Mel Menzies is the author of a number of books, one a Sunday Times bestseller. An experienced keynote speaker, she has led family forums, marriage enrichment courses and writers' workshops, in addition to appearances on TV and Radio chat shows. She has also written under the names of Merrilyn Williams and Meg Scott.

Coming Soon...

... in the Evie Adams series:

Chosen?

A client seeking counselling in respect of illegitimacy and adoption triggers unforseen and tragic consequences.

Other Books By The Same Author...

A Painful Post Mortem: A Novel

'After reading your book, we felt it would be good to add it to the Bereaved Parents' Network library.'
–Mike Coulson, Bereaved Parents' Network Co-ordinator
www.careforthefamily.org.uk/bpn

'I have read A Painful Post Mortem with much interest and I am greatly impressed with the book and, not least, your actual written style.'
–Michael Saward, Canon Treasurer St Paul's Cathedral

'I loved the bereavement poem in the book. It was so moving...'
–J. Long Crendon

'Started your book last night – finding it most compelling.'
–Celia Bowring of CARE www.care.org

'I'm not normally a reader; however, I could not put this book down.'
–Penny (works in drugs rehab)

'Not only is this a good read but it would probably prove an invaluable help to the parents of teenagers/young adults who are causing their family heartache. I warmly recommend it.'
–USA Reader review, via Barnes & Noble

'Skilfully handled, a most moving book.'
–Author, Jessica Stirling

'The book is riveting. I could not put it down.'
–Sue Jenner via Facebook

'A beautifully written book with strong characterisation. The ending leaves an open verdict with sinister implications.'
–Sheila Johnson, Woman Alive Book Club

Non-Fiction Titles

Healed Within

Grace and wholeness when a brain tumour and disability strike. Published by Hodder & Stoughton.

The Last Mountain
Sunday Times No4. Bestseller

Enduring love in the midst of anguish when HIV and AIDs result in death for a talented young scientist who is a haemophiliac. Published by Hodder & Stoughton.

Stepfamilies

How-to book; part author-experience, part anecdotal material from families whose successes and failures have helped them to create warm, loving relationships. Published by Lion Hudson.

All titles are available from Amazon or www.melmenzies.co.uk